Show me

OTHER BOOKS BY ABIGAIL STROM

Winning the Right Brother

The Millionaire's Wish

Cross My Heart

Waiting for You

Into Your Arms

Almost Like Love

Nothing Like Love

Anything but Love

Tell Me

ABIGAIL STROM

This is a work of fiction. Names, characters, organizations, places, events, and incidents are either products of the author's imagination or are used fictitiously.

Published by Montlake Romance, Seattle

www.apub.com

ISBN-13: 9781542048804
ISBN-10: 154204880X

Cover design by Damon Freeman

Printed in the United States of America

For Robert A. Heinlein, who introduced me to the Red Planet, and for my father, who introduced me to Heinlein

Chapter One

She was free.

Airin Delaney looked over her shoulder for the tenth time, just to be sure. No sign of her mother; no sign of anyone who worked for her mother; no sign of anyone but tourists, strolling around Waikiki on a beautiful evening in February.

Her tense muscles relaxed. She was just a person in a crowd now. Ordinary and unremarkable.

Normal.

She was only a few blocks away from her luxury hotel, but it felt as though she were in a different world. Bars, restaurants, souvenir shops, neon lights—all combining to create a kind of honky-tonk atmosphere, brightly colored and a little seedy.

She loved it.

Taking a deep breath, she inhaled a hundred different things—the smell of beer coming from the open door of a bar, steam rising from a dish of Chinese dumplings on an outdoor cart, the scent of plumeria from a stand selling leis. On an impulse, she stopped and bought one, bending her head as the proprietor placed the lei around her neck.

When she continued down the street, the scent went with her.

She'd stopped to stare at the sign above a strip club—the first time in her life she'd seen an actual strip club, outside of TV and movies—when someone bumped into her from behind.

"Oops! Sorry, ma'am."

A strong hand closed around her upper arm, helping her recover her footing. She turned and found herself looking into the hazel eyes of a very tall, very good-looking man.

They stared at each other for a few heartbeats.

She wasn't used to being touched by strangers—except, of course, for the medical professionals who'd drawn her blood and changed her IVs and poked and prodded her for so many years.

This was different.

There was nothing professional or antiseptic about this man's touch or the way he was looking at her right now. His eyes widened as he took her in, his gaze neither blatant nor furtive. A slow smile lifted one corner of his mouth.

"Or maybe I'm not sorry," he went on, his voice low and husky and intimate.

Her heart began to beat faster. Her pulse throbbed at her wrists and the base of her throat. There was a prickling under her arms—adrenaline, she knew. She'd experienced all these things in hospitals, waiting for people to do things to her body that she couldn't control.

But while the physical sensations might be the same, the emotions that went with them were utterly different. It wasn't panic she was feeling, or dread, but exhilaration.

With a little nervousness mixed in.

The man was wearing a brown leather jacket she recognized as the kind worn by fighter pilots. Her father had been one. He'd died when she was twelve years old, but her mother had kept his jacket.

Of course, plenty of men who weren't pilots wore jackets like this. But something about the way this man held himself—not to mention the close-cropped military-style haircut—made her think he might be the real deal.

One of the things she remembered about her father was how *present* he always was. In the moment, ready for anything, with a grasp on everything happening around him.

This man was like that. Intensely alive, with an energy that seemed to crackle in the air.

And right now all that energy was focused on her.

He was flirting with her. There was actual flirting happening here, and she was the object of it.

How did women respond in situations like this? How would *she* respond?

She wanted to find out.

But before she could, they were interrupted. A big blond man came up beside them, shooting her a grin as he slung a heavy arm around the hazel-eyed man's shoulders.

"No beautiful women, Hunter. Not unless they're onstage wearing a lot less than that."

His name was Hunter.

A third man joined them now, this one with longish brown hair and a Stetson.

"Not onstage, either," the third man said. "I promised Jane no strip clubs. Anyway, why go out for hamburger when you've got steak at home?"

The second man looked at him. "Caleb, my dude, this is your last night of freedom. You don't belong to Jane yet."

"Yeah, I do. I'm whipped like you've never seen a man whipped before. No naked women, Stu. But I'm in favor of drinking whiskey until we can't stand up."

"I guess we can start there. Pick a bar. Any bar."

This must be a bachelor party. Which meant that the man who'd bumped into her—Hunter—had plans that didn't include flirting with her.

It was probably just as well. She'd come out tonight looking to be part of normal life, but that didn't mean she had to jump into the deep end of the pool right off. She had another week in Hawaii, after all. Maybe tomorrow she could look into the whole man/woman thing.

Still, she felt a twinge of regret. If she were going to try her hand at flirting, she couldn't imagine a sexier man to experiment with than this one.

It might have been her imagination, but she thought she saw a twinge of regret in Hunter's eyes as well. He hadn't moved yet, and he was still looking at her.

The other two men were looking at her, too, and she was starting to feel awkward.

She took a step back, and Hunter took his hand from her upper arm.

"I hope you enjoy your evening," she said. She didn't know if that was what an ordinary woman would say in these circumstances, but if she second-guessed herself too much she wouldn't make any progress tonight.

Feeling more awkward by the second, she decided to exit the scene as quickly as possible. She turned her back on Hunter and found herself facing the strip club and the building next to it—a bar. A few steps took her to the door of the latter. She started to open it, but a man and woman came out before she could.

They had to be tourists. They were wearing plastic leis, their Hawaiian shirts looked brand-new, and the man's bald spot was pink with sunburn. They seemed very happy and a little drunk.

This was what she'd come out tonight to experience. She wanted to be a normal person doing normal things, carefree and happy and sunburned.

Not literally sunburned, of course. But metaphorically.

Why not start with a drink, like this couple had? That would be the shallow end of the pool, as opposed to the deep, dark, sexy waters represented by the hazel-eyed Hunter. And since she'd never been in a bar before—other than the fancy ones in hotels, where she'd always drunk club soda or Perrier—it would count as a brand-new experience.

The sound of someone tuning a guitar floated out through the open door. She knew from talking to the musicians who performed nightly at her hotel that it was a steel guitar, played slack-key style. She'd fallen in love with the uniquely Hawaiian sound, and hearing it now was the final push she needed. She smiled at the couple holding the door for her and stepped across the threshold.

◆ ◆ ◆

Hunter watched the black-haired beauty until she disappeared inside the bar. Leilani's, according to the sign in the window.

Her eyes had caught him first. They were big and lustrous, dark brown with deep red notes like cinnamon or teak or mahogany. Incredible eyes.

But it was the whole package that had held his attention.

She wore a crisp white collared shirt, the kind professional women wore to business meetings, and a pair of gray pinstripe trousers. Her shoes were expensive leather with chunky square heels. Her hair was loose, but the elegant perfection of the black satin waves made her look as though she'd just come from the hairdresser. Surrounded as she was by tourists and locals in shorts, T-shirts, flip-flops, and bathing suits, she looked as out of place as it was possible to be.

Was that what had intrigued him most? Or was it the fact that she was one of the most gorgeous women he'd ever seen?

"I think she has the right idea," Caleb said. "This place looks as good as any. May as well start our bar crawl here."

It was his brother's bachelor party, so he got to decide where they went. The fact that Hunter wanted to get another look at the woman he'd bumped into was completely irrelevant.

Stu, Caleb's best friend from college, led the way into the bar. It was big, dimly lit, and crowded, with a local musician tuning up on the small stage. Stu snagged them a table in the back.

"I'll grab us some drinks," Hunter said. "Whiskey all around?"

"Sure, but there's a waitress," Caleb said. "She'll make it over here eventually."

"Nah. Why wait? I'll be right back. If she does come by, order some food. Chicken wings for me if they've got 'em."

Of course, the real reason he wanted to visit the bar was to get another look at his mystery woman.

She was perched on a stool near the door. Hunter came up behind her in time to hear her conversation with the bartender, a skinny Asian man with tropical flowers tattooed on his arms.

"What'll it be, Snow White?"

Not a bad nickname for a black-haired, fair-skinned beauty.

She put her elbows on the wooden bar and rested her chin on her folded hands. Her eyes traveled slowly from left to right, reviewing the array of liquor bottles.

"What would a normal woman order?" she asked after a moment.

Okay, that was weird. She sounded like an alien visiting Earth, tasked with the mission of trying to fit in with the local population.

The bartender was taken aback. "A . . . normal woman?"

She seemed to realize how odd her question sounded.

"Sorry. I mean, what do most women order when they come in?"

"Well . . . if you're talking tourists, I guess a Blue Hawaii or a mai tai."

His mystery woman looked intrigued. "What's in those?"

Rattling off drink ingredients put the bartender—Kaleo, according to the name tag on his faded Hawaiian shirt—on more familiar ground.

"A mai tai is light and dark rum, orange curaçao, lime juice, and simple syrup. A Blue Hawaii is rum and vodka, blue curaçao, pineapple juice, and sweet and sour."

She thought for a moment. "A blue drink sounds lovely. I'll have that one. A Blue Hawaii."

Kaleo grinned at her. "No problem, Snow White, but you look about eighteen. ID, please."

Hunter was standing a little behind her and to the right, but he wasn't close enough to see the name on the card she handed over. Kaleo gave it a long squint before saying, "A-I-R-I-N? I've never seen that before. Pronounced *Erin*?"

She nodded.

"Irish?" Kaleo asked as he began mixing her drink.

"My father was Irish, but my name is Kurdish. My grandmother came here as a refugee from Iran in the seventies. I was named for her." She sighed. "*Airin* means 'fiery and passionate.'"

Why the sigh? Did she think her name didn't fit her personality? Did she wish it did?

Kaleo started to say something, but a man standing to the left of Airin interrupted.

"Waaaaaait just a minute," the guy said. He was maybe forty years old, big but out of shape, and something in the tone of his voice put Hunter on high alert. "You're a refugee? Did I hear that right? From Iran? You're a goddam Muslim?"

It only took a split second for Hunter to insert himself between the man and Airin.

"Hey there," he said pleasantly, keeping his broad back to Airin and giving the guy his full attention. "Where are you from, friend?"

He held out a hand, and when the other man took it automatically, Hunter gave him the kind of shake he'd still be able to feel tomorrow.

The guy looked bellicose and intimidated at the same time, which was as good an indicator as any that he was well lubricated with alcohol.

"I was having a conversation with a Muslim bitch," he said, articulating his words carefully. He tapped Hunter on the sternum. "If you see something, say something. Who the hell knows what she's planning? These people are animals."

Anger shot through him, but he controlled his impulse to strike. This asshole was his size but older and out of condition—reason enough not to smash his face in.

"Hey, man," Kaleo said, taking the empty glass that had been sitting in front of him. "You finished your drink, you're all paid up, and now you're gonna leave."

The guy turned his belligerence on the bartender. "Was I talking to you, Chopstick? I'll leave when I'm done with this Muzzie."

Then he actually raised a fist.

Hunter grabbed him by the wrist and spun him around, twisting his arm behind his back.

"I think you'll leave now," he said, and marched him out to the Waikiki street.

Once he was free, the man turned and began to sputter at him. Hunter leaned in close, and the man got real quiet real fast.

"Here's a pro tip at no charge," Hunter said, his voice low and controlled. "If you ever get yourself arrested for assault with hate crime charges attached, you'll find out what happens to racist cowards in prison."

He turned away without waiting for a response and went back inside the bar.

His intervention had taken less than a minute. Airin and Kaleo were exactly where he'd left them, the bartender with a bottle of blue curaçao in his hand and Airin sitting frozen, her brown eyes enormous and her soft lips pressed together in a thin line.

Seeing the shock and fear that still lingered in her expression, Hunter regretted the restraint that had kept him from punching the guy in the teeth.

Kaleo nodded at him. "Thanks, brah. What are you drinking? It'll be on the house."

Hunter shook his head. "That's all—"

Then he heard his brother's voice from behind him. "Three shots of Jack Daniel's."

The bartender laid three shot glasses out in the blink of an eye. Then he reached behind him without looking, grabbed a bottle of Jack, and filled them up.

"And here's yours, Snow White," he added, handing the finished Blue Hawaii to Airin. "This one's on the house, too."

Another customer was calling for his attention, and he went to take the order.

Caleb held a hand out to Airin.

"My name's Caleb Bryce. You've already met my brother, Hunter."

She took his hand automatically. "I'm Airin."

"Nice to meet you, Airin." Caleb nodded toward the other side of the room, where they could glimpse Stu through the crowd, sitting at their table in the back. "That's a buddy of mine from college. I'm getting married tomorrow, and this is my bachelor party. How'd you like to join us while you drink that blue thing?"

Hunter gave his brother a what-the-hell-are-you-doing look, but Caleb kept his eyes on Airin.

Airin looked from Caleb to him and back again. "But . . . I couldn't. You're having a bachelor party. That's men only, isn't it? Except for strippers." Her eyes widened. "You don't think I'm a stripper, do you?"

"I'm pretty sure you're not a stripper, ma'am," Caleb said gravely, though Hunter spotted the quirk at the corner of his mouth. "But you are a beautiful woman, and Stu keeps telling me I'm supposed to have beautiful women around tonight. If you join us for a drink, he'll shut up about that for a while. So you'd be helping me out."

She frowned a little. "That's not your real reason. You're making fun of me."

Caleb shook his head. "No, ma'am. That really is my reason—or one of them, anyway." He glanced at Hunter. "The other reason is my brother. He just kicked some guy out of here for bothering you, and knowing the weight of the hero complex he labors under, I know he won't be able to enjoy himself if he's worried about you. So if you join us for a round or two, you'll help me solve that problem, too."

Airin's expression relaxed. And then, after a moment, she smiled.

As soon as she did, Hunter felt a kind of swoop in his stomach that he knew was bad news.

But it was Caleb's night, and he could invite whomever he wanted to join them. And what did it matter, anyway? It wasn't like he'd ever see this girl again.

"Give us some space, little brother," he said, making a shooing motion. "Airin and I will be over in a minute."

"I'll hold your drink hostage till then," Caleb said, picking up the shots and ambling away toward their table.

Then, finally, Hunter was able to give his full attention to Airin.

"Are you okay?"

She swiveled on her stool to face the bar, reaching out to pluck the yellow paper umbrella from her drink.

"I'm not even Muslim," she said, twirling the umbrella between her thumb and forefinger. Then she turned her head to look at him. "But that shouldn't matter. Should it?"

Hunter shook his head. "No, it shouldn't matter. I'm sorry you had to deal with a jerk like that—especially when it's your first night on our planet."

Her dark brown eyes widened. "My first night on . . . what do you mean?"

He leaned against the bar and grinned at her. "You just seem like a stranger in a strange land, that's all. I heard you ask the bartender what a normal woman would order to drink." He paused. "And if you'll excuse my mentioning it, you're not exactly dressed for Waikiki."

She looked down at herself and back up at him. "I wasn't really sure what to wear, to be honest. And anyway, all my clothes look like this."

"See what I mean? That's what I'd expect an alien explorer to say. It's like you're a scientist from another planet, here to observe the earthlings up close and personal."

That made her smile. "Maybe that's what I am," she said, and he knew she wasn't going to tell him any more.

But then, why the hell should she? They didn't know each other. And after tonight, they'd never see each other again.

"So come do some observing," he said, holding out a hand to help her up from the bar stool. "You can study three human males in their natural habitat."

Chapter Two

Three human males in their natural habitat.

How could she refuse an offer like that? Especially since being around Hunter made her feel safe after that ugly encounter.

I told you so.

She could practically hear her mother's voice saying those words. Dira Delaney prided herself on responding to every situation with cool logic, but a threat to her daughter would get her blood up like nothing else could.

I told you you're not ready for the world out there. You need more time to heal, to get stronger. Let me keep you safe.

But the doctors had said she was fully healed. *No restrictions*—those had been their exact words. She was strong, she was healthy, and she was sick of feeling safe.

And yet, wasn't that why she wanted to join Hunter for a drink? Because he made her feel safe?

Airin took his hand as she slid off the bar stool, and a jolt of electricity made her catch her breath.

"Are you all right?" he asked, his eyebrows drawing together.

"Yes, I'm fine," she said quickly, withdrawing her hand from his and picking up her drink from the bar.

The ice had made water condense on the outside of the glass, and she tried to concentrate on the sensation of cool wetness against her fingers.

Hunter's skin had been warm, his palm calloused, his grip strong and confident. And the touch of his hand had made her knees weak.

Was it possible for something . . . for someone . . . to feel safe and dangerous at the same time?

"I can carry your drink for you," he said.

As inexperienced as she was, and in spite of her instinct that Hunter was a man she could trust, she knew better than that.

"I'll carry it myself," she said. "Just in case you have Rohypnol or something."

A slow smile spread across his face. "Fair enough."

The guitarist started to play as they made their way toward the back of the bar. As people began to crowd onto the floor in front of the stage, filling the tables and the spaces between them, Hunter took her elbow in a protective grasp.

Caleb grinned when she took a seat at the round wooden table in the corner, and he introduced her to his college friend.

"It's very nice to meet you, Stu," she said, leaning across the table to shake the large blond man's hand.

All three of them were large, and even though Hunter was definitely the handsomest, they were all good-looking. She wasn't doing too badly for her first night of real freedom. She was in a Waikiki bar with three good-looking guys, and slack-key guitar music was playing behind her.

She took a sip of her Blue Hawaii and discovered that it was delicious.

Caleb was sitting on her right. "So, Airin," he said after a moment, "tell us what you—"

She shook her head. "You don't have to do that."

Caleb looked puzzled, and she elaborated. "It's nice to be here after what happened with that tourist, but you don't have to make polite conversation with me or anything. I'm very happy just to drink my drink and listen to the music. This is your bachelor party, and you're here with your brother and your friend. You should drink and laugh and carouse.

I can be just another part of the background." She remembered what Hunter had said. "Think of me as an anthropologist, here to observe three human males in their natural habitat."

Caleb threw back his head and laughed, and Stu almost choked on a piece of chicken. Hunter, sitting on her left, shook his head.

"I meant that as a joke," he said, but he was smiling. Then he took one of the shot glasses from the table and held it up. "But Airin's right about one thing. This is, first and foremost, my little brother's bachelor party. To Caleb, who got hooked and hooked hard by one hell of a woman."

Stu held up a glass. "To my old buddy for finding someone crazy enough to marry him, and to Hunter for having a job in Hawaii so we had to do the wedding here." He winked across the table at Airin. "And to you, the hot chick who's giving me something better to look at than either of them."

In all her twenty-four years, nobody had ever called her a hot chick.

Caleb picked up the third glass. "To all of you. With this whiskey, I thee salute."

He tossed his shot back, and the other two followed suit.

The waitress brought them another round. After downing their second shots, Hunter and Stu started trading stories about Caleb, which was perfect. She could listen without feeling like she had to contribute anything, and some of the stories were so funny she laughed until her stomach hurt. Her Blue Hawaii was wonderful, and she made it last until the men were on their fifth round of Jack Daniel's.

She assumed because she had such a feminine, fruity drink—and was drinking it so slowly—she wouldn't get intoxicated. But as she sipped her way to the bottom of her glass, she found herself feeling distinctly . . . happy.

Wait a minute. She wasn't happy.

She was drunk!

Or possibly both.

She noted the symptoms as the three men decided to make use of the dartboard hanging on the wall behind them. A kind of lightheadedness that felt good, not bad. A tingling in her fingers and toes. A general sense of well-being that suffused every cell in her body.

Then Hunter brushed against her as he got up from his chair, and the contact made something tighten deep in her belly. She put her hand over the spot.

"Do you want to play, Airin?" Caleb asked.

She shook her head. She'd never played darts in her life, and she would have more fun watching them play.

Especially Hunter.

The more she drank, the less self-conscious she felt about staring at him.

He'd taken off his bomber jacket and was playing darts in a navy-blue T-shirt and jeans. The shirt was old and faded, but she could still make out the NASA logo on the front, just over his heart.

NASA? Well, why not? He was probably a fan. Plenty of people were. Maybe he'd been to the Kennedy Space Center in Florida or the Johnson Space Center in Houston.

But as Hunter leaned forward to make a perfect throw, her attention was captured by something more compelling than his T-shirt.

His body.

A lifetime of medical care had given her an odd relationship with the human body, including her own. There were so many representations of it in hospitals and doctors' offices—MRIs and X-rays and medical charts; model skeletons and model brains and model hearts; framed diagrams showing layers deconstructed, bones and muscles and skin. But here in this Waikiki bar, staring at a man she'd only met an hour ago, she was having a very different viewing experience.

All the muscles she'd seen illustrated in anatomy posters were perfectly defined in Hunter. His deltoids, pectorals, biceps, and triceps flexed and released in flawless harmony. Powerful bands of muscle slid over the bones beneath, and the whole incredible infrastructure was covered by smooth, tanned male skin.

Even the simple act of throwing a dart became poetry when Hunter did it. Caleb was fun to watch, too—his movements were deceptively lazy, like his smile. But there was nothing lazy—deceptive or otherwise—about Hunter.

His focus was intense. His energy and physicality were intense. His movements were powerful and graceful at the same time, and he seemed so darn *healthy* it was impossible to imagine him needing to see a doctor or take a pill or have an operation.

He radiated strength. She remembered how sure and fast he'd been at the bar, stepping between her and the tourist and getting him outside before she had a chance to feel truly afraid. Hunter was a man who trusted his instincts and acted on them, and who was used to taking responsibility for his decisions.

Stu had mentioned a job that kept Hunter in Hawaii. There were, she knew, a lot of military bases here. Could he be in the military? That would account for his haircut, his jacket, and the way he carried himself.

Or was it possible he really did work for NASA? They were partnering with the University of Hawaii for several projects, including the biosphere study that had brought her mother here this week.

But that wasn't very likely. There were close to fifty thousand active-duty military personnel in Hawaii, compared to maybe five hundred people working with or for NASA.

Her glass was empty. She set it down on the wooden table beside the last round of shots and gave her whole attention to Hunter, leaning forward and staring at his broad, powerful back as he took careful aim with his last dart and let fly.

His throw—which was, apparently, enough to win the game—caused Caleb and Stu to groan in unison.

Caleb went to the board to gather the darts. Stu said something she didn't catch and headed off in the direction of the restrooms. Hunter clapped Caleb on the shoulder, turned back toward the table, and met her eyes.

Whenever Hunter had glanced her way in the last half hour, she'd ducked her head briefly before meeting his gaze, hoping to hide the fact that she'd been staring at him. It was doubtful she'd fooled him, since his sharp eyes didn't seem to miss much, but it had made her feel a little better.

This time she didn't look away.

She couldn't. She'd been staring again, of course, but this time she'd been fathoms deep, caught in an undertow of fascination impossible to escape.

A wave of heat traveled from her toes to the top of her head. Her heart began to pound as Hunter walked toward her, his eyes never leaving hers, until he was standing right in front of her.

"Hey," he said.

She cleared her throat. "Hey."

He was too tall. She had to tilt her head back to look at him, and it felt like a surrender, somehow . . . the way her body curved toward him like a flower in sunlight.

She was being pulled into his eyes. His pupils were dilated, pools of black within hazel.

"So should we play again, or—"

She and Hunter jerked their heads around at the same time, startling Caleb into silence.

For a moment the three of them were frozen in an awkward tableau. She and Hunter were just inches apart, connected by heat and electricity, and Caleb stood a few feet away with a bunch of darts in his hand.

"Why do you guys look so weird?"

Now there were three people jerking their heads around, this time to look at Stu, who'd just returned from the restroom.

Another moment went by, and then Caleb cleared his throat. "So I've had a great time tonight. I've laughed, I've played darts, I've drunk whiskey. That's carousing, right? Bachelor party mission accomplished. I think I'm going to call it a night."

"What are you talking about, man?" Stu protested. "It's not even midnight."

Caleb glanced meaningfully at Hunter and Airin. "I guess you and I could toss back a few more, but I think my brother has other plans."

Other plans? Meaning . . . her?

Oh no. No, no, no. She'd spent too much time already observing these males in their habitat. It was time to head back to her world.

She jumped to her feet. "I have to go," she said. A sudden wave of dizziness made her grab the back of her chair. "The three of you should"—she made a vague gesture with her free hand—"keep doing the bachelor party thing." She focused on Caleb. "I hope you have a wonderful wedding. Your Jane sounds like a lovely person."

She took her hand from the back of the chair, tested her balance, and decided she was okay to walk.

She pulled off her lei and handed it to Caleb. "For you," she said. "Congratulations." She smiled at all three men. "Thank you for letting me join you."

Then she turned and walked quickly away, pushing through the crowd toward the entrance, which suddenly seemed very far off.

She bumped into someone—an older woman swaying to the guitar music.

"Watch where you're going," the woman snapped.

"I'm so—"

She bumped into someone else.

"Damn it, lady."

"I—"

A big hand closed on her upper arm, and then Hunter was guiding her the rest of the way through the crowd to the door. He held it open for her, and the two of them stepped outside.

The air was cool and delicious. In spite of all the cars and tourists going by, it tasted of the ocean, which was just a few blocks away.

Airin took in a deep breath and let it out slowly.

"Thank you," she said to Hunter. "I'm sorry you had to rescue me so much tonight." She nodded toward the bar. "You should go back to your brother."

"Caleb will be okay for a few minutes. Why don't you let me walk you back to your hotel? I assume you're staying somewhere around here."

She imagined her mother spotting the two of them together, and the long, unpleasant discussion that would inevitably follow.

No. She'd go back to her room by reverse engineering the way she'd left it: skirting the dolphin enclosure, sneaking past the kitchens, and squeezing behind the dumpsters near the side door that led to the housekeeping staircase. From there, it was an easy journey to her suite.

But she didn't want Hunter to witness any of that. How in the world would she explain herself?

She shook her head. "I'll be fine. I know you don't have reason to believe it based on the hour we've known each other, but I'm not completely helpless."

Hunter looked down at her. They were standing to the left of the door, out of the way of the crowds, in their own little pocket of privacy.

"Okay," he said. "If you're sure." He paused. "It was nice to meet you, Airin."

She stared at him for a long moment. He was, without a doubt, the handsomest, sexiest man she was ever likely to meet.

She'd hit the jackpot on her first night of freedom.

"I'm never going to see you again, am I?" she asked, half to herself.

"Probably not. Strangers who bump into each other in Waikiki don't usually meet again, and in my case, the odds against it are even higher."

"Why is that?" she asked, intrigued.

He grinned. "In three days, I'm going into a sealed biosphere on the Big Island. I'll be living with seven other people in a simulated Mars habitat for eight months."

She stared at him.

It was obvious from his expression and tone that he didn't expect her to know what he was talking about—or even to believe him.

But she did know what he was talking about. And it made perfect sense.

He was an astronaut.

He was smart, decisive, in perfect physical condition, and a natural problem-solver. His background was probably military—fighter pilot, if she had to guess. Of course he was an astronaut.

I know all about the biosphere, she could say. *That's why my mother came here to Hawaii. She's meeting with the scientists who designed the Mars simulation project, because she runs a private aerospace company that contracts with NASA.*

But that was the kind of conversation you had at the beginning of a relationship or a friendship. And this wasn't the beginning of anything. Not for the two of them, anyway.

Timing really was everything.

Her fingers curled into her palms. Was there a chance she could make the timing work for her instead of against her? A chance that the very temporariness of this connection could give her the nerve to ask for something she wanted?

"So you're an astronaut," she said after a moment, reaching out to touch the faded NASA logo on his T-shirt.

He sucked in a breath. "Yeah." He covered her hand with his, trapping it against his chest.

She could feel the powerful beat of his heart, and her own pulse began to race.

"And you're going into a biosphere for eight months."

"Yeah."

She took her courage in both hands. "I wonder if you'd do me a favor. It would only take a few minutes."

"Sure. I already said I'd be happy to walk you back to your—"

"That's not it."

To the left of the bar there was a narrow alleyway. Airin pulled Hunter into it, leading him halfway down to a door she assumed led into the kitchen or back room of the bar they'd just left.

The alleyway was deserted. There were no lights, except for the ambient illumination from the streets on either end.

Perfect.

Hunter looked amused as he leaned back against the wooden door. "Okay, now you've dragged me into the shadows. Are you a spy? A beautiful assassin? A member of Hawaii Five-0?"

If only she were anything that interesting.

"No." She hesitated. "What if I told you that your first guess was right? That I'm an alien here to observe Earth?"

"Then I'd say your Blue Hawaii really did pack a wallop."

She plowed on. "If I were an alien . . . someone who was here for the first time . . . you wouldn't think it was weird if there were things I'd never experienced. I mean, of course it would be weird that I was an alien, but it wouldn't be weird if I'd never kissed someone before."

He stared at her, and she was very grateful for the shadows that hid her face. Her cheeks were probably bright red.

He put his hands on her shoulders. "Airin. I'm pretty sure you're under the influence of rum and blue curaçao, but let's forget that for a moment. What is it you want to ask me?"

It was harder to think clearly with his hands on her shoulders. And in the darkness, his face was more inscrutable. The lines of his cheekbones and jaw were harsher, more rugged.

More alien.

"I want—"

She stopped, took a deep breath, and started again.

"I want—"

A moment of silence, and then Hunter squeezed her shoulders.

"Spit it out, Airin. What do you want?"

"I want you to kiss me."

Chapter Three

The electric jolt in his chest traveled straight to his groin.

What was with all that alien stuff? Was it really possible Airin had never kissed anyone before? As in ever?

It couldn't be true. She was so goddamn beautiful. Her skin was like cream, and her hair was black silk. Those big soulful eyes were gazing up at him, and her expression was . . . doubtful? Wistful? Hopeful?

"You don't have to give me a reason to kiss you," he said gruffly, his pulse already in high gear. "I'm standing here looking at you."

She licked her lips, which drew his attention to her lush, beautiful mouth.

"But you'll need a reason for why I don't know what I'm doing. I'm twenty-four years old and I—" She swallowed. "I want . . . I need . . . I want you to show me what it's all about. I want to understand . . . to experience . . ." She trailed off.

Was this some kind of role-playing thing? Or was she really so inexperienced she was worried about what he'd think of her?

"Airin."

She shook her head, looking frustrated. "I'm sorry."

"Don't be sorry."

"You must think I'm some kind of freak. Do you want to say good night and walk away? Do you—"

His hands seemed to move of their own accord, sliding up from her shoulders to frame her face.

She stopped talking abruptly, her lips still parted.

Her skin really was as soft as it looked. It was so soft it felt like he shouldn't be touching it with his rough, calloused hands . . . and yet he never wanted to stop.

The bones of her face were so delicate. Her temples, her cheekbones, the lines of her jaw.

And that mouth. Soft and rose-pink, with a cupid's bow up top and a full, luscious lower lip begging to be kissed.

It was impossible to believe she hadn't been. Who was she, this mystery girl? What was her story?

"Maybe you are from another world," he murmured, his thumbs moving over her cheekbones.

Her eyes fluttered closed.

"I am," she whispered, tilting her head back a little. "And I'm doing research."

"Kissing research?"

"Kissing research." Her eyes opened. "You and I will never see each other again. Kiss me, Hunter. Show me what I've missed."

There might be reasons not to, but hell if he knew what they were . . . or cared.

But he couldn't give free rein to the heat firing his blood and making his pulse pound. He had to treat this moment as though Airin were telling the simple truth: that she'd never done this before.

"A kiss starts a long time before the actual mouth-on-mouth action," he said. His voice sounded a little rough, and he cleared his throat.

"It does?"

He nodded. "Remember in the bar, when we were looking at each other? You know what I'm talking about."

He was so tuned in to her he saw her pupils dilate.

"Yes," she said. "I know."

"That's when this kiss started. That's when I knew you wanted me."

Her lips parted, and he had to clamp down on the raw lust gripping him.

"And you?" she asked, her voice a whisper that went right to his groin. "Is that when you knew you wanted me, too?"

He let his hands settle on her shoulders again.

"No," he said. "I wanted you from the moment I saw you."

He felt her shiver. "You did?"

"Yeah. But that look we shared in the bar . . . that was when we both knew we wanted each other."

Her shoulders were as delicate as the bones of her face. His hands felt huge and clumsy as they gripped her, and he had to work to keep his touch gentle.

Then she moved a little closer to him, and he had to work harder.

"What happens after that? After two people know they want each other?"

She was only inches away. Every time he took a breath his senses were filled with her—the rich, intoxicating scent of the lei she'd worn, the faint spiciness of whatever shampoo she used, and the salty tang that came from the sheen of perspiration that made her skin glow.

"After that, I'll show you how revved up I am . . . and I'll get you revved up, too. So revved up you have to kiss me or explode."

Her hands rose and settled on his chest. "I feel that way now."

He could feel the warmth of her palms through the thin cotton of his T-shirt. The heat of her seeped through his skin to his very bones and the pounding heart beneath.

"You're not where I want you yet," he said.

Her eyes, just inches from his, looked enormous. A guy could lose himself in those eyes.

"How will you get me there?" she asked breathlessly.

He took hold of her wrists and moved her hands to his shoulders, which brought their bodies closer. Then he grabbed her hips and turned them 180 degrees, putting her back against the wooden door.

She gasped, and her grip on him tightened.

"I wasn't expecting that."

"I want you to feel surrounded," he told her, putting his hands on either side of her head.

"Surrounded by what?"

"Me."

He leaned in close, letting her feel the whole length of his body from his knees to his chest. When his erection brushed against her and then settled against her belly, she made a new sound . . . half breath, half moan.

He brought his mouth to her ear and spoke softly. "I don't want you to be able to think about anything but me. I want you shivering and quivering. I want your heart pounding. I want you wondering if I'll taste as good as I feel, and if I can make you feel better than you've ever felt before."

She was already quivering. And as he pressed even closer, he felt her nipples harden against his chest.

"Please," she said, her voice so faint he could hardly hear it.

Her ear was right there, and it was so damn tempting.

He caught her lobe in his teeth, and she gasped. He nibbled and licked and blew a cool breath over her damp skin. Then, as she let out a little squeaking breath, he dragged his mouth down her throat and pressed a kiss into the hollow above her collarbone.

Her head fell back to give him better access, and something in him responded to the surrender in that movement. He nipped the soft, delicate skin over her jugular, and when she gasped and shuddered, he pressed his lips against the place to feel the wild thrum of her pulse.

"Oh. Oh. Ohhhhhh . . ."

The raw honesty of her response made it seem possible this really was her first kiss. Logic said it couldn't be true . . . but it felt true.

It felt like he was the only man in the world who'd ever touched Airin this way.

He pulled back and stared at her. Her eyes were closed, her head thrown back, her lips parted.

He had a hundred other weapons in his arsenal to drive her wild before their mouths ever touched. But as he looked at her flushed, beautiful face, the last of his restraint went out the window.

He slid his hands into her hair and kissed her.

◆ ◆ ◆

Airin's whole world was reduced to one thing: Hunter's lips on hers.

Nothing had ever felt so good. But "good" didn't do this justice. Hot baths felt good. Massages felt good. Morphine felt good.

This was good and terrifying and overwhelming and electrifying, and she never, ever wanted it to end.

His lips teased hers open. Then his tongue was in her mouth, and oh God, it was glorious.

He tasted like the whiskey he'd been drinking and something else—something that made her feel hot and restless and wild.

She'd been afraid it was too late for her to have a first kiss. Who had a first kiss when they were twenty-four? You got to fumble around not knowing what you were doing when you were a teenager. At twenty-four, that kind of inexperience made you a freak.

But Hunter wasn't treating her like a freak. He was treating her like a woman—a woman he wanted.

She'd watched kissing scenes in movies as a form of research, hoping that when she finally got to kiss someone herself, she'd be able to act like she knew what to do. But with Hunter, she didn't need to act.

She didn't need to know anything. He was in charge, and all she had to do was go with it.

He pulled back just long enough to make her miss him. Then he was kissing her again, nipping at her lower lip and licking where he'd bit, and using his hands to change the angle of her head before diving in for another wet, carnal, oh-God-that-tongue encounter.

When he finally broke the kiss, she was panting and shivering, her blood leaping, and there was an aching throb between her legs.

She opened her eyes and stared at him. "How does anyone do anything but this, ever?"

His laugh sounded a little shaky. "That good, huh?"

"That was the best thing that ever happened to me."

He gazed down at her for a long moment. Then, as if he couldn't help himself, he reached out and traced the line of her lips with the knuckle of his index finger.

"I've kissed a lot of women in my time, and none of them ever said that."

"I bet they thought it, though."

He smiled. "Man, you're good for my ego." He paused. "I don't even know your last name. I know we said we'd never see each other again, which seemed to be a selling point for you, but . . . hell, why don't we at least exchange phone numbers? I'll be out of touch for a while, but once I'm free again I—"

"No."

She spoke sharply, and Hunter looked startled.

"Sorry. It's just, like you said . . . we're supposed to be two ships passing in the night."

He nodded slowly, but she could see the curiosity in his eyes.

"Okay, mystery woman." He cocked his head to the side. "Will you at least tell me where you live?"

Western Massachusetts, she started to say . . . but that might be too much information. A lot of people, especially people in the astronaut business, knew that her mother lived in splendid isolation in the Berkshires. He might put that together with her first name, which was a bit unusual. She hadn't been in the press much—certainly not like her mother had—but he still might figure out who she was.

"I'm from New England," she said.

"New England," he repeated, reaching out and twining a finger in a single lock of her hair. "Okay, that's something. At least I know you really are an earthling."

There was a melting feeling in the pit of her stomach. Her scalp was tingling, and she wished he'd go on touching her forever.

But it was getting late, and if she kept dragging this out she'd end up doing something stupid, like telling him exactly who she was and giving him her phone number. Then she could spend the next eight months wondering if he'd call her after he got out of the biosphere.

She remembered something her mother had said once. *The problem with being a woman is that the very men who attract us—the ones who are brave, daring, heroic—are also the men most likely to abandon us. Soldiers, aviators, astronauts.*

Her father had been an aviator. He hadn't exactly abandoned them, though. He'd been killed in action.

But maybe her mother thought of that as abandonment.

"Stay far away from heroes," Dira Delaney had concluded.

An unnecessary caution, Airin had thought at the time. It wasn't likely she'd ever meet such a man—at least not while her mother kept such a close watch on her.

And yet, here she was.

Hunter unwound that single strand from his finger, and she felt relieved and disappointed at the same time. But then he slid his whole hand into her hair, and the tingles in her scalp spread over her entire body.

A thousand pinpricks of pleasure.

She closed her eyes. "You should go," she whispered. "Your brother must be wondering where you are."

He slid his other hand into her hair. "I don't want to go," he said, his voice husky, and his words sent even more pleasure coursing through her.

She opened her eyes and smiled at him. "That's a nice thing to say. When I think back on tonight, I'll remember you saying it."

"I'll remember feeling it," he said.

There was a long, electric pause. Then, very deliberately, he let his hands drop to his sides as he stepped back.

"You're sure you don't want me to walk with you?"

"I'm sure."

She took a deep breath and ran her hands through her hair, trying to reassert ownership over herself after Hunter had planted his flag so thoroughly. Then she took a step, and another, until she'd reached minimum safe distance.

She started to turn away. "Thank you," she said over her shoulder. Then, without waiting for him to respond, she began walking toward the main road.

She didn't look back until the alley was two blocks behind her. But Hunter was the type who might follow her to make sure she got home safely, and she turned once to make sure he wasn't there.

There was no sign of him.

"Good," she said out loud.

But as she continued on to her hotel, she knew she'd been hoping for one more glimpse of his face.

Chapter Four

"It's a bad idea," her mother said.

"But I'm interested in the biosphere project. And I'd love a chance to see the volcanoes on the Big Island."

"I'll be too busy to look after you properly. You should stay here on Oahu." Dira took a sip of her espresso. "This is an excellent hotel, Airin. You haven't even tried the spa and wellness center yet. You know I don't go in much for that sort of thing, but I always keep an open mind toward innovation, and they do have a remarkable reputation. There's a Himalayan salt chamber and some other avant-garde treatments."

They were having breakfast together—coffee and a croissant for her mother, a ham-and-cheese omelet for her. Dira Delaney always insisted her daughter start the day with a high-protein breakfast, although she never followed that advice herself.

Airin had lain awake for hours the night before, reliving every minute of her time with Hunter. That was the reason for her request this morning.

Hawaii was a chain of eight islands, and the one they were on now—Oahu—was a forty-five-minute plane ride from the Big Island, where NASA and the University of Hawaii had built their Mars simulation center. The biosphere itself sat on the slopes of Mauna Loa, the world's largest volcano.

If she went with her mother to the Big Island, there was a chance she could see Hunter again. And even if she didn't get to see him, she'd still be closer to him. They were going into the biosphere in two days, right? If she went with her mother to meet the project engineers, there'd probably be video feed of the astronauts inside the habitat. She could observe Hunter, at least.

She paused with a bite of omelet halfway to her mouth.

Observe him?

Good Lord, what was happening to her? One kiss had turned her into a stalker.

"All right," she said, setting her fork back down on her plate. "I'll stay here."

Dira nodded briskly. "Good."

They were having their breakfast out on Airin's lanai. It was a beautiful morning, with a deep blue sky above them and the turquoise ocean below. The air was warm and soft, touched with the scent of flowers—bougainvillea and other plants she couldn't name.

The lanai was beautiful, too. The chairs were beige wicker with snow-white cushions, and their table was covered with crisp white linen, fine china, and silver. If there was trouble or misery anywhere in Hawaii, they were far from it, safe in the most elegant, rarefied bubble money could buy.

Dira Delaney looked as rarefied as her background. Her coal-black hair was cut in a no-nonsense bob, and though Airin knew she chose that style because it was easy to care for and she hated fussing with her appearance, the effect was one of untouchable elegance.

Airin had always accepted that her mother was a remarkable woman. After the death of her husband—naval aviator Frank Delaney—Dira had devoted her life to Frank's lifelong dream: sending a human being to Mars.

She'd started by putting her degrees in aeronautical engineering, electrical engineering, and applied physics to work. Partnering with two other scientists, she'd created an ultralight, extremely powerful rocket fuel that had the potential to revolutionize space travel. Her invention had other potential applications as well, including as a room-temperature superconductor that could transform energy production and storage here on Earth.

Her first patent, granted years before in the field of nanowire technology, had already put her on the map as an energy innovator. But the new rocket fuel was an even bigger breakthrough. It made Dira Delaney one of the wealthiest women in America, and it enabled her to start her own privately held company. DelAres was accountable to no one but her, leaving her free to pour money into her pet project: sending a manned mission to Mars.

A female Elon Musk.

That was what the *New York Times* had called her in their profile a few years back.

"They should call him the male Dira Delaney," her mother had muttered when she saw the story.

People who met Dira through work described her in many different ways. They said she was brilliant. Obsessed. A visionary. Ruthless. Airin was one of the only people in the world who had ever seen a different side of her. She'd seen a mother desperate about her daughter's heart condition, at times frantic, despairing, enraged, and, in the end, humbly grateful for the course Airin's treatment had taken.

Airin knew the deep well of feeling that lay behind her mother's very thick skin. But ever since the doctors had declared her last surgery to be a complete success—and Airin herself to be completely recovered—her mother's two sides had been merging into one. Airin was seeing more and more of the scientist and businesswoman and less and less of the mother.

At first, she'd thought Dira might be preparing herself emotionally to let her sheltered daughter finally experience the world. But over the course of the last few months, it had become clear that the opposite was true. Dira was still determined to protect her. This time, though, her desire was fueled by all her ruthless efficiency and unrelieved by any softer emotions.

Softer emotions.

For some reason, the phrase made her think of Hunter. As a sudden, overwhelming memory of their kiss in the alley flooded her, she gripped her fork hard enough to turn her knuckles white.

She took a deep breath and let it out slowly. Hunter was a guy she'd met at a bar. It was the kind of thing that happened to normal women all the time, and it had finally happened to her.

But normal women didn't make a single sensual experience the center of their lives.

What she was feeling now wasn't just about Hunter. It wasn't just about the romance she hadn't experienced in her twenty-four years.

It was about the *life* she hadn't experienced.

"I want to talk about grad school again," she said abruptly.

She'd attended college from home. Her mother had negotiated a special arrangement with MIT, and she'd earned her degree—a double major in biology and computer science—remotely. Dira insisted she could get a graduate degree the same way.

Maybe she could, if she wanted to pursue computer science. That was a field that lent itself to distance learning. Biology, though, had been much more challenging. And a field like medicine—which was at the top of her interest list right now—would be impossible to study remotely.

Her mother, of course, had different ideas about her future.

"Have you thought more about software engineering?"

Airin shook her head.

Her mother's lips tightened. "If you're still considering that absurd idea of becoming a doctor . . ."

"It's not absurd."

Dira used her crisp white linen napkin to wipe an invisible crumb from the corner of her mouth. Then she laid the napkin precisely in the center of her plate and rose to her feet.

"I don't care to have this conversation right now, Airin. I hope you enjoy yourself while I'm gone. I'm leaving Thomas here to . . ."

"Babysit me?"

Thomas was one of her mother's assistants, but he'd started out as a bodyguard. Dira trusted him implicitly. Airin did, too, but that didn't mean she wanted him dogging her movements like a Secret Service agent.

A single line appeared between her mother's arching brows. "Protect you. And, of course, assist you with anything you may need during my absence."

Of course.

She'd learned long ago to pick her battles, and this one didn't seem worth fighting right now.

"I hope you have a good trip, Mom."

Dira nodded. "Thank you. All indications suggest that I will."

Airin spent the morning researching medical schools online and the afternoon swimming in the ocean. The ubiquitous Thomas, a decent guy who probably wished he could do something more valuable with his time than chaperone his boss's daughter, was thankfully out of sight during both of those activities. She locked the door to her suite while she did her online research, and in the ocean she could feel alone even surrounded by people—including Thomas, who watched her like a private lifeguard as she dove and swam and floated in the Pacific.

She opted to go to bed early. Hours of sun and sea had left her deliciously tired, and between that and a really comfortable bed she expected to drop off within seconds of her head hitting the pillow. Her windows were all open, and a cool, salt-tinged breeze wafted through the room. It was a perfect night for sleeping.

But as she lay with her eyes closed and the covers up to her chin, she felt more and more awake with every passing moment.

Finally she gave up. She threw off the covers and rearranged her pillows, leaning back against them with her arms wrapped around her shins.

The windows showed a star-filled sky above a wine-dark sea. She stared out at the night with her chin on her knees, wondering where Hunter was right now.

Caleb's wedding had been that afternoon, she remembered. The reception would probably go on into the wee hours.

She bet they were having fun. All three of those guys had been fun, and Caleb was such a sweetheart she was sure the guests at his wedding would be the kind she'd want to spend time with.

The thought of laughing, happy people—normal people—celebrating a wedding made her feel wistful. Her mother didn't enjoy weddings and rarely attended them, and the last one Dira had gone to had been for DelAres's CFO. That had been two years ago, during a period when Airin had been hospitalized, and she hadn't been able to go. The pictures she'd seen afterward had made her wish she'd been there, if only so she could've reminded her mother to smile a little more often.

There'd been a time when Dira Delaney had smiled a lot. Before her husband was killed, before her mother passed away, before her daughter was diagnosed with a heart condition.

The day Airin experienced her first episode of tachycardia, Dira had been smiling like a sunrise. They all were. They were at Cape Canaveral to watch a NASA shuttle launch, and aviator Frank and engineer Dira were explaining the experience to their nine-year-old daughter. She hadn't really needed the information to appreciate the coolness of a rocket launch, but information had always been her parents' first language.

"The hardest part of a space journey is breaking away from Earth's gravity," Frank told her as they waited for the countdown to begin. "A craft leaving the surface of our planet needs to travel at seven miles per second, or nearly twenty-five thousand miles per hour, to reach escape velocity. It takes a lot of fuel to generate that kind of speed, and fuel is heavy. The more fuel, the more weight, and the more thrust it takes to lift. A catch-22 we'll need to solve if we really want to become a spacefaring species."

Dira was looking at the shuttle on the launch pad. "Those astronauts are sitting on eighty-eight tons of rocket fuel right now," she said. "It takes a special kind of crazy to do that."

"And a special kind of cool," Frank added, squeezing Airin's shoulders. "You think you've got enough crazy and enough cool to go into space, kiddo?"

"Yes," she said with complete confidence. She and her dad had decided long ago that she'd be the first human being to walk on Mars.

"The project I'm working on now could be a possible solution," Dira said, her thoughts turning to science. "If we can compress hydrogen to the point where it becomes a metal, it would conduct electricity even at low temperatures."

"But how could you turn a gas into a *metal*?" Airin asked.

Frank grinned. "Your mom will figure it out. She's an engineering badass."

Dira rolled her eyes at that, but she was smiling, too.

That smile was the last thing Airin remembered before her life changed forever.

It didn't seem like a big deal at first. Her heart began to beat faster—that was all. But then it was beating faster and faster and *faster*, until she was dizzy and gasping and terrified.

The worst part was seeing her terror reflected in her parents' faces before she finally blacked out.

A week later, they had a diagnosis and a treatment plan.

The diagnosis had been the easy part. Wolff-Parkinson-White, all the doctors agreed—also known as WPW syndrome.

In a normal heart, an electrical signal starts near the top and travels through a pathway across the entire muscle, causing it to squeeze and pump blood through the body. In a person with WPW, there's an abnormal extra pathway. If the electrical signal follows that pathway, the heart short-circuits and beats much faster than it should. This can cause dizziness, fainting, and in rare cases, sudden death.

Treatment, they were told, depended on the severity of the condition. Sometimes medicine could take care of the problem. They tried that first, and for a while it seemed like her condition was under control.

Until it wasn't anymore.

The next step was to try radiofrequency catheter ablation. That was a procedure where a surgeon threaded wires along her blood vessels, from her inner thigh all the way to her heart, to disconnect the extra pathway. They were told this was almost always effective . . . unless there was more than one abnormal pathway. Then the ablation had to be performed again.

And again.

By this point in her treatment, her father had stopped talking about her becoming an astronaut. He stopped talking about Mars, too. He spoke instead about heart-healthy diets, exercise, and physical therapy programs. Her mother made the decision to pull her out of school so they could better control her environment, monitor her condition, and respond to the ever-more-frequent episodes of tachycardia.

Being homeschooled was the first step toward an isolation that only grew worse after her father's death. She and her mother retreated into their own private worlds of misery, and when they emerged, the dynamic between them had changed. Dira's overriding mission now was to shelter and protect her daughter from anything that might harm her . . . which seemed to include the entire world.

Doctors continued to discover abnormal pathways in her heart, and her tachycardia grew more severe. Finally, it developed into atrial fibrillation. When her heart rate reached six hundred beats a minute during one episode—and after multiple ablations had failed to solve the problem—the decision was made to perform open-heart surgery.

During the months that led up to this procedure and the months after it, it felt like her mother controlled every molecule of air she breathed. Even after the doctors pronounced the surgery a complete success and her WPW syndrome completely cured, her mother had barely relented. It had taken a week of badgering to convince her to let Airin come to Hawaii.

This trip was her first true taste of freedom in years. And then last night, with Hunter . . .

No. If she started thinking about Hunter, she'd never get to sleep.

She slid back down in bed, curling up on her side and closing her eyes. Hunter was participating in a biosphere project. He wouldn't have any contact with the outside world for eight months. Thinking about him was an exercise in futility.

There was, however, a solution to her thinking-about-Hunter problem. She needed to sneak out again. She had to prove to herself that her encounter with Hunter wasn't the only interesting thing that would ever happen to her. Tomorrow night she'd make another expedition to Waikiki, and she might even try her hand at flirting.

But as she tried to imagine herself talking to another man, his eyes were always hazel. And when she finally drifted into sleep, it was Hunter she dreamed of.

Chapter Five

Caleb's wedding was like something out of a chick flick, designed to make men gag and women swoon. Jane was beautiful, the vows made Hunter tear up, and there was even a damn rainbow in the sky.

He loved every minute of it.

That had been yesterday. This morning, he'd driven Jane and Caleb to the airport. Now he was in Waikiki for one last hurrah, because tomorrow he was going inside a two-room Martian habitat for eight months, with seven other people for company.

Forty-eight hours ago he'd celebrated Caleb's last night of freedom. Tonight it was his turn.

People asked him all the time how he would handle living in isolation for so long, eating freeze-dried food and drinking recycled urine and only going outdoors in a Mars suit. The truth was, he looked forward to it.

Well, maybe not the recycled urine part. But the rest would be okay.

He wasn't claustrophobic. He could get along with just about anyone. And as long as he had a mission to focus on, one that was a stepping stone to his goal of walking on Mars, he could put up with anything.

What he couldn't handle was being aimless. He couldn't take being a useless no-load with nothing to work toward. Going to Mars was the kind of goal he could sink his teeth into, and being part of the first manned mission would be worth any sacrifice.

Humanity's future lay in space exploration. And to be there at the beginning of that journey was all he'd ever wanted.

Even so, spending eight months in a sealed biosphere was a hell of a thing. He deserved to give himself a sendoff. So here he was in Waikiki, footloose and fancy-free and ready to make the most of the next several hours.

He couldn't go *too* crazy, of course. The helicopter taking him to the Big Island was leaving at six o'clock in the morning. He'd given himself a midnight curfew and a one-drink limit, but that didn't mean he couldn't enjoy himself.

Caleb and Jane were on their honeymoon. Stu was off God knew where with a girl he'd met at the wedding. There were a few other people on Oahu he could have partied with, but since both solitude and strangers would be in short supply for the next eight months, he decided to go out on his own.

He parked in the Halekulani garage and started walking. He didn't have a particular destination in mind; he just wanted to people watch and take in the sights.

After a while, he recognized the block he was on. This was where he and Caleb and Stu had ended up two nights ago. Another few minutes brought him to Leilani's, the bar where he'd met—

Airin.

He stopped short in front of the window. There she was, sitting on the same bar stool, having an animated discussion with the bartender.

She was dressed very differently tonight. It looked like she'd gone shopping in her hotel's boutique for resort wear or island wear or whatever they called it. She was wearing a gauzy floral dress with spaghetti straps and no back, and when he realized that probably meant she was wearing no bra, something happened in his body.

Shit. He'd been telling himself to stop thinking about Airin for forty-eight hours now, and he hadn't had much success until this afternoon, when thoughts about his upcoming mission had finally taken their rightful place at the forefront of his brain. And now here she was in that dress.

He swallowed hard. Blood was rushing to his groin, and every nerve ending in his body was on fire. Why the hell had he come back here? Why had *she* come back here?

The only thing to do was turn his ass around and go somewhere else. Anywhere else. A last night of freedom before an eight-month mission was one thing, but going inside that bar and talking to that woman was something else.

If he got pulled into her like he had two nights ago, it wouldn't be good for his state of mind. What you wanted before a mission was a palate cleanser. A pleasant and forgettable distraction.

There was nothing forgettable about Airin. His mystery woman had managed to get under his skin with one kiss, and spending time with her tonight was the last thing he should do.

So why wasn't he turning around? Why was he still standing here, staring through the window like a lovesick teenager?

Danger, Will Robinson.

Airin leaned forward to say something to Kaleo, and a lock of that satiny black hair fell forward across her face. She lifted a hand and tucked the strand behind her ear, and everything about that one simple movement mesmerized him.

Her unconscious sensuality went straight to his cock. He remembered the way she'd responded to him two nights ago, as though their kiss really had been her first.

He still wasn't sure that was the truth. But standing here staring at her, unable to make his feet take him in the other direction, he knew he wanted her next kiss to come from him, too.

Bad idea. Terrible idea. Get the hell out of here.

But he would never know how that internal struggle might have played out. Because at that moment, something made Airin turn her head. She saw him, and her face lit up, and the sight went straight to another part of his body.

His heart.

She wasn't even trying to play it cool. She was surprised and happy to see him, and both emotions showed on her face. And even though the smart move might still be to turn around and walk away, he just didn't have it in him to do that.

He went to the door and pushed it open.

Airin swiveled on her stool to face him, her back to the bar, as he closed the distance between them.

Now that he was seeing her up close instead of through a window, he became fully aware of how much of a mistake this was.

It was funny. All day yesterday, thinking about Airin even when he tried not to, he'd had trouble remembering exactly what she looked like. Even though he'd spent so much time staring at her—he hoped she hadn't realized how much—what he'd been left with was more an impression than a memory: black hair, brown eyes, lush body.

What he did remember was what it felt like to look at her, to talk to her . . . and to kiss her. The feeling had been soft and electric at the same time, and it was like nothing else he'd ever experienced.

Now he was feeling it again.

"Hunter!" Airin said, surprise and delight in her eyes and her smile.

"Hey," he said, sliding his hands into the pockets of his jeans to stifle the ridiculous impulse to touch her hair or cup the side of her face.

"I thought you'd be on the Big Island by now. Don't you go into the biosphere tomorrow?"

"Yeah. I'm taking a helicopter over in the morning. We leave at six a.m."

"Oh."

Neither of them said anything for a minute after that. They just looked at each other, her sitting on the bar stool and him standing a foot away.

Her eyes were like polished teak, the kind you found on really beautiful boats. Or like chestnuts or chocolate or cinnamon.

He'd never felt such a pull toward another human being. The urge to touch her, to take her hand, was like the urge to drink when he was thirsty.

What the hell was going on? Was this some kind of reaction to the mission tomorrow? Some kind of internal rebellion, a need for distraction?

He was a guy who liked sex, after all. And while it wasn't explicitly forbidden in the biosphere—there were two married couples participating in the project, and he was pretty sure they'd be getting it on at some point—the idea of starting a relationship under those circumstances seemed nuts. Hunter fully expected to be celibate for the next eight months.

Maybe that's what this was. His libido, annoyed at the prospect of a long abstinence, was making itself felt in a big way.

But what an object for his desire. If Airin had been telling the truth two nights ago, she was a virgin. If you wanted a wild last night of debauchery before a long haul of celibacy, a virgin was the very last sexual partner you'd pick.

"I'm sorry," Airin said suddenly, reminding him of how much he liked her voice. It was low and sweet, the kind of voice he'd never get sick of hearing.

"Sorry for what?"

"For just sitting here staring at you. You must think I'm very strange. The truth is, I've been thinking about you for two days even though I tried not to. And just now, seeing you through the window, I felt like I finally understood why women make such stupid decisions when it comes to men."

He stepped in closer, parking himself between her stool and the one beside it and leaning against the bar. She swiveled a quarter turn and tipped her face up to meet his eyes.

"What do you mean?" he asked. "What kind of stupid decisions?"

She shrugged, and the movement made him aware that she was, indeed, going braless under that dress.

"My mother works with someone whose daughter got into Princeton. I met her a few times, and she seemed so smart and so excited about her future. But then, a week before her first day of classes, she decided to run off with some guy to Arizona. I thought she was crazy. Absolutely nuts. I couldn't understand why she would do such a thing." She smiled at him. "But if you asked me to run off with you to Arizona, I might do it. And I don't even know you."

Normally if a woman said something like that—especially a woman who was a virtual stranger—all his warning bells would go off and he would run, not walk, in the opposite direction. But hearing Airin say it didn't scare him.

Although, come to think of it, that fact should have scared him even more.

She frowned a little. "I don't mean I'm hoping you'll ask me to run away with you to Arizona," she said. "That would, of course, be insane."

"Of course," he echoed, and then, unable to resist any longer, he reached out and slid a hand into her hair.

He knew right away he'd made a huge mistake.

God, it's so soft.

And then it got worse. Because Airin closed her eyes and leaned into his caress, and he saw her nipples harden beneath the thin material of her dress.

Shit.

She opened her eyes. "I can see it now," she said, her voice a little breathless. "I can see why a woman would give up anything to have this feeling. It's extraordinary. Although," she added thoughtfully, "I have to remember it's extraordinary for me because I've never experienced it before. I mean, I assume you're not feeling anything unusual. You're not, are you? Feeling anything you haven't felt before?"

If she were another woman, he would have suspected her of fishing for compliments. But that didn't seem Airin's style, somehow. She was just looking for information. That's what was so unusual about her: the combination of an instinctive sensuality with a scientific approach to the world.

Just the way he'd expect an alien anthropologist to act.

In a sexy sci-fi movie, anyway.

He pulled his hand from the silken waves of her hair and slid it back into his pocket.

"Where are you from?" he asked, partly to avoid answering her question and partly because he really wanted to know. "What do you do? Are you a student? A scientist? A musician? What?"

She tilted her head to the side. "Does this mean we're going to talk instead of kiss? Because, to be absolutely honest, I really, really want to kiss you again."

Jesus.

He swallowed. "Right back at you, angel. But here's the thing. I've got a pretty big day tomorrow, as you know, and I don't want to go too wild. I'm not saying kissing is totally off the table, you understand. But I think it'll be best for both of us if we pace ourselves. So how about we start by talking and see where things go?"

In his experience, wanting to have a conversation with a woman was usually a selling point. It often led to the bedroom part of the evening being even hotter.

But Airin actually looked disappointed.

"I guess we could do that," she said slowly. "But I don't really like to talk about myself. If there are some questions I don't want to answer, will that be all right?"

"Sure," he said, wondering if this was a new psychological warfare thing women had figured out. A way to intrigue a man to the point of fascination.

Because he was fucking fascinated.

Airin glanced over his shoulder. "He left," she said.

"Who left?"

"The man who was sitting behind you. You can sit down, if you want. Then we could do the talking thing. Especially if I can ask you more questions than you ask me."

He thought for a moment.

"Tell you what," he said. "I set myself a one-drink limit for tonight, and I'd like to save that for later. How about we stroll around town for a while and then sit down for a drink?" He nodded toward the glass in front of her, which was empty. "It's good timing for a break, since you just finished one."

In answer, Airin slid off her bar stool. She stumbled a little when her feet hit the ground, and he caught her by the upper arm, and then it was like two nights ago but worse. A hundred times worse.

She put her palms flat against his chest and met his eyes. She wasn't looking as far up tonight, which meant she was wearing heels. Maybe that was why she'd stumbled.

He still had a hand on her upper arm, and his other hand, without his even realizing it, had gone to her hip. As they stood staring at each other, Airin's hands curled into the material of his T-shirt.

"Jesus," he said, not even realizing he'd spoken out loud until Airin's eyes widened.

"You feel it, too?"

What use was there in pretending?

"Yeah, I feel it. Let's get moving before I do something about it."

"But I want to do something about it. I want to—"

"Talk," he said firmly, stepping back. "We're just going to talk. At least for the next hour or so," he amended.

Airin nodded reluctantly. "All right."

"Can I tell you something?" he asked as the two of them left the bar and joined the throngs of tourists and locals out on the sidewalk. Figuring the crowds made it sort of necessary, he reached for Airin's hand and held it firmly.

"Yes," she said. "You can tell me something."

At the next crosswalk he took a left onto a less crowded street, but he kept hold of her hand.

"Women usually like a man who wants to talk. They think it means he wants more than sex."

"It's not that I object to talking," she said, pausing at a lei stand. "I just want to kiss you so much it's hard to focus on anything else."

He wished she would stop staying shit like that. How was a guy supposed to hang on to his self-control under these circumstances?

"Do you want a lei?" he asked, wincing at the unintended double entendre.

She shook her head. "I just wanted to smell them. I'm in love with plumeria," she added as they started walking again. "That's the lei I was wearing when we met."

He doubted he'd ever forget the scent. "Yeah, that was nice."

For a moment they walked in silence. There were more boutiques on this street than restaurants or bars, and most of them were closed for the night. It was quieter and less crowded here.

"I thought you wanted to talk," Airin said finally. "May I start by asking you some questions?"

He smiled at the hint of formality. "Sure."

"What made you want to do this biosphere project? What would make you willing to give up your freedom for eight months?"

He glanced down at her. "That's a big question."

"I don't have anywhere else to be."

"Fair enough. Okay. Well, I don't love the idea of going into a sealed environment with seven other people as my only company. But

I do love the idea of going to Mars—or at least furthering the research that will get someone to Mars—and I'm willing to make sacrifices to achieve that goal."

Airin was quiet, and after a moment he looked down at her again. Her expression was thoughtful.

"You look like you're mulling something over," he said. "What is it?"

"I was thinking that you remind me of my mother," she said. "She's a very, um, driven person. And she would sacrifice anything to achieve her goals."

That intrigued him. "Including you?"

She looked up at him, startled. "Oh, no. In fact, there have been several times I got in the way of a project. She put me first every time."

"What does your mother—"

"I have another question," she said quickly. "Why do you care so much about getting to Mars?"

He shook his head. "That one would take a lifetime to answer."

"Well, make a start, anyway. What's wrong with Earth?"

"Nothing at all. But there wasn't anything wrong with dry land when explorers went out to sea. There wasn't anything wrong with the valleys when people decided to climb mountains. Exploring is part of who we are."

Airin was quiet again. Then, after a moment, she spoke.

"May I make an observation?"

He really got a kick out of the way she talked. "Go for it."

"That's kind of a philosophical explanation for wanting to go to Mars."

"Yeah?"

She hesitated. "I hope this doesn't sound rude," she began.

"Won't know till you try."

"Well . . . it's just that you don't seem like a very philosophical person to me." She went on in a rush. "I don't mean you're stupid or selfish or not very deep or anything like that. But you seem like someone who would have to have a personal reason for doing something. I mean, did you want to be an astronaut when you were younger?"

"For as long as I can remember."

"Well, what made you want to travel into space back then?"

People didn't usually press him after his first answer to this question, which of course he got all the damn time. Why would you subject yourself to years of isolation and confinement and all the untold dangers of a Mars mission?

For the good of humanity was a true answer, as well as one he believed in, and it usually satisfied anyone who asked him why he wanted to go into space.

But it was his last night of freedom, and he was with a beautiful, mysterious, completely adorable woman. Maybe if he opened up a little he could get her to do the same.

"We're heading *makai*," he said, shifting his hand to thread their fingers together. "What do you say we keep going and walk along the beach? I'll tell you all about my childhood dreams of space travel then."

"That sounds lovely. I don't think I've ever been on the beach at night." She paused. "*Makai.* Is that Hawaiian for 'south'?"

"Not exactly. It means 'toward the ocean.' *Mauka* is the other word you'll hear; that means 'inland.' It makes sense, if you think about it. Seaward and inland are more useful points of reference on an island than north, south, east, and west."

"I like that," Airin said. "I mean, it's really interesting, don't you think? I wonder if that correlates with any differences in the way Hawaiians conceive of space and geography. It's such a different scheme from the four points of the compass and latitude and longitude, which lead to a kind of grid thinking, right? Whereas conceiving of directions as going *in* toward the center of the island or *out* toward the sea might lead to a different orientation."

There she went, thinking like a scientist again. She'd fit right in at NASA.

He almost stopped walking as a thought occurred to him. Was it possible she *did* fit in at NASA? Could she be one of their scientists?

No, that didn't make sense. During the last year he'd met everyone who worked in the Hawaiian field offices, and if there'd been a new hire—especially a hire like this woman—he'd have heard about it. And why would she hide a NASA job, especially once she'd learned who he was?

Whatever her mystery was, it wasn't that.

He refocused on their conversation.

"I suppose that's possible. I'm used to thinking of direction and space differently than other people do, from training as a pilot. You have to deal with an extra dimension. On land you can go forward or backward, left or right, but up and down aren't really an option. It's different when you're flying."

"Like being in free fall," she said as they reached the end of the street and made their way down the sandy path that led to the beach. "Or in the water," she added, looking out at the moon-silvered ocean.

"Yeah."

The path came to an end, and rippling sand lay before them. This part of the beach was well lit, close as it was to the hotels and nightlife of Waikiki, but out toward the ocean it was much darker.

He looked down at Airin's feet. The high heels she wore—white leather sandals—looked brand-new. She hadn't given any indication of it, but he wondered if they were hurting her.

"Do you want—"

"Yes," she said, smiling up at him. "I do want."

She let go of his hand and bent down to undo the straps. A moment later and three inches shorter, she straightened up again with her shoes in one hand.

They started forward. He'd kicked off his flip-flops, too, and the soft sand felt great on his bare feet.

Sand always felt better at night. But then, everything did.

When they reached the water's edge, he pointed up at the sky.

"That's why," he said.

Airin followed his gaze. "That's why what?"

He took off his jacket and laid it down on the sand. "Care to sit, my lady?"

She did, and he dropped down beside her.

"But now you're getting all sandy," she objected. "There's room on your jacket for both of us."

"I'm happy to get sandy. I'm going into a biosphere for a year. The messier I can get tonight, the better."

More unintended innuendo, but Airin didn't react to it. Instead, she leaned against him as they watched the gentle lapping of waves on the shore. The moon made a path of silver toward the horizon, and he remembered the first time he'd ever seen that phenomenon. It had been on a lake, not an ocean, but the effect on his imagination had been the same.

He'd wanted to run along that path until he could leap off the edge of the earth.

"You pointed at the sky and said, 'That's why,'" she reminded him. "That's why what?"

With his jacket off, the bare skin of his arm was against the bare skin of hers.

"That's why I wanted to be an astronaut," he said. "Because of the way I felt every time I looked up at the night sky."

"You wanted to be up there?"

"Yeah. To be honest, I don't understand how anyone can look up and not feel that way. Don't you want to see what's out there? To experience being in space? To stand on another planet? To explore?"

Airin was quiet for a moment. In the silence, the sound of the ocean was like music.

"My father loved the idea of space travel," she said finally. "He used to tell me bedtime stories about a little girl who stowed away on a rocket ship and went to Mars."

He chuckled. "Sounds like the kind of stories I'd tell if I was a parent. But your dad didn't inspire you in that direction? You never wanted to be an astronaut yourself?"

"I actually did, for a while. But my mother . . ."

She trailed off.

"Your mother what?" he prompted after a moment.

"Nothing. Tell me about your parents. They must be so proud of you."

He wondered if he'd ever reach a point where a question about his parents didn't feel like a gut punch.

"Not exactly," he said. "What do you say we rule our parents out of bounds for tonight?"

There was a short silence. Then: "With pleasure."

Chapter Six

Airin had found Hunter's bio online yesterday. First in his class at the Air Force Academy, fighter pilot, joined NASA three years ago. Nothing about his family or childhood, although some of the other astronaut bios had been more personal.

Now he'd cut off conversation about his parents. So she wasn't the only one with topics she'd rather avoid.

Well, that was fair enough. It wasn't like they were going to become friends or anything. He was about to go into a sealed biosphere for eight months. And he was an astronaut. After the Mars simulation ended, all his time and energy would be focused on getting into space.

The two of them had tonight, and that was all.

A wave of sadness went through her. She was out on her own for the first time in her life, sitting on a beach in Hawaii with a man who made her bones turn to water, and it was as though the universe were dangling things in front of her she could never have.

Hunter would never know her secrets, and she would never know his. They would never grow close, never become friends, never—

He shifted beside her, putting an arm around her shoulders as they looked out at the ocean.

She closed her eyes.

His arm was heavy. Her mother put an arm around her sometimes, and her favorite nurse from the old days used to as well. They were both small women, and their arms had felt light.

The weight of Hunter's arm made her cognizant of the size of him. It made her think of dense bone and heavy bands of muscle and a kind of physical capability that was fundamentally different from her own. It made her imagine him in bed, that big body over hers, overwhelming her.

Her heart was pounding in her chest. She remembered her surgery a year and a half ago and the doctor saying after her last follow-up appointment, "You're completely recovered. No restrictions. You can do anything anyone else can do."

Tell that to my mother, she'd thought at the time.

But maybe it wasn't her mother who was holding her back. Maybe she was holding herself back.

Because right now, with the heavy promise of masculinity beside her, the weight of it palpable, she didn't know if she was feeling excitement or fear.

But what was there to be afraid of? She didn't have to worry about making a fool of herself or not knowing what she was doing. It hadn't mattered two nights ago, had it? And after tonight, she'd never see Hunter again.

Right. She'd never see him again. A moment ago that had seemed a terrible negative, but maybe, like two nights ago, she could view it as a positive.

Her heart was beating so hard and so fast the vibrations seemed to reverberate through her whole body.

Your heart is as strong as anyone else's, the doctor had said. *Maybe stronger, since you've done so much work in the exercise room.*

All the times she'd repeated those words to her mother, she'd believed them. But now that she was saying them to herself, suddenly she wasn't so sure.

Stay strong, heart. You've been through a lot, but I need you now, okay?

Hunter's hand began to move against her bare skin. It was a small and subtle movement, a caress that made goose bumps spring up everywhere.

"Airin?"

"Yes?"

"Was our kiss that night really your first?"

"Yes."

He took his arm from her shoulders, and she felt forlorn. But then he shifted, turning to face her, and she turned to face him.

"How can that be?" he asked. "I mean, damn. I'm sitting here looking at you, and you're one of the sexiest women I've ever seen in my life."

His words sent a thrill through her. But what could she tell him? Not the whole truth—if she told him who she was, the focus would all be on Dira Delaney. He was an astronaut, after all, and Dira was a rock star in the aeronautical world.

But she could tell him part of the truth.

"I had some medical issues growing up. They're solved now, but I had a really sheltered childhood, and it's been hard to break out of that." She took a breath. "I wondered so many times if it was too late to have a first kiss. If it would ever happen. And then, with you . . ."

His eyes, already dark in the moonlight, seemed to grow darker.

"Yeah," he said. "That was a pretty good kiss."

All she could do was nod.

He leaned in closer. "Hey, Airin?"

"Yes?" she whispered.

"I'm going to kiss you again."

He was so close she could smell the clean male scent of him, and it went to her head like wine.

"You are?"

"I am."

"Well, I think—"

And then his arms were around her and his lips were on hers and her breasts were crushed against his chest, and she was so, so glad she wasn't wearing a bra, because it was one less layer between them.

Before she knew what was happening, his weight, that glorious masculine weight, was bearing her down until she was on her back and he was above her, kissing her, his tongue in her mouth and his hands in her hair and oh God, it was more perfect than she could have imagined.

Everything in her yearned to open to him. Her mouth, her heart, her body. His kiss was deep and then deeper, wet and electric and so, so carnal.

Carnal.

The scrape of his teeth against her lips. The scrape of his stubble on her skin. The way his tongue stroked and teased and assaulted and soothed.

Open. Open.

Everything he was doing demanded that of her.

Open your mouth. Open your body.

She wanted to. She needed to.

And then, responding to the most primitive urge that had ever swept through her, she parted her legs.

That one movement changed everything.

Hunter made a low, rumbling, growling sound that was like nothing she'd ever heard. And then his weight shifted, taking immediate advantage of the opening she'd given him, and his lower body sank into the cradle she'd created.

Her whole being responded with a primal *yes*.

Her dress was rucked up around her waist, and only Hunter's jeans and her cotton panties separated them. But more important than clothing or anything else was the sensation that had become the center of her universe. The long, thick, rigid erection pressing against her.

Hunter broke their kiss and rested his forehead on hers.

Now that they weren't kissing, there was nothing to distract her from what was happening below her waist, and all she could think about was how to get him closer.

She wrapped her legs around his hips, and he made the growling sound again. And then he was moving, pressing hard against her center and pulling away, pressing hard and pulling away, in a motion that made her feel desperate and frantic and helpless and feverish all at the same time.

The friction. The pressure. The . . .

Oh God.

When she froze, Hunter did, too.

He pulled back and looked down at her, his dark eyes wild.

"Am I hurting you?"

She stared up at him, panting.

"I just . . . I just . . ."

"What?"

"My panties are wet. Soaking wet. I—"

Hunter closed his eyes. "Airin."

"What?"

"I didn't think I could get any harder. Jesus fucking Christ, I think you're trying to kill me."

"I want you so much," she whispered. "I didn't know it was possible to want anything this much."

He opened his eyes again, and his expression was equal parts lust and tenderness. "I know the feeling. I want you so much right now I'm fucking wrecked."

He leaned in and pressed a quick, hard kiss to her lips. Then he rolled away, surged to his feet, and reached down to help her up.

She felt weak and shaky. "What's happening?"

"Nothing. Not one goddamn thing, for about a hundred different reasons. Not the least of which being that we're on a public beach."

She was leaning against him so she didn't fall, her hands fisted in the material of his T-shirt. Now she looked around, and there were, indeed, other people on the beach. There was a couple walking hand in hand toward them, another couple kissing by the water's edge twenty yards away, a few people in the water enjoying a night swim.

They were in public. And she'd been lying on her back with her dress up around her waist, her panties soaking wet, writhing like an animal in heat.

"Oh my God."

"Yeah."

"Hunter, I'm so sorry."

He grinned at her. "For what? I was the one who started all that craziness. I was the one ready to do you on a beach."

She still felt shaky. But there was something else she still felt, too.

Desire.

She gripped his T-shirt harder. "Hunter."

"Yeah?"

"Is there somewhere we can go that's not a beach?"

He stared at her. "Airin—"

"I want you," she said, the words tumbling out. "I know we're never going to see each other again. I don't care. I want you. I want—"

"Airin."

He was going to say no. Of course. She was out of her mind, and he recognized that, and he was going to save her from herself. Or something.

"How far away is your hotel?" he asked gruffly.

He wanted her, too.

"Not my hotel."

"Why not?"

This was definitely not the time to explain about Thomas.

"Family stuff." Her head was spinning, her heart thudding against her ribs. "Let's go to your hotel."

"Angel, nothing would make me happier. But I'm not staying in a hotel. I've got a place in Kailua."

"Kailua?"

"It's sixteen miles away. Half an hour by car."

That desperate, feverish feeling between her legs was only getting more intense. She wanted to twine herself around him like a vine around a tree.

"Let's go. Do you have a car? Do we need to get a taxi or an Uber or—"

"Airin."

"What?"

Her hands were still against his chest, and she felt his rib cage expand with a deep breath.

"I am more than willing to take you to my place in Kailua. But I drive a Mustang convertible, and you'll be feeling the cool breeze on your face as we cross the mountains, and there's a chance that you'll come to your senses between here and there."

What was he saying?

"I—"

He covered her hands with his. "Airin, if you want me, I'm yours. Just for one night, but I'm yours. I won't change my mind. But if you change yours, that's one hundred percent okay. I just want you to know that."

A sudden wild affection swept through her.

"Deal."

◆ ◆ ◆

Hunter had told her he wouldn't change his mind, but as he drove the most beautiful woman he'd ever met along the winding, climbing Pali Highway, he wondered if he'd *lost* his mind.

He was doing everything he'd told himself he wouldn't do. He was going to be a virgin's first time, and he was going to do it the night before he went into the biosphere.

But every time he questioned his sanity, he looked over at Airin in the passenger seat and knew it wouldn't make a damn bit of difference.

This would be his last chance for a long time to make a crazy decision, and he couldn't think of one he'd rather make.

They'd driven the last few minutes in silence. Pali Highway was spectacular even at night, with the dense, lush forest scenting the air, and he wondered what Airin was thinking.

"Talk to me," he said after another minute. "You've gotten kind of quiet. Are you experiencing a wave of regret, or are you enjoying the drive?"

Airin turned to look at him, and even though it was nighttime he could tell her smile was radiant. "I'm enjoying the drive. It's so beautiful up here in the mountains. I almost wish it was daylight. It smells like heaven." She paused. "What about you? Are you having second thoughts?"

"Not a one. But I like the sound of your voice, and I want to keep hearing it. Tell me something."

"What should I say?"

"Anything you want. Tell me about yourself. Not the things you don't want to talk about," he added, downshifting as the road climbed higher.

The air was getting cooler. Beside him, Airin tilted her head back and let the wind blow her hair. It flowed behind her like a black silk banner.

"My favorite movie is *Rear Window*," she said. "What's yours?"

"*Mad Max*."

"Seriously?"

He grinned. "Yeah. Ever seen it?"

"Yes. I hated it."

"Well, I hated *Rear Window*. I thought it was boring. I mean, the whole damn thing happens in that guy's apartment."

Highway 61 wasn't well lit, and he slowed down before taking a curve.

"Let's keep going," he said. "I bet there are a ton of other things we don't have in common. What's your favorite music?"

"Bach. You?"

"Metallica."

Airin laughed, and the sound went to his head like whiskey.

His groin, which had calmed down a little since the raging inferno on the beach, was rising to attention again.

"What do you fantasize about?" he heard himself asking.

Shit. Did I ask that out loud?

There was a short silence.

"You mean like . . . sexual fantasies?"

"Yeah," he said, his voice sounding husky.

"Well. That's a pretty dramatic change of subject."

"We can go back to music if you want. But all I can think about right now is making love to you, and I guess it's coming out in my conversation."

There was another silence, and then she put her hand on his thigh.

"It's all I can think about, too."

If she was going to touch him so close to his hard-on, he needed to slow down and focus on the road.

He pulled his foot off the gas a little. "For a woman who's never had sex before, you know exactly how to turn me on."

"I do?"

She sounded delighted.

"Yeah. So tell me, Airin. Does a woman who's never had sex fantasize about it? Do you ever think about it late at night when you can't sleep?"

Her hand squeezed his thigh, and he slowed down even more. He was damned if he'd get into an accident on this winding road before he had a chance to make love to this woman.

"I do think about it sometimes," she said. "And . . ." She paused. "Can I tell you something I always thought I'd be too embarrassed ever to tell anyone?"

"Hell yes. If you can't tell stuff like that to your soon-to-be one-night stand, who can you tell?"

They'd had the highway to themselves for the last several minutes, but now he saw the flash of headlights in his rearview mirror. They came up pretty quickly, which meant the driver wasn't going to be thrilled that he was taking it slow. On a one-lane highway, his only option was to pull over so the guy could pass, and he started looking for a place to do just that.

"I read erotica. While I, um, masturbate."

Holy hell. He was harder than a fucking diamond right now.

"Yeah?"

"Yes. But I haven't . . . it doesn't . . . that is, it's never worked."

The glare of the headlights was right behind him now. Where was a spot to pull over? He needed to focus 100 percent on Airin.

"What do you mean, it's never worked?"

"I've never been able to make myself . . ."

"Come?"

"Yes. I mean, I've tried. Believe me, I've tried. I've read sexy stories and touched myself and thought about things, but I've never . . ."

The fucking asshole behind him honked.

Okay, fine. There wasn't a place to pull over, exactly, but he'd squeeze as far as he could to the side of the road and wave the guy past.

He put on his blinker and started to slow down, but just as he began to move to the right, another pair of headlights flashed—coming toward them this time.

The guy behind him honked again.

"Hold your horses, asshole," Hunter muttered under his breath. "Let me pull over while this other guy goes by, and then you can—"

The disaster happened so fast he barely had time to react.

The car behind him pulled out and tried to pass before the other car reached them. But he miscalculated, badly, and the two vehicles slammed into each other.

In the split second before the squeal of brakes and the crunch of metal and Airin's scream, all Hunter could do was hit his own brakes and pray.

Chapter Seven

Hunter didn't lose consciousness, but he had a pretty hard head.

Airin wasn't so lucky.

The two other vehicles took the brunt of the damage. He and Airin might have been out of it completely if one of the cars hadn't spun into them, forcing them off the road and into a tree.

Once the dust settled, Hunter ripped off his seat belt and crouched over Airin.

Their airbags hadn't deployed. Except for bruises from his seat belt, he wasn't hurt at all. The impact had all been on Airin's side of the car.

She was out cold.

He had to call on every bit of his discipline not to panic. He moved his hands gently over her arms and legs, looking for broken bones. He didn't find any. But the passenger-side door was crumpled up pretty good, and there was a cut on Airin's temple.

Her breathing was labored, but her pulse was steady. The heartbeat was a good sign, but he knew how dangerous head wounds could be, and he knew there might be internal injuries he couldn't detect. He pulled his phone from his pocket and dialed 911, his movements and his voice so calm it felt like he was two different people.

"Are you okay? Fuck, are you okay?"

It was one of the other drivers, stumbling out of his own car and hanging on to Hunter's door.

"I'm fine. I've called the ambulance and the police. Go check on the other car."

He should probably do the same—the other vehicle looked to have taken the worst of the crash, and he couldn't detect any movement in the front seat. But he couldn't make himself let go of Airin's hand after he'd pressed his fingers to her wrist to take her pulse, and he knew he wouldn't leave her side until the ambulance came.

◆ ◆ ◆

Twenty minutes later, Airin was strapped to a stretcher and Hunter was riding beside her.

"Take us to Kamehameha Medical Center," he told the driver.

"Whitney Hospital is closer."

"Only by five minutes. Take us to Kamehameha."

He'd told the paramedics he was Airin's brother, but that wouldn't fly at a hospital. The only place he had a shot at staying with her was Kamehameha, where the wife of a fellow astronaut worked in the ER. Dr. Sue Jackson would vouch for him and let him stay with Airin.

He hoped.

Because here was the kicker: he had no fucking clue who she was.

Her dress didn't have pockets, and she didn't have a purse with her. He thought he remembered one from when he first saw her at the bar—small, with a long leather strap—but if she'd had one then, she'd left it there or at the beach. God knew they hadn't been paying a lot of attention to details when they'd decided to go back to his place.

He called the bar, but no one had turned in a ladies' purse. He asked the bartender if he recalled carding a woman named Airin and what her last name was, but no dice. The guy remembered her but not the name.

That made her a Jane Doe—or at least an Airin Doe. And he had to go someplace where they'd let him stay with her.

But when they arrived at the ER, it turned out that even if you knew someone, HIPAA regulations were still the supreme power in the universe. Dr. Jackson told him to stay in the waiting room while they assessed Airin's condition, ran scans and tests, and made sure she was stable.

"But I don't know her last name. I don't have her phone or ID. I have no way to reach her family. Jesus Christ, Sue. Shouldn't there at least be a familiar face there for her? I don't want her to wake up alone and confused and—"

"I understand what you're saying, Hunter. We'll tell Airin you're here once she wakes up, okay? The rest will be up to her. Now leave me alone so I can do my job."

He was a pilot, and that was an instruction he understood. He let go of Sue's lab coat, which he'd been hanging on to like a goddamn child, and went out into the waiting room.

The next three hours were the longest of his life.

He sprang to his feet when Dr. Jackson finally came through the doors to the waiting room. She was frowning, and for a few awful seconds he was sure Airin was dead.

"She's stable," Sue said when she saw his face. "My God, you look terrible. Are you sure you won't let me look you over?"

"I'm fine," he said brusquely. "Is Airin awake?"

Sue shook her head. "She regained consciousness, but she's asleep right now. While she was awake, I asked permission to discuss her condition with you, and she agreed. She also said she'd like you in the room with her if you're still willing."

"Willing? That's what I want. But how is she doing? She was in there a long time. What's going on?"

"She has a mild concussion and two broken ribs, which resulted in a pneumothorax."

His hands, stuffed in his pockets, tightened into fists.

"English, Sue. What's a pneumothorax?"

"Basically, a collapsed lung."

He stared at her. "Jesus."

She put a hand on his arm. "It sounds worse than it is. We've reinflated the lung, and once we remove the chest tube and sew up the incision where it went in, that part of her injury will heal entirely within a couple of days. The broken ribs will take longer—at least four weeks."

"And her concussion?"

"Very mild. We'll keep her in the hospital for a few days, and we'll be monitoring the head injury as well as the injuries to her thorax." She hesitated.

"What?" he asked immediately. "What aren't you telling me?"

"It's nothing medical. But when she regained consciousness, we asked for her last name. She wouldn't give it to us."

"You mean she has amnesia or something like that?"

"No. She could tell us if she wanted to. She refused."

He frowned. "Refused to give her name? Why?"

Sue raised her eyebrows. "I was hoping you might have some insight into that, Hunter. You say you've only known her a few days, but even in that short amount of time you might have expected to learn her last name. But she didn't give it to you."

"No. She didn't."

"Do you think she could be running away from something? An abusive partner or family member?"

Christ. Was that possible?

He forced himself to think about it, recalling every one of their interactions. She'd told him she'd never had a romantic partner, and he believed her. But what about family? Could there be something wrong there?

Whatever the problem was, he didn't think it was physical abuse. Airin definitely had her secrets, but nothing she'd said or done had given him any hint that she was dealing with that kind of trauma.

"She told me she'd had medical issues as a kid. She said her childhood was really sheltered because of that."

"That makes sense. There's a heart surgery scar."

Heart surgery. Jesus.

"I think she's interested in breaking away from her family, but I don't think she's the victim of abuse." He paused. "But the truth is, I don't really know. I don't really know *her*."

Sue nodded. "We'll table that for now, then. Come with me."

She led the way through the swinging doors and down the hospital corridor.

It didn't take them long to reach their destination. Sue opened the door of a private room and ushered him inside.

His heart clenched in his chest.

He remembered what Kaleo had called Airin. This was Snow White at the end of the story, lying in a glass coffin with her face deathly pale and her black silk hair scattered on the white pillowcase . . . if Snow White had been attached to monitors and stuck full of tubes.

"She'll probably wake up soon," Sue said. "I should mention that finding herself in a hospital seemed to cause distress." She paused. "I mean, more than the usual distress of someone finding herself in a hospital."

Hunter nodded to show he understood.

"When she wakes up, try to keep her calm. Try to convince her to tell us who she is. Find out if there's anyone we can contact for her— or anyone she wants protection from. I know you can only give us a couple of hours, Hunter, but I do appreciate it. If you need anything or if there's any change, just—"

"Wait a minute. A couple of hours? Why only a couple of hours?"

Sue was staring at him. "Doesn't your helicopter leave at six?"

Shit.

As Hunter stared back at Sue, he felt the color draining out of his face until he must have looked as pale as Airin.

"Right," he said. "Of course."

Sue's eyes narrowed. "You *forgot*? Damn it, Hunter, I want to check you over."

He shook his head. "I only forgot for a minute. I'm fine, Sue. Just a couple of bruises. And the medicos will give us all a final checkup before we go in. Don't worry about it."

Her lips were pursed. "Did you get any kind of blow to your head? Lose consciousness for any time at all?"

"No. Go do your job, okay? I'll stay here and watch over Airin."

"All right. Hopefully by the time you have to leave, we'll know a little more about her situation."

Once Sue was gone, silence fell in the room.

There was an upholstered chair over by the window. Hunter grabbed it and set it down by the head of Airin's bed. He sat down, leaned forward with his elbows on his knees, and stared at her face.

This was his fault.

He'd gone to Waikiki tonight instead of staying in Kailua. He'd had no reason to do that—no bachelor party for his brother, no one he was meeting, nothing in particular he wanted to do. It had been his choice to drive across the mountains to the place where he'd met Airin.

Had he been hoping to see her again?

What a fucking sap he was.

But even after going to Waikiki, even after seeing her in that bar, everything could still have been okay. He could have bought her a drink like a normal human being and had an hour's conversation with her. They could have shared one more kiss before saying good night, goodbye, and good luck.

Instead, he'd taken her to the beach and practically screwed her in public.

Even then there'd been an opportunity for a happy ending. *I had a great time with you tonight, but now I have to get ready for the next phase in my career.*

But he hadn't said that. He'd said, *Come back with me to Kailua and let's fuck. I know it'll be your first time, and I still don't know your last name, and in less than twenty-four hours I'll be sealed in a biosphere, but what the hell. It's only both our lives, right? Let's be reckless.*

And now here they were.

He replayed that moment on the Pali Highway. As inclined as he was to blame himself for everything right now, he couldn't honestly claim responsibility for the crash. He'd been focused on driving safely even in the face of his lust for the woman in his passenger seat, and he'd done the right thing in trying to pull over and let the guy behind him pass. What had followed had been sheer bad luck, helped along by the impatience and carelessness of the driver behind him.

The police had supported that conclusion when they'd come to interview him during his long hours in the waiting room. He'd also learned that everyone involved in the crash had pulled through, thank God.

So no, the accident itself hadn't been his fault. Years of training in the precise analysis of mechanical events forced him to admit that, and the police had confirmed it. But everything that had led up to the accident?

That sure as hell was his fault.

Airin was lying in this hospital bed because of him.

He studied the lines of her face, the feathery black lashes on her cheeks, the graceful arch of her eyebrows. Even the tubes stuck in her body and the bandage on her temple didn't detract from her beauty.

He remembered what Sue had said. When she'd regained consciousness, Airin had refused to give her name—and she'd panicked when she saw she was in a hospital.

What was she afraid of? He still didn't think she was fleeing from any kind of physical danger. He'd been in the theater of war, and he knew what that particular fear looked like. He'd also known abuse victims, and he knew the signs of that kind of trauma as well.

No, he didn't think Airin was afraid for her safety. But she was afraid of something, even if it was just the memory of whatever medical shit she'd gone through when she was younger. She'd had heart surgery, after all. That was pretty damn scary.

And now she was all alone . . . except for him.

As the minutes ticked by, a depressing predawn malaise settled over the room. After what felt like an eternity, he looked up at the wall clock.

It was four thirty in the morning.

He needed to leave right now, collect his things from Kailua, and get his ass to the helipad.

Then he looked back at Airin.

He didn't know her last name. They were practically strangers. But she'd been in his car when the accident had happened, and even if he hadn't caused the crash, it was because of him that she was lying here.

He put his head in his hands. His crew was supposed to enter the biosphere at nine o'clock that morning. The eight of them had been in Hawaii for a year, working on joint NASA-UH projects. They'd done other, shorter mission simulations together. They were, right now, the elite of NASA's potential Mars mission astronauts.

They'd all made sacrifices to get where they were. The biosphere project itself was a sacrifice. But there was no question in any of their minds that it was worth it.

When he thought about going to Mars, a fierce longing flamed up inside him. He'd wanted to travel for as long as he could remember. A journey of 140 million miles—and the chance to stand on an alien world—would satisfy even *his* wanderlust.

There was a backup crew for this simulation. A group of eight astronauts with equivalent skills and specialties, as dedicated to the Mars mission as the first team. There wasn't one of them who wouldn't do a backflip off a rooftop for the chance to go into the biosphere. That included his counterpart, Liam Jones—a good man and an even better pilot.

He pulled out his phone and made a call to Ted Barkley, the chief project engineer.

A few minutes after he hung up, Sue came through the door.

"Airin hasn't woken up yet," she said—a statement rather than a question.

"No. Not yet."

She sighed. "You have to get going, Hunter. When she does wake up, I promise to let you know her status. I'm sure she—"

"No."

Sue blinked. "What?"

"I'm not going. I'm staying."

She stared at him. "You're not serious."

He wished to hell he wasn't.

"Yeah. I am."

"Hunter." Sue shook her head slowly. "I just got off the phone with my wife, who's leaving me for eight months to pursue the one thing she's wanted since she was a little girl. A chance to be part of the first manned mission to Mars."

"Sue—"

She held up a hand. "If you tell me you don't want that as much as Courtney does, I'll call you a liar. We're going to take good care of Airin. Now get the hell out of here."

"No."

"Goddamn it—"

"It's done. I phoned Barkley. They're calling up Jones from the backup crew." He paused. "At least someone's having a good day because of me."

"I don't believe it. If you do this, I swear to God you'll regret it the rest of your life. It's not too late. Call Barkley back."

He dragged a hand through his hair. "Sue, the only thing you're accomplishing right now is making me fucking depressed. I'm staying, so get over it."

"Hunter—" Her beeper went off, and she glanced at it. "I have to go. Please reconsider this decision while I'm gone."

And then, thank God, she left.

Chapter Eight

When Airin woke up, she was plunged into every nightmare she'd had since she was nine years old.

Hospital bed. Hospital smell. Hospital sights and sounds and sensations.

She jerked upright as panic clawed at her chest.

"No, no, no, no, no—"

"Airin."

A hand on her wrist, squeezing. She turned her head and saw—

Hunter.

It took her only a moment to remember who he was. But that still didn't explain where she was or why they were here.

"Is it . . . is it my heart?" she asked, almost too terrified to finish the question.

"No, angel. Do you remember the accident?"

Accident? Had there been an accident?

She shook her head. "We were at the beach," she said slowly. Images of kissing him flooded through her mind, and she felt her face heating. "Is that what happened to my heart? Was it too much?"

He squeezed her hand again. "Your heart's fine. It's your rib cage we're worried about. We were driving to Kailua and we crashed, and you broke a couple of ribs and collapsed part of your lung. Do you remember the doctor telling you any of this? Dr. Jackson? She talked to you when you first woke up."

She shook her head again. "I want to get out of here."

"Not an option," Hunter said. "They're going to keep you a few days for observation."

Panic rose. "They can't make me stay."

His eyes narrowed as he looked at her. "Airin—"

She licked her lips, which felt dry. "My ribs don't hurt. If I broke them, why don't they hurt?"

"They gave you pain medication."

"Through my IV?"

"Yeah."

There was an IV in her left arm and a chest tube between two of her ribs on her right side. Down below, hidden by the blanket, there was a catheter. The rawness in her throat meant that she'd had a breathing tube in there at some point, though that at least had been removed.

She remembered the technique her favorite nurse had taught her once, for whenever she felt overwhelmed by hospital-induced panic. She breathed in through her nose and out through her mouth, slowly and evenly, and after a few moments she could speak calmly again.

"I don't remember a car accident. The last thing I remember is being on the beach with you and . . ." A sudden flush swept over her, and she worried her quickening pulse would set off the heart monitor.

In through the nose, out through the mouth.

"I remember that, too," Hunter said.

She cleared her throat. "How long ago was that? I mean, how long have I been in the—" She didn't want to say *hospital.* "In here?"

"The beach was last night. It's ten in the morning now."

Ten in the morning.

There was something about that. Something important . . . something . . .

Realization flooded through her.

"Oh God," she said, staring at Hunter.

His jaw was shadowed with stubble, and he looked like he hadn't slept. He leaned in closer, his face concerned.

"What's wrong?"

"You. You're supposed to be in the biosphere. Oh God, Hunter. Are they waiting for you?"

He reached out and brushed the backs of his knuckles over her cheek. "Don't worry about that, angel. It's not an issue."

"Not an issue? Damn it, answer me! Are they waiting for you? Do you have time to get there?"

He took her hand again. "Airin—"

She sat up straighter. "You tell me right now, Hunter. And you tell me the truth."

He sighed. "All right. If you calm down, I'll tell you."

In through the nose, out through the mouth.

"I'm calm."

He studied her for a moment before speaking.

"No, they're not waiting for me. But it's fine. My backup is going in. A really good guy named Liam Jones. You'd like him."

She leaned back against the pillows and closed her eyes. Tears pricked behind her lids, and as hard as she fought to hold them back, they leaked slowly down her cheeks.

Hunter had missed his window because of her. He'd missed out on the biosphere.

If there was one kind of person she understood, it was a person with a mission. Hunter had wanted to go into space all his life. The biosphere project was a crucial step on that journey.

She'd wrecked his career. And even if he thought otherwise right now, eventually he'd see what she'd done to him.

And he'd hate her for it.

"Airin. Don't think about it, okay? This is not your problem. What I need you to do now is tell me your last name and how to reach your family. You lost your purse somewhere, angel. Nobody knows who you are or who your emergency contact is."

Her eyes flew open. "My family," she said.

"That's right. We have to let them know what happened to you."

"Oh God."

Her family. Her mother. What time was it? Ten in the morning. Was there a chance in the world they hadn't noticed she was gone yet? She was usually a very early riser. But maybe Thomas and the others would think she was sleeping in today. They wouldn't go into her room, would they?

Of course they would. Who was she kidding? If they were worried about her, they would absolutely go into her room. They wouldn't even have to ask the hotel for help, since they could get in through the connecting door to her mother's suite.

Unless, please God, they weren't worried. Her mother was on the Big Island, after all, and they all had plenty of other work to do. Maybe they'd give it a while longer before going in to check on her and sounding the alarm.

But even if she'd gotten lucky so far, noon would be the outside limit of her window of privacy. She had to get back to her hotel room now, and she had to do it without anyone seeing her.

"Hunter. Can you do me a favor?"

He leaned forward, and something in his eyes made her stomach do an odd little flip.

"You're lying in this bed because of me. Hell yes, I'll do you a favor. Anything. Name it."

"I need you to get me out of here. I mean, they can't keep me here against my will, can they? Then I need your help to get back to my hotel. Only . . . no one can see me. You'll have to sneak me in somehow. I know the layout pretty well, but I've only ever snuck back at night, and—"

"Airin."

Hunter's quiet voice stopped her. After a moment he spoke again, his voice gentle.

"Is there someone you're afraid of? Someone in your family?"

She started to laugh, and it turned into a cough. Hunter handed her a cup of water, and she took a swallow.

"Yes, there's someone I'm afraid of. But not for the reasons you're thinking."

She put the cup down on the table beside her. Then she started to run a hand through her hair, stopping when she encountered the bandage on her temple. She explored its dimensions, noting without emotion that they'd shaved off a small portion of her hair—no more than an inch or two.

"In case you're wondering, you're still gorgeous as hell."

"That's not what I'm worried about right now, but thanks."

She turned to look at him again, noting the shadows under his eyes. He'd endured a sleepless night and missed out on the biosphere mission because of her. If nothing else, she owed him the truth.

"There's something I have to tell you."

"You can tell me anything, Airin. I mean it."

"It's about my family. Well . . . my mother. She's the only family I have. She's not—that is—I . . ."

There was a commotion out in the hall. Voices yelling, growing closer. One voice in particular, a deep and scathing contralto.

Oh God.

The door was flung open with sudden violence, and Dira Delaney stood on the threshold. She was flanked by three of her staff and a gaggle of hospital people.

At the sight of her daughter, Dira held up a hand imperiously. Airin wasn't surprised when everyone who'd been yammering at her fell silent.

Her mother had that effect on people.

"Airin. There you are."

Her voice sounded almost matter-of-fact, but Airin knew better. Beneath Dira's tightly controlled exterior was a tangle of panic and fury.

She took three steps into the room, turned her eyes on Hunter for a moment, and looked back at Airin.

"Congratulations on not being dead yet." She took another step. "Now tell me what the hell is going on."

Chapter Nine

Hunter was a fighter pilot, and he'd been through NASA's astronaut program. That meant he was trained to respond to all kinds of crazy situations, to analyze circumstances with cool precision, and to make the best decisions possible. His mind and his body had been disciplined for years to deal with the unexpected.

And yet, at the sight of Dira Delaney, his thought processes stuttered to a halt.

Dira.

Delaney.

Genius scientist, genius businesswoman. Nanowire technology pioneer. The inventor of a new process that was already beginning to revolutionize energy use here on Earth and had the potential, in the field of jet propulsion, to make it possible for humans to explore farther in space than they ever had before.

The woman who'd started a company with the sole purpose of beating NASA to Mars.

The woman who, apparently, was also Airin's mother.

Holy fuck.

He could see the resemblance. But while Airin looked soft and vulnerable, her lips trembling, her mother looked fierce and implacable and a little bit terrifying.

She wasn't a blusterer, though. After asking Airin for an explanation, she didn't say anything else. She simply waited for her daughter to speak.

He looked at Airin. Like anyone interested in space, he'd read about Dira Delaney, and although she seldom spoke about her family or private life, it had gotten out that her only child had heart problems that had necessitated a series of surgeries. That tied in with what Airin had told him and what Sue had said.

Is it my heart? Airin had asked when she first woke up.

His own heart tightened in his chest. Dira Delaney would have taken on her daughter's medical situation with the aggressive, take-no-prisoners approach that had gotten her where she was today. That was why Airin had led such a sheltered life. That was why she'd never had a romantic relationship or even kissed a man before.

And why she'd been so excited at her first taste of freedom.

She was a grown woman, and she'd said her medical issues were behind her. Why did she have to sneak out of her hotel room to see the world? Was her mother still so overprotective, even after her daughter was no longer in medical danger?

"Mother."

Hearing that little tremble in her voice, he wanted to leap to his feet and stand over her. It was the same thing he'd felt after the car accident and when he saw Airin lying unconscious in her hospital bed. It was a fierce need to protect her—from everything.

His hands tightened on the arms of his chair. He might have an unaccountable desire to fight Airin's battles for her, but he needed to stay out of this one. This was family shit, and he had no right to stick his nose in.

But he had no intention of leaving this room, either. Not until he was sure Airin was okay.

Airin cleared her throat. "Mother," she said again, her voice stronger this time. "Please allow me to introduce—"

"I know who he is," Dira said, turning her piercing black eyes on him.

She did?

"I was just on the Big Island, Mr. Bryce. I happened to be meeting with the people in charge of the biosphere project. I was there when Ted Barkley received your call. Of course I had no idea your unexpected withdrawal from the first team had anything to do with my daughter. Nor did I know you were involved when I learned she was missing. My staff discovered her location while I was en route back here, but they made no mention of you." She looked back at Airin. "I'm still waiting for your explanation."

Airin lifted her chin. "We were in a car accident. It wasn't Hunter's fault. I'm perfectly fine."

"Perfectly fine?" Dira's voice rose a little, and she stopped.

Her lips firmed for a moment and then relaxed. She turned to Sue Jackson, who had moved to the front of the hospital staff group. "My daughter says she's perfectly fine. I'd like some medical confirmation of that, please."

Sue raised an eyebrow. "Your daughter is an adult." She looked at Airin. "Do I have your permission to discuss your medical information with your mother? Including the results of CT scans and other tests?"

Airin looked both surprised and grateful to be asked. "Yes," she said.

Sue turned back to Dira. "If you'd like to come with me, Ms. Delaney, I'd be happy to fill you in."

Dira frowned. "Why can't we discuss it here?"

"Because, to be quite frank, I don't think your presence is very soothing for your daughter right now."

Dira's nostrils flared. "That's an impertinent remark. There's no one who cares more about my daughter's well-being than I do. That includes you as well as this"—she looked at Hunter again, and there was venom in her expression—"person."

"I would like a break, Mom," Airin said, more firmly than she'd spoken yet. "If you'll go with Dr. Jackson, I'll be able to rest for a few minutes."

"Your time would be better spent saying goodbye to Mr. Bryce. Then he'll be free to focus on salvaging the remnants of his career." She leveled those black eyes at him. "NASA isn't very pleased with you at the moment, as I'm sure you can imagine. My daughter and I will be heading home soon, but we'll be in touch if we decide to sue you for anything."

Dira Delaney was going to sue him?

"No."

Both Hunter and Dira jerked their heads around to look at Airin. He hadn't known her for very long, so the fact that he'd never heard her speak so forcefully wasn't too surprising. But Dira, who'd presumably known her daughter for her entire life, looked just as startled as he felt.

Within a few seconds, Dira had her expression back under control.

"Fine, we won't sue him."

"That's not what I meant."

"Oh? What did you mean, then?"

"I meant I won't be going home with you. Not to our hotel, and not to Stonebridge."

Stonebridge, he remembered, was the name of the town in western Massachusetts where Dira had built a mansion.

Her delicate black brows were exactly like Airin's. Now they drew together slowly, creating the kind of frown you might see in your nightmares.

"What are you talking about? What do you mean, you're not coming home with me?"

Airin turned to look at him for the first time since her mother had entered the room, and there was something close to desperation in her expression. But what was she desperate about? What did she need him to do?

"I'm going to be staying with Hunter for a while," she said, and her eyes pleaded with him.

What. The. Hell?

All he could do was stare back at her. He managed to keep his jaw from dropping, but he hoped Airin would elaborate on this plan before Dira started asking him questions.

Airin seemed to take heart from the fact that he didn't immediately contradict her, and she turned back to her mother.

"I've decided it's time to leave the nest. I want to consider my options for graduate school, and I'd like to do that away from—" She hesitated. "Away from home," she finished, though Hunter was pretty sure she'd been about to say *away from you.* "Hunter has a place here on Oahu, and he's very kindly offered to let me stay there while I consider my, um, next steps."

He didn't have a place anymore. He'd sublet his Kailua rental for the duration of the biosphere mission. The new tenants would be moving in at the end of the month, which was only two weeks away.

But he had a feeling Airin didn't care about details right now. She was making a move to break away from her mother, and those big brown eyes of hers, back on him now, were begging him to help her.

Jesus.

Dira looked from her daughter to him and back again. Judging by the fury behind her eyes, he could only guess at what it was costing her to keep from yelling.

"We'll discuss this after I speak with Dr. Jackson."

And with that she turned and left, her staffers going with her.

The hospital people filed out as well. Sue, though, paused at the door.

"Everything all right here?" she asked.

For a doctor who'd just discovered her Jane Doe was the daughter of one of the most powerful women on the planet, she seemed calm and composed.

Airin nodded. "I'm sorry my mother is so . . . um . . ."

"Forceful?" Hunter suggested.

"That's one way to put it," Airin muttered.

"I asked about you two," Sue reminded them.

Airin looked groggy but game. "I'm fine."

"We're both good," Hunter added. "I hope you'll be able to say the same in ten minutes."

Sue smiled. "Don't worry about me. I work in an ER, and I just said goodbye to my wife for eight months. I can handle anything—up to and including the forceful mother of one of my patients."

When the door closed behind her, a short and extremely awkward silence ensued.

Then he said, "What do you—"

"I'm so sorry I—"

They both paused. After a moment, Hunter said, "You first."

Airin took a deep breath. "Okay. So. I obviously took a liberty just now. I didn't mean to put you in such a bad spot."

Bad spot was an understatement. But the truth was, something happened when she looked at him. Those brown eyes were so earnest and vulnerable . . . and everything inside him just kind of melted.

What the hell was it about this woman that made him willing to fuck up his life? That made him want to do anything—*anything*—to keep her safe?

He tried to stay focused. "Let's start with the fact that you didn't tell me your mother is Dira Delaney."

She looked down at her hands, which were twined together on her lap. After a moment, she started to fiddle with the medical bracelet on her left wrist.

"I know I should have told you who I am. But when people find out, it tends to . . . color everything. My mother has always been the most interesting thing about me. I guess I liked being around someone who wasn't looking at me and thinking about her."

Was that a fair point? Maybe. But: "You can't honestly think that your mother is the only interesting thing about you."

"I didn't say the *only* interesting thing. Just the *most* interesting thing."

"That's not—"

She looked up and met his eyes. "I was just trying to explain why I didn't tell you who I am. One reason was that I liked being with someone who didn't know. The other reason . . . well. The other reason is that I had to sneak away from my mother and all her henchmen just to be at the bar that night." She shook her head. "I shouldn't say henchmen. That's not fair. She has a bodyguard—that really large man who was just in here—but he's not a thug. His name is Nathan, and he's actually really nice. Thomas, too—he's an assistant-slash-bodyguard. Everyone else is just a regular employee. PR assistants, personal assistants, that kind of thing. No henchmen. But I had to sneak around to get away from them, and I didn't want to make you a party to that."

"I would've helped you sneak around if you'd asked me to."

She smiled for the first time since she'd woken up. "Really?"

"Yeah. But that doesn't explain *why* you had to sneak around."

She looked back down at her hands. "It's kind of a long story. My mother is sort of . . ."

"Controlling?"

"Overprotective." She paused. "Well, and controlling, too, I guess. I don't know if you've read a lot about my mom, but if you have you might know that I—"

"Had heart problems growing up. Yeah, I read about that. And you told me you'd had medical issues." A sudden pulse of anxiety went through him. "You said you're recovered now. Is that true?"

"Yes, it's true. The doctors told me last year that they didn't anticipate any future surgeries and that there's nothing stopping me from living a normal life. My heart is as strong as anyone else's, maybe stronger. There are no restrictions on my activities at all. It's as though it never happened." She took a breath. "But my mother never seemed to get the memo. She still treats me like a heart patient. Like a little girl who needs to be protected and sheltered from everything."

"So that's why you—"

He stopped abruptly. He'd been about to say, *So that's why you've never kissed anybody.*

But of course Airin knew exactly what he was talking about. Pink came into her cheeks, and she looked away for a moment.

"Yes," she said. "That's why. I've never really been out in the world on my own. I got my college degree remotely. Of course, my mother being my mother, she set up an arrangement with MIT." She looked back at him. "I mostly interact with people online, which makes me like those bloggers who live in their parents' basements and never see the sun. Well, except that we live in the Berkshires where it's really beautiful even if it's in the middle of nowhere, and I always do a lot of walking and hiking."

"But except for that, you're a basement-dwelling millennial."

She smiled. "Pretty much. And that's why I hope you might . . . maybe . . . be willing to help me." She bit her lip. "You wouldn't have to spend any time with me. I mean, as long as I can tell my mother I'm staying with someone and not just wandering around on my own . . ."

"I think I get it."

"You don't have to take care of me or anything. I have my own money. And once I've taken the first step out of the nest, I think it'll be okay."

"You think what will be okay?"

"Things with my mother. She just needs to see that I can survive on my own. I've been trying to talk to her for months about leaving home, but she hasn't listened. If I go back with her now, after a car accident and an injury . . . I don't think I'll ever convince her I'll be safe away from home. Don't you see?" Her voice rose a little. "It has to be now. And the only person I can think of who might help me is you."

"But, angel—"

Suddenly her eyes filled with tears. "Oh my God, I just heard myself talking to you in my head. I mean . . . you know what I mean. I sound crazy. Your whole life is wrecked because of me, and I've just asked you for help with a problem that's none of your business. We don't even know each other. We—"

Hunter leaned forward, grabbed her hand, and squeezed it.

"You haven't done anything to me, Airin."

"Yes, I have. You're not in the biosphere, and that's my fault."

"I'm not in the biosphere because of decisions I made and decisions other people made—especially the guy in the car behind us. But my life isn't wrecked."

"You've wanted to go into space since you were a little boy. Now that's derailed. How can you say your life isn't wrecked?"

"Because it isn't over yet." He paused. "You know part of NASA's astronaut training is learning to speak Russian?"

Airin looked a little thrown by the change of subject, but she nodded. "Because of the International Space Station. In case you have to talk to Russian mission control."

"Right. Well, I had a Russian tutor at the Johnson Space Center a couple of years ago. He loved chess, and he taught me to play while we were working together. He told me something about chess strategy once that I never forgot. He said, 'Play the position you have, not the one you think you should have.'" He leaned toward her again. "Neither of us expected to be here. But let's deal with the circumstances we're in, not the ones we wish we were in. Okay?"

Airin's eyes were bright with tears, but she nodded. "Okay."

With her hand in his, he felt that rush of tenderness that had been wreaking such havoc with his thought processes. For a guy who'd just been counseling clear, strategic thinking, he needed to make sure he was doing that himself.

He released Airin's hand and sat back in his chair. "So let's take stock of where we are. You'd like some time away from home and your mother to figure out what you're doing next. I need to figure out what I'm doing next, too—and I still work for NASA, which means I'll be taking over Liam Jones's job at the university field office while he's in the biosphere. I don't see any reason why you and I can't share expenses while we're doing those things. Now, my place in Kailua is only available for a couple more weeks. After that—"

"After that, we'll play the position we have."

He smiled at her. "Yeah. So we have a plan, then."

"We have a plan."

But the good feeling flowing between them only lasted another minute. Because after that, Dira Delaney came through the door.

She was by herself, and she didn't waste any time getting to the point.

"I'd like to talk to my daughter alone, Mr. Bryce. If you'd give us half an hour?"

Airin spoke before he could. "No. I know you'll try to talk me out of my plan, and I'd rather Hunter stayed."

Dira's lips pressed together in a look Hunter was starting to become familiar with. It was a look that seemed to say, *I'm pissed as hell, but it won't do any good to shout, so I'm going to think of something constructive to do instead.*

"Fine," she said crisply. She turned to him. "Then perhaps you'll take a walk with me, Mr. Bryce. Unless you're afraid to be alone with me as well."

Airin frowned. "Mother—"

Hunter gave her hand a squeeze. "I'd be delighted to take a walk with you, Ms. Delaney."

Airin hung on to his hand as he rose to his feet. "I'm not sure this is a good idea. I don't see why we can't all—"

He spoke low enough that Dira, still in the doorway, couldn't hear him.

"She won't talk me out of anything, if that's what you're nervous about. I've dealt with tougher cookies than your mother."

"No, you really haven't," Airin muttered, but she let go of his hand.

"You don't have to be concerned about your new friend, Airin. He's an astronaut. He should be able to survive a conversation with me."

And with that, Dira turned and led the way out of the room.

Chapter Ten

She took him down the hall to what looked like a nurses' lounge. It was empty, and once they were inside she shut the door.

And then it was just the two of them, face-to-face.

If someone had told him yesterday that within the next twenty-four hours he'd miss his window to go into the biosphere, put Airin in the hospital, and be standing in a room with billionaire industrialist Dira Delaney, he would have said they were crazy.

Dira was smaller in person than she seemed on TV. But that didn't make her any less intimidating.

They looked at each other in silence for a good thirty seconds. He had a feeling that Dira was waiting for him to speak first, and he remembered something else his chess teacher had taught him.

When you seem to play your opponent's game, it can make them overconfident.

"Ms. Delaney, I know you're worried about Airin. But I think you're underestimating her."

Dira's lips tightened. "And you're basing this analysis of my daughter on what? The deep knowledge you acquired during three days' acquaintance?"

Not even three days. Two separate—and relatively brief—encounters.

But there was no need to mention that.

"I'm basing it on a perspective you've never had when it comes to your daughter. The perspective of an objective observer."

One corner of her mouth went up slightly, and it was the first sign of humor he'd seen in her.

"You'll forgive me, Mr. Bryce, but I've seen the way you look at Airin. I might call you many things when it comes to my daughter, but 'objective observer' is not one of them."

Score one for Dira Delaney. But he didn't have to acknowledge the hit.

"I'm still more objective than you are, ma'am."

Dira glanced away from him for a moment. There was a standard-issue hospital poster on the wall, an anatomical diagram of the human heart. She looked at it for a few seconds and then back at him.

"I know you've read about me, Mr. Bryce. Every aspiring astronaut has. The media likes to highlight the optimism of my vision. Dira Delaney wants to send humans to Mars. She wants to reignite the American fervor for innovation and exploration."

She huffed out a breath. "I've worked hard to keep the focus on that aspect of my personality, because it helps me achieve my goals. It's also true. I do want all those things for America and for the human race. But other things about me are true as well."

She took a step toward him, and it was as if she let a mask drop. Some of her brutal self-discipline fell away, and he saw the flash of fire in her eyes.

"To get where I am, I've had to take on giants. I compete with Boeing and Lockheed Martin and every aerospace CEO who sees rockets as an extension of his genitalia. I compete with nations. Russia, China, the USA. I've taken on these challenges because I believe the mission is worth it and because I believe I can accomplish the goals I've set for myself. I've made sacrifices along the way that most people wouldn't dream of making. There are those in my industry—and in the media—who say that even in a field that attracts fanatics, I seem uniquely obsessed. So keep all of that in mind when I tell you this, Mr. Bryce."

Her voice hardened. "I would give it all up to protect Airin. I would turn my back on my company, my mission, everything else, if doing so would save Airin's life. Do you understand?"

Hunter was almost a foot taller than Dira and a good hundred pounds heavier, but it took no small effort to stand his ground in the face of her emotional and intellectual force.

"You're a mother who loves her daughter. That doesn't make you unusual, Ms. Delaney. In fact, that's probably the most ordinary thing about you."

Her eyebrows went up.

"Touché," she said after a moment. "I suppose that's true. But bear in mind that behind my 'ordinary' love for my daughter is a lot of money and a lot of resources—and the ruthlessness of a woman who's succeeded in the most male of worlds."

He nodded his acknowledgment of those facts.

"You're telling me you're a tough opponent and a bad enemy. Believe me, Ms. Delaney, I have no desire to be your enemy. But your daughter asked for my help, and I'm going to give it to her." He paused. "And there's something you should know about me. To get where I am, I've had to take on deserts and dust storms, catastrophic equipment failure, and air defense artillery. I've risked my life in prototype aircraft no one else would fly. I took on more crazy-ass missions than anyone in my unit. And once I left the military, I had to negotiate my way through NASA. Bureaucracy can beat the toughest pilot, but it didn't beat me."

He saw that flash of humor in her for the second time. "Are you telling me you're a bad enemy, too?"

"Nope. I'm just telling you that once I make a commitment, I see it through."

"Didn't you have a commitment to the NASA biosphere project?"

Ouch.

Yeah, that one would leave a mark. But it would be a mistake to let her see it.

"I had a backup for that mission. Qualified and ready to go. But there was no backup here for Airin. She was so eager to get away from you, to be with someone who didn't know she was your daughter, that she didn't tell me who she was. She didn't have ID on her. I didn't know her last name. She was unconscious when we got here, and I had no way to contact her family or anyone else she might know. If I left her, as far as I knew I'd be leaving her as a Jane Doe among strangers. I had a decision to make, and I made it."

Dira nodded once, slowly, her eyes never leaving his.

"I do know all that, Mr. Bryce. And believe it or not, I respect it. I'm in a position to know exactly what astronauts in training go through . . . and I know what fighter pilots go through, too."

He remembered suddenly that her husband had been a fighter pilot—until he was killed in action.

"I know only the most extraordinary men and women make it as far through the program as you have. But as rare as you are, there are still hundreds like you, with the same résumé of bravery, intelligence, leadership, and problem-solving ability. You're not unique, Mr. Bryce. But you do have something those other men and women don't have."

"Which is?"

"The trust of my daughter."

And where, he wondered, *are you going with that?*

"I have a proposal for you, Mr. Bryce. I propose that you let my daughter stay with you for a few weeks while she spreads her wings. Figures out what she wants to do next."

"You're proposing I do what I already told Airin I would do?"

Another twitch of humor at the corner of her mouth. "Yes, as far as that goes. But there's something else I want you to do for me. Something you will not tell Airin about."

She lifted her chin, and there was something familiar about the movement. After a moment, he realized he'd seen Airin lift her chin exactly like that.

"I want you to communicate with me every day without my daughter knowing that you're doing so. I want you to give me complete reports as to her physical health and mental state. I want you to tell me how she's doing emotionally. Most importantly, I want you to tell me what you talk about. What she's thinking about her future. What she wants to do next."

He stared at her. "You have to be kidding."

"I assure you I'm not."

"You want me to spy on your daughter for you."

"In essence, yes. That's exactly what I want you to do."

He shook his head slowly. "You can't honestly believe I'd agree to that."

"Under ordinary circumstances, you wouldn't. But I'm going to bribe you."

His lip curled involuntarily. "You can't bribe me."

Her eyes appraised him coolly. "Not with money, no. Didn't I tell you I understand astronauts? I know you're not motivated by greed. But you see, Mr. Bryce, I know what *does* motivate you. And I'm in a position to offer you the one thing you want more than anything else." She paused. "A chance to go to Mars."

Whatever he'd been expecting, it wasn't this.

"What are you saying?"

"I'm saying that I'm going to beat NASA to the Red Planet. They're fifteen years away from the first manned mission. I'm ten years away. I know you'd give almost anything to be a part of the first crew to step foot on Mars. I'll be putting my crew together over the next decade, Mr. Bryce. How would you like to be a part of it?"

Well, fuck.

It was a damn good thing he had experience keeping his cool. He got a grip on his self-control, but it took a hell of an effort not to let his jaw drop.

"I'm a NASA astronaut, Ms. Delaney. I already have a chance to go to Mars."

"A chance that, I would imagine, decreased dramatically after you pulled out of the biosphere mission."

Another shot home. "Maybe. But in spite of your assessment that I'm not unique, NASA's crew selection committee doesn't agree with you. They seem to be under the impression that I'm one of the best pilots they've ever seen. I've also gone through their program with higher marks than any other candidate they've ever tested."

Her eyebrows lifted. "I guess we can't count modesty among your many fine qualities."

"You said you understood fighter pilots, Ms. Delaney. We're self-confident. Some people mistake that for arrogance, but I know you're not one of them."

"Very well. We'll agree that you're an outstanding pilot and an excellent candidate for NASA's Mars mission. But you'll also agree that you're not, by any means, irreplaceable . . . and that your star is not exactly in the ascendant at the moment."

Had he ever met anyone with sharper eyes than this woman?

He shrugged. "I'll concede that."

"And you'll agree that what I'm offering you is more than what NASA would ever dream of offering you. Barring some kind of disqualifying event—medical or otherwise—you can have a spot in my crew. The crew that will beat NASA to Mars."

There was no such thing as a guarantee in the space program—especially when it came to Mars. Every astronaut knew that.

The world's best in every field wanted in on that mission. The best roboticists, planetary scientists, aerospace engineers, computer scientists, geochemists, and pilots. And in spite of his words to Dira, he knew she was right about one essential fact: when it came to NASA, no one was irreplaceable.

There'd be six or eight or ten spots on that first manned Mars spacecraft and a million people, give or take, who wanted one. Out of those, maybe a hundred thousand were qualified. And the further you whittled down that hundred thousand, the more rarefied the air became.

It was the ultimate seller's market.

He thought he'd done a decent job of hiding the fever that had gripped him at Dira's offer, but after a moment he realized his hands had clenched into fists. It was as though a lifeline had been thrown from the Red Planet down into the gravity well of Earth, and he'd taken it in a death grip.

Dira's eyes on him were shrewd. She probably knew exactly what he was thinking and feeling right now, damn her.

And like any good saleswoman would, now that she knew she had him on the hook, she began to reel him in.

"I'm not asking you to do anything dishonorable," she said, her tone shifting from sharp to persuasive.

"Spying is pretty damn dishonorable."

"I let you put it that way to show you I'm not afraid of stark realities. But I don't think it's an accurate description of what I'm asking you to do. Yes, Airin is an adult. But she's been sheltered and protected her whole life, and with good reason. Until last year we didn't know if she'd live or die. Her heart condition could have killed her at any time."

"But it didn't. And according to Airin, her last surgery was completely successful. She's fully recovered with no restrictions on activity. It's as if it never happened."

"That's where you and Airin are both wrong. Because it did happen, and Airin's childhood was unusual because of it. For her to want to leave the nest now, as she puts it . . ." Dira pursed her lips. "Quite frankly, I'm afraid for her. But if I offer to accompany my daughter on her journey into the real world—or offer the company of someone who works with me—she'll reject that offer. She's determined to do this without me, and I suppose that's natural enough. So what I need is someone to look after her. Someone my daughter trusts and someone I can trust as well. Someone who will let me know what's going on with her." She paused. "I'm not asking you to violate anything truly private. If she keeps a diary, I don't need to know about it. I just want you to tell me the kind of things she once told me herself."

Airin, he thought. *Stay focused on Airin.* What she needed, what she wanted, and what she would think about this offer.

But the images that flooded his mind were of Mars.

The Red Planet.

He could be one of the first human beings to set foot on it.

He forced himself back to the present. "You said you weren't afraid to lay out the 'stark reality' of what you want. But now you're trying to make it sound as innocent as possible."

"I want you to accept my offer. So yes, I want to make it palatable to you."

"How long would this arrangement last?"

"Six weeks seems a reasonable amount of time. Airin will have made her decisions by then . . . and, hopefully, be ready to come home." She looked at him keenly. "You can't tell me you don't want to accept. I can see the glow of Mars in your eyes."

No shit.

"There's something else, Mr. Bryce."

"Another condition?"

"No. A compliment. You see, I don't trust many people. Of that small number, there are perhaps three or four I would trust with my daughter's safety. But you chose to stay with Airin at the cost of your own career advancement. I imagine you bring that same quality—a willingness to put another's well-being above your self-interest—to all your endeavors. So even if you weren't in a position to do me this service, I would consider you worthy of a place in my crew."

She was laying it on pretty thick.

"But if I accept your offer, wouldn't that be out of self-interest? What would you think of a man who would spy on your daughter for a chance to go to Mars?"

She shrugged, her expression opaque. "I would hope he'd agree it was for Airin's own good. And that he'd simply be doing what he already agreed to—keeping her safe during a difficult transition—while helping her mother with an equally difficult transition. I would also hope he might recognize that I'm motivated by love."

Maybe she thought she was. But whether she realized it or not, she was also motivated by a need for control.

Up until this point, Dira had been able to manage her daughter's safety to an extent few parents could . . . and that many might wish for. Now she was losing that control, and she was desperate to hang on a little longer.

Well, that was probably natural, too. How would he know? The truth was, he was the last person who could speak to what a normal parent might wish for or struggle with. His own parents had been the opposite of normal. Compared with them, Dira Delaney was a fucking paragon.

But that didn't mean he should accept her proposal.

He turned his back and walked over to the window. It overlooked a parking lot, and he watched people come and go without really seeing them.

Dira was a determined woman. If he didn't help her, she'd find some other way to get what she wanted. Wouldn't it be better for Airin if he was the one talking to her mother? As opposed to someone else?

Even as he voiced that thought in his head, he knew it was a rationalization. But that didn't mean it wasn't true.

He wanted to go to Mars. He also wanted to protect Airin. If he agreed to Dira's proposal, he could do both those things.

There was really only one thing he couldn't do if he made this deal.

He couldn't act on his attraction to Airin.

However he justified this arrangement, he'd still be betraying her trust. It might be better for her in the long run than whatever alternative her mom came up with, but she wouldn't see it that way if she ever found out.

There was no way they could be involved under those circumstances.

But wouldn't that be for the best, too? The one-night stand he and Airin had planned was one thing. The chemistry between them was off the charts, and it was something they'd both wanted. But if they were living under the same roof? It was easy to imagine things getting intense, emotionally as well as physically . . . and intense meant messy.

There was a reason he'd decided a while back that pilots and astronauts were better off single. Those were jobs that took all of your focus, and being married or in a serious relationship could only get in the way.

Not to mention how unfair the life was to your partner or spouse. Look at Sue Jackson, saying goodbye to Courtney for an eight-month mission. And if Courtney ever went to Mars? They'd be saying goodbye for two or three years.

Airin was looking to spread her wings for the first time. He needed to get back on track with NASA. If he and Dira went through with this agreement, he'd be joining DelAres. The last thing he or Airin needed was some kind of emotional entanglement . . . especially when it would be Airin's first.

She needed to figure out her life before she started dealing with romance. And when she did, she deserved more than he'd ever be able to give her—even if he weren't going behind her back to talk to Dira.

So once again, he was rationalizing. He was telling himself that making this deal would be the best thing for everybody.

Maybe it was even true.

He turned around. "I accept."

He spoke abruptly, and Dira looked almost startled. Then she smiled—the first full-out, no-holds-barred smile he'd seen from her.

"I'm glad," was all she said, but he knew she meant it.

She had what she wanted, and if things worked out as planned, he'd have what he wanted, too.

The thing he wanted most in the world, as Dira had said.

But for a man who'd driven his career off the rails a few hours ago and now had a realistic shot at being one of the first humans on Mars, he wasn't feeling euphoric or ecstatic or any of the things he ought to feel.

He was feeling like shit.

Chapter Eleven

Three days later, Airin stepped out of Hunter's truck—the one he was renting while his convertible was in the shop—in front of a small white house nestled in a tropical garden. The backyard was a little forest of trees whose names she didn't know, some of them bearing fruit.

But the extraordinary thing about the backyard was where it ended up. Behind all the houses on this side of the road, the mountains of the Manoa Valley rose in lush green folds to a perfect blue sky.

They weren't in Kailua. Instead, they'd be staying in the four-bedroom house Hunter's replacement had shared with two other members of the backup team. They'd been using the fourth bedroom as an office, but after Hunter had talked to them about Airin, they'd cleared it out for her.

The house was only two miles from the University of Hawaii at Manoa, where most of the team was involved in joint NASA-UH research projects. It was only four miles from Waikiki.

When Airin remembered her luxurious hotel on the beach and the honky-tonk atmosphere a few streets away, it was hard to believe this was the same island.

They were definitely *mauka* here. Inland. Nestled in the most beautiful valley she'd ever seen.

A thrill of happiness went through her, in spite of the dampening her spirits had gotten that morning. When Hunter had picked her up at the hospital he'd been . . . something. Reserved, maybe? He'd been a little different with her ever since he'd spoken with her mother, but since Dira obviously hadn't been able to talk Hunter out of helping her, Airin hadn't worried about it too much.

Her mother had flown back to Massachusetts last night. With Dira out of the picture and her hospital stay over, Airin had been hoping she and Hunter could get back to the dynamic that had seemed so natural when they first met . . . as though they'd known each other for years instead of days.

But it was clear from the formal, almost distant way Hunter was speaking to her today that things between them weren't going back to the way they'd been. Not right away, at least.

Maybe he still felt guilty about the accident. Maybe Dira had said something awful to him. Maybe it was what she'd been afraid of all along, and he was beginning to resent her for derailing his career.

Whatever the reason, Hunter was treating her as a housemate or a colleague, not as a friend—much less a friend he'd wanted to have sex with a few days ago.

She could table that problem for now, though. Because here she was, on her own in Hawaii, about to move into the first place she'd ever lived apart from her mother.

And it was beautiful.

Even the pain of her ribs and the stiffness in her torso couldn't lessen the enjoyment of this moment. She looked at the shrubs and flowers in the front yard—there was even a plumeria tree at the far end—while Hunter grabbed her suitcases from the trunk.

"This is a lot of stuff for a ten-day trip to a tropical climate," he commented.

"I didn't pack it," she said. "One of my mother's assistants did, back in Massachusetts before we came here."

She turned away from the yard in time to see him swing her heavy case as though it weighed nothing at all.

Whatever she'd been going to say next was forgotten.

Hunter's T-shirt and jeans were like the T-shirt and jeans of any other man in the world. The jeans were old and faded, and his navy-blue NASA T-shirt looked like it had been washed a thousand times.

But it was the man inside the clothes who had her staring.

Up until now, she'd only seen him at night or in the hospital. This was the first time she'd seen him in full sunlight, looking like some kind of pagan god in modern clothing.

His shoulders were so powerful. Wide, with those thick bands of muscle that could lift heavy objects like they were nothing. And his arms . . . the flex and release of his biceps, his triceps . . .

"Airin?"

She swallowed. "Yes?"

"Are you okay? You're just kind of standing there. Do you feel all right? Is it your ribs?"

She put a hand to her torso as though that were, indeed, the source of her hesitation. She'd dressed carefully that morning, thinking of her environment as well as her injury. She'd never seen Hunter in anything but jeans, and though she didn't own any denim herself, she'd wanted to dress as casually as possible.

She'd picked a pair of gray linen slacks and a blue silk shirt—loose so there would be no constriction of her rib cage, and thick enough that it would do something to hide the fact that she wasn't wearing a bra. She'd meant to wear one, but trying to put it on had been so painful that she'd given up.

So there was nothing between her skin and the air but her silk shirt. She'd assumed that her ribs would be wrapped before they sent her home, but the nurse had told her that they didn't wrap that type of injury anymore.

"Compression increases the risk of lung infection and pneumonia," she'd said. "We want you to be able to draw a deep breath even if it's painful. You can use an ice pack for up to twenty minutes three times a day, just as we've done here in the hospital. Other than that and pain medication, there's really nothing else we can do."

After a childhood spent in and out of hospitals and months of her life spent in recovery from surgical procedures, Airin had grown to hate the effect of pain medication on the clarity of her thought processes. With her body the province of doctors, it had felt like her mind was the only thing that truly belonged to her, and she was unwilling to do anything to dull its faculties.

She'd taken what they'd given her during her three days in the hospital, but now she was relying on ibuprofen and acetaminophen to ease her discomfort. That meant she was in enough pain to have an authentic reaction to Hunter's question.

"It hurts a little, but I'm getting used to it," she said.

He nodded. "We'll get you some ice as soon as we're inside. Come on in and meet your other housemates."

She'd read their bios on NASA's website while she was in the hospital, and she recalled the details as she followed Hunter along the path to the front door. Dean Bukowski was a mechanical engineer and roboticist. Valerie Ames was a triathlete as well as a scientist, and her fields were planetology, geology, and hydrology.

Hunter held the screen door open for her.

The house was designed very simply. She walked into an open kitchen with a big living room beyond it, the two areas separated by a granite-topped counter with bar stools on either side. Along the right side as she entered were two bedrooms behind closed doors.

The living room was the heart of the house. It had a light and airy feel, with big open windows and fluttering gauzy curtains and casual, comfortable furniture. When she and Hunter came in, Dean was sitting at a computer desk and Valerie was curled up on the sky-blue sofa with a laptop. They both looked up from their work to say hello.

Dean's shaggy hair and wiry physique was a marked contrast to Hunter's military bearing and athletic body. That, of course, was a contrast she'd expect to find in a Mars crew. The mission needed a mix of strengths and abilities and personality types, from geeks to jocks and everything in between.

Valerie represented the in between. She was powerful physically—a product of her triathlon training—and an equally formidable scientist. She told Airin to call her Val.

In addition to reading their bios, Airin had done some Googling. Now she was able to say to Dean, who was clearly itching to get back to his computer, "I'm impressed by what I've read about your helicopter drone project. Do you really think the counter-rotating propellers you're working on will help you cope with Mars's thin atmosphere?"

Dean's eyes lit up. "Yeah. I've been running lab tests at Mars air density, and we're showing some real progress. Of course, staying aloft isn't our only challenge. There's also the problem of the rough terrain the drones have to land on."

"That's my department," Val put in. "I've been working to set up a lab environment that mimics the different surface elements on Mars. Once Dean solves the lift problem, we'll be ready to tackle the terrain problem."

A moment ago, Dean and Val had seemed friendly enough, if distracted. But now the two of them wore an expression Airin recognized easily after growing up with her mother: the look of scientists who've just been given an excuse to talk about their work.

I can do this. I can relate to people. I can be a person in the world outside my mother's shadow.

And then Dean said, "Are you interested in Mars stuff because of your mother?"

So much for getting away from Dira Delaney.

Yes, she started to say—because that was the expected answer.

And yet, she realized suddenly, it wasn't true.

"No. I've been fascinated by Mars since I was a little girl."

Space had been her thing long before her mother had made it her life's work. She remembered her dad's stories about the little girl who'd stowed away to Mars and her own dreams about traveling to the Red Planet.

Dira didn't own the copyright to passion about interplanetary travel. Hadn't Dira herself said something like that in one of her speeches to investors? *Mars belongs to all of us. The push to establish a self-sustaining colony on another planet represents the hope and future of all humankind.*

Dean turned his computer monitor so she could see the screen. "Do you want to take a look at the drone blades I'm working on?"

"I'd love to."

Dean grinned at her. He seemed so eager and likable, like a shaggy puppy of some superintelligent variety. "Are you sure you know what you're getting into? Offering to look at an engineer's designs is like coming upstairs to look at a guy's etchings. Only you're thinking he's got something else in mind, when he really does want to show you his etchings. For hours."

She laughed. "I'm the daughter of two engineers. I know exactly what I'm getting into."

"Okay then, gorgeous. Just remember that I warned you."

But before she could cross the room, Hunter spoke up. "How about you two geek out a little later? I'm going to get Airin settled in her room, and then she needs to rest. Val, would you grab us an ice pack from the freezer?"

Val raised an eyebrow. "It's like Jones never left. You sound exactly like him when you give orders, Bryce. Mission commanders are all alike."

Hunter smiled. "It's not an order, it's a request. We'll be in Airin's room, okay?"

"Aye-aye, Captain."

Airin followed Hunter up the stairs to the second floor, which consisted of a hallway, two bedrooms, and a bathroom.

The whole house could have been tucked into a corner of her home in Massachusetts and no one would have noticed it.

"This is you," Hunter said, leading the way into the room on the right. She followed, and the first thing she noticed was the plumeria tree right outside her window. The scent wafted through the screen, and she closed her eyes as she took a deep breath.

The room was small but lovely, with the polished wood floors of the rest of the house and walls painted a pale apricot. There was a ceiling fan, a double bed covered in a Hawaiian-print quilt in shades of cream and green, a big wicker chair with cushions of the same pattern, and a desk and bookcase along one wall.

When she saw the books in the case—scientific tomes, a shelf full of Japanese manga, and another shelf full of horror novels—she remembered that they'd been using this room as an office. She was willing to bet that the manga belonged to Dean. Were the horror novels his, too? Or could they be Val's?

Val herself came in then, holding ice packs and a towel. She was tall, close to six feet, and Airin could easily imagine her running the Ironman triathlon here in Hawaii.

"Here you go," she said, laying down the towel before setting the ice packs on the desk.

She was turning to leave when Airin asked, "Who reads all the Stephen King? Is that you, Val?"

The other woman turned back and nodded. "Yep. I've been into horror since I stole my big brother's books to read with a flashlight under the covers. Are you a fan?"

"I've read him, but he's a little intense for me. I prefer—" She started to say *romance novels*, but she wasn't sure she was ready to admit that to a houseful of astronauts and scientists. "Mystery novels," she finished instead, which was also true. Romance was her favorite, but she'd read anything. "Is the manga Dean's?"

Val nodded. "Don't get him started on all that stuff, or you'll get an earful. Of course, that's true of any topic you pick."

Airin was about to say something else when Hunter spoke. "Thanks for the ice packs, Val. I was thinking of ordering pizza for dinner tonight. How does that sound? It'll be my treat."

"I never say no to a free meal. I need to eat by six, though. I'm giving a lecture at eight."

"Got it."

Once she was gone, Hunter turned to Airin. "You seem to be getting along with your new housemates."

His tone was neutral, but sort of carefully neutral, as though he wasn't really saying the thing he wanted to say.

She spoke tentatively, trying to feel him out. "That's good, isn't it?"

"Yeah. I guess." He turned away for a moment, going to the desk for one of the ice packs. "You should sit down and ice your ribs for a while. How long did the doctor say?"

"Ten to twenty minutes."

She went over to the bed and propped the pillows against the wall, sitting cross-legged against them. Hunter came over and handed her the blue pack, and the clammy wet chill of it was depressing somehow.

"Did I do something wrong?" she asked abruptly.

Hunter paused as he was hoisting one of her suitcases onto the end of the bed. "What?"

"It's just that you seem . . . I don't know. Disapproving? It made me wonder if I said something wrong."

"Of course you didn't say anything wrong," he said gruffly. "Just the opposite, in fact. You sure made a big hit with Dean."

She was more confused than ever. She was tempted to let it go, but a sudden wave of determination stiffened her spine. If she was going to make this whole living-in-the-world thing work, she had to face uncertainties—and people—head-on.

"You make it sound like that's a problem," she said. "What exactly bothers you about me making 'a big hit' with Dean?"

Hunter lifted her other case onto the end of the bed. Then he went over and sat on the desk chair, swiveling it around to face her.

"Here's the thing. You want to live on your own, right? Have a chance to experience the world?"

"Yes."

He rested his hands on his knees and leaned forward. "Then you can't be naïve."

She stared at him. She was holding the ice pack against her rib cage, and the feeling of numbness spreading outward was an exquisite relief.

"What are you talking about? How am I being naïve?"

"Dean is attracted to you, Airin. A lot of guys will be. You need to start adjusting to that reality if you want to keep yourself safe. I mean, not every guy is going to be as harmless as Dean. You need to be aware of the ulterior motives of the people around you."

She blinked. "I see."

"You just need to—"

"I want to show you something," she said, reaching into her pocket and pulling out her phone—the new one her mother had given her to replace the one she'd lost.

"What are you doing?"

"Just hang on a minute."

It took her less than that to find what she was looking for. She centered the relevant paragraph in the screen and held it out toward Hunter.

"Read that."

He rose from the chair, came over to the side of the bed, and took the phone from her.

"'Dean Bukowski lost his husband to cancer in 2013. After that tragedy, he—'"

Hunter broke off, looking down at the phone for a moment. Then he handed it back to her, went back to the desk chair, and sat down.

There was a short silence.

"Dean's gay," he said finally.

She nodded. "Dean's gay."

"I didn't know that," he muttered, frowning at the floor.

"Why didn't you? Don't mission team members get to know each other really well?"

He looked up again, his expression almost defensive. "Not always the personal stuff. And Dean and I weren't on the same crew."

"Right."

Was she enjoying this moment a little too much? This was the first time since she'd met Hunter that he'd seemed in the least embarrassed. He was always so in control, so cool and competent.

She had seen him angry, though—that first night in the bar, when the racist tourist had threatened her. Remembering that, she sat up a little straighter and spoke.

"If this is going to work—me living here, I mean—then you can't always be thinking of me as someone who needs to be protected. Not everything is going to be a threat to me. Not every guy I meet is going to look at me through some kind of sexual lens. Even the straight ones might see me as a person first and a woman second—even if you don't."

There was another silence, this one a little more tense.

Hunter's eyes were full of things, but she didn't know what they were. What was he thinking? What was he feeling?

"Airin," he said finally. "This probably goes without saying, but . . . you know nothing's going to happen between us, right? Physically, I mean."

Actually, no. She hadn't known that. But based on the way he'd been acting the last few days, she probably should have guessed.

"Because of my injury?" she asked, hoping she sounded cool and detached.

"Not only because of your injury. I just think it's a bad idea. It was one thing when I was some kind of adventure you were having, a one-time thing with a guy you'd never see again. But things aren't like that now."

"Right," she said, nodding. "Because now you'd have to actually see the woman you slept with. After the fact, I mean."

He didn't like that. She could tell by the way his brows drew together.

"I'm not some kind of player. I've been in relationships. But only when—" He stopped.

"Only when what? When the woman wasn't a virgin?"

"When both of us knew the score."

"The score," she repeated, drawing the word out. "Of course. The score. Which is what, exactly?"

His gaze shifted away as he dragged a hand across his short hair. He looked like a man who didn't want to be where he was right now.

"I've always thought astronauts are better off single," he said finally. "I've had relationships, but only when both of us understood it wasn't going anywhere. Anywhere long-term, I mean."

"And you think I wouldn't understand that?"

He met her eyes again. "That night at the beach, things were different. I was going into a biosphere for eight months. We both knew one night was all we had. But now . . ." He shook his head. "Now you'll think I have a choice. And you could get attached."

Attached. Like she was a stray puppy.

Her skin smarted, as though she'd been scraped raw by something.

Well, she'd wanted real life. Real interactions with people. What could be more real than a guy saying he wasn't into commitment?

But that wasn't the whole story. She was sure of it.

"My mother said something to you at the hospital. She told you to stay away from me. She threatened you or yelled at you or—"

"No. She didn't."

"Then what *did* she say to you that day? You never told me. In fact, you've kept your distance from me ever since."

He looked stung. "Kept my distance? I was in the hospital with you every day."

That was true.

What she'd meant, of course, was that the dynamic between them had changed. But how could she put that into words without sounding . . . desperate? Clingy?

One of those girl things men didn't like. Especially when they thought she might get "attached."

"I know she said something awful to you," she said instead, reverting to a subject she was sure about: her mother's instinct to be interfering and overbearing where her daughter was concerned.

"No, she didn't." Hunter rose to his feet and looked at the two suitcases on the bed. "Do you need me to unpack for you?"

So much for getting an answer out of him.

"No, I'll be fine. The doctors said I can do most normal tasks if I take it slow."

"Okay. But if you need anything at all, you text me. I'll be downstairs."

"I could, you know, just call out for you."

"Don't do any shouting. That might hurt your ribs. Just text *I need you*, and I'll come. All right?"

Something about that sentence was way too appealing—especially after the conversation they'd just had.

"All right."

And then he was gone, closing the door behind him.

Chapter Twelve

Hunter couldn't sleep.

He had Liam's room, which was across the hall from Airin's. He wished like hell he was downstairs. He'd made a fool of himself today, and being twenty feet away from her wasn't helping.

He was jealous, and not for the reasons she thought.

He remembered meeting Airin that first night and feeling like he really was her first contact on this planet. That she'd come from afar to visit Earth, and he was the lucky human being who got to meet her and talk to her—and kiss her.

And now here she was interacting with other people, and they had one important advantage over him in being part of Airin's life.

They weren't going behind her back to talk to Dira.

Of course that wasn't their fault. The corner he'd backed himself into was all of his own making. His choices, his decision, his betrayal.

It's not a betrayal, he told himself for the hundredth time. He was just letting Dira know how Airin was doing. He wasn't going to advocate for her mother's point of view or mediate that relationship or try to convince Airin to do what her mother wanted her to do.

So why did he still feel so shitty about it?

Because it *was* shitty.

He'd called Dira to give his first "report" after dinner, letting her know that her daughter was eating lightly—she'd only had one piece of pizza for dinner—but that she was in good spirits. She liked her housemates, she liked the house, and she'd managed to put him in his place within ten minutes of their arrival.

Okay, he hadn't actually mentioned that last part. But to his mind, that moment was the best indication yet that Airin was going to be okay . . . and that she might not be the helpless babe in the woods he still worried—and her mother believed—she was.

It had also been a wake-up call in another way.

Not every guy I meet is going to look at me through some kind of sexual lens.

For her sake, he hoped that was true. But the fact was, at the very moment she'd said that to him, at least 80 percent of his brain had been focused on one thing and one thing only.

She was holding an ice pack against her ribs, and the coldness, while hopefully easing the pain of her injury, was also having another effect on her body.

Her nipples hardened.

The fact that she wasn't wearing a bra—which he'd noticed the first instant he'd seen her that morning—meant that he could watch it happening with only the thin blue silk of her shirt in the way.

He'd never seen a woman with more perfect breasts.

Not that he was picky when it came to breasts. If a woman he liked was willing to get naked with him, he was pretty much good to go.

The same went for legs and butts. He didn't have a "type" the way some guys did. A woman either did it for him or she didn't, and if there was an algorithm to that—tall or short, curvy or flat-chested, plus-size or skinny or whatever—he hadn't yet figured out what it was.

But there was one thing he was sure of. If there was an algorithm, Airin Delaney had broken it. She turned his crank like no woman ever had before.

From this point forward, she would define his type.

A woman taller than five foot six would be too tall, and anything less than that would be too short. He would never again be able to call a blonde or a redhead the ideal of female beauty. Only jet-black hair and dark brown eyes could lay claim to that.

And only breasts of that shape—soft, on the small side, perky as hell—could ever be called perfect.

That night at the beach, he hadn't gotten to feel them against his palms. But the sight of her hard nipples under her blue silk shirt made it all too easy to imagine the contrast they'd make with her butter-soft skin.

And right now, lying in bed staring up at the lazy movement of the ceiling fan blades, imagining that sensation was enough to get him hard.

Fuck.

He'd told himself his arrangement with Dira would make Airin so off-limits it wouldn't even be an issue. But apparently his body didn't care about the moral reasoning his mind came up with.

He tried to think about other things. He thought about his meeting with the Mars project team tomorrow, to talk about the next eight months. He'd be doing pilot simulations and hardware evaluation and all the experiments the scientists had lined up for Jones. And then, of course, there were the inevitable presentations and interviews—most via Skype since he'd moved to Hawaii—that astronauts were always expected to make.

"Our job is half PR," he always groused—though never to anyone with the power to make flight assignments.

You didn't grouse about anything to them. There were too many people who wanted to take your spot in the food chain. Candidates who didn't complain, ever. Candidates who scored high on the psych chart for "adapts successfully to situations without trying to change them."

This was a critical skill for astronauts, who had to solve problems using limited resources and without any backup.

Play the position you have, not the one you think you should have.

That made him think about the DelAres deal. When he and Dira had spoken after dinner, she'd suggested he not quit his job with NASA while Airin was staying with him. That, she'd said, would make Airin ask questions.

"Why would I quit my job with NASA?"

Dira had sounded surprised at the question. "Because you no longer need them to reach your goal. I've offered you the chance you want to go to Mars, and once things with my daughter are resolved, you'll be working for me." She'd paused. "Unless you don't trust me to fulfill my side of the bargain."

"No," he'd said. "I trust you."

Dira Delaney had a reputation for impeccable integrity and for keeping her word. But even so: "I trust you, but I don't have a signed contract or job offer in hand."

"You can't expect me to generate that kind of paperwork during the Airin situation. I can't take the risk she might learn of our arrangement."

"I get that. But I'm planning to operate like nothing has changed. After the 'Airin situation' is resolved, I'll expect to see a contract from you. We can figure out a transition then." He'd paused. "And anyway, you contract with NASA. I know you want to beat them to Mars, but they're your ally more than your enemy. It'll be in everyone's best interest if I'm in good standing with them. And that means working out a transition that satisfies both parties—when the time comes."

Yeah, he'd keep working for NASA. He'd work his heart out for them, doing his best to redeem himself after bailing on the biosphere mission. He'd take whatever they threw at him, including all of Jones's responsibilities.

That seemed to be doing the trick. Thinking about all the shit he'd have to do in Jones's place was boring enough that he was actually starting to feel a little sleepy. Maybe if he closed his eyes and—

A scream of terror ripped through the night, and he sat bolt upright in bed.

The voice was Airin's.

He was on his feet before he could blink, out of his room and into the hallway. There was a light on in the bathroom, and he lunged for the doorway.

Airin was naked.

She was standing in the middle of the bathroom floor, her hands pressed against her mouth, her whole body rigid with horror. He followed the line of her gaze to the bathtub and saw two of the immense winged cockroaches that flourished in the tropical climate of Hawaii.

Ah.

Feet were pounding up the stairs, and he stuck his head out into the hallway to say, "It's okay, guys. Airin's first encounter with *Periplaneta americana.*"

Dean and Val, pajama-clad and disheveled, understood immediately. Val merely nodded and padded back downstairs. Dean asked, "You want me to get them out?"

He shook his head, conscious of Airin's nakedness. "We're good."

"All right. Good night," Dean said, turning to follow Val downstairs.

Trained as he was to react quickly under pressure, it nonetheless took Hunter at least three seconds to make his next decision.

It wasn't even a complicated one. Did he allow himself one more look at the most perfect naked female body he'd ever seen, or did he respect Airin's privacy?

After a brief struggle, he came down on the side of honor and decency. He stepped into the room, keeping his back to Airin as he grabbed a towel. He kept his back turned as he held it toward her.

"Here."

A beat went by. Then she took it from him, and after another moment, he figured it was safe to turn around again.

The white towel was wrapped tightly around her torso, and she held it closed with a hand at her sternum. She was trembling.

"What are they?" she asked. "My God, what are they? What the hell is a *Periplaneta americana*?"

"Cockroaches," he said, wishing he hadn't been so damn honorable. Seeing her in a towel that covered her from just above her breasts to just below the juncture of her thighs was doing terrible things to his peace of mind.

Airin stared at him. Then she looked back at the two insects, every detail of their brown bodies visible against the white enameled surface of the bathtub.

"They're too big to be cockroaches. They're . . . giant. Like something out of a nightmare."

He moved slowly toward the tub. There was a window above it, and he raised the screen, his movements still measured. Then he crouched down and his hands shot out, grasping the bugs lightly but firmly.

He rose to his feet, a cockroach in each hand, and tossed them through the open window out into the night. Then he lowered the screen and went to the sink to wash his hands.

He leaned back against the sink as he dried his hands. "See? They're gone. Nothing to worry about."

Airin was still frozen in the middle of the floor, her brown eyes huge as she stared at him.

"You didn't kill them. You released them. Like . . . like they were birds or squirrels or something. How can you stand to touch those things?"

He grinned. "I don't look at bugs the way I look at birds, but I try not to kill things when I don't have to. And cockroaches actually play an important role in the ecosystem. They have a taste for decaying organic matter, which means they recycle fallen and dead vegetation. If you think about how prolific the plants are in Hawaii, we'd probably be up to our necks in vegetable debris if it weren't for cockroaches and other insect scavengers."

She stared at him for a moment. Then, slowly, some of the tension eased from her shoulders.

"They're still disgusting."

"No argument."

He saw the muscles in her throat jump as she swallowed. "When I first saw them, do you know what I thought?"

He shook his head.

"I thought, *That's it. My mother wins. Experiment over. I'm going back home.*"

She went over to the toilet and sat down on the lid, closing her eyes for a moment and then opening them again.

There was an empty feeling in his stomach.

Was this really it? Was she going to call it quits without even giving it a full day?

He ought to be rooting for that outcome. If she left Hawaii, that would satisfy his bargain with Dira. Airin would be safe at home with her mother, he wouldn't be a spy anymore, and he'd find out if Dira intended to honor her side of the deal with a written contract.

He spoke abruptly. "Are you really going to let a cockroach stop you from doing what you want to do?"

She blinked. "Actually, no. But I thought about it."

He was surprised at the strength of the relief that flooded through him.

"I'm sorry I screamed so loud," she went on. "I heard you talking to Dean and Val. Are they mad at me for waking them up?"

He shook his head. "Nah. As far as they know, this is one of NASA's psychological tests. Sometimes they'll call us at three in the morning to see if we get annoyed—or if we show it, anyway. Can we control our emotions under stress? Not only when we're expecting it, but when we're not?"

Airin smiled a little. "One of my mother's research partners ran an isolation experiment last year. It was a week long. On day three, the toilet in the pod broke. The five people in the experiment assumed it was a genuine mechanical failure and figured out ways to cope. They didn't find out until the experiment ended that the designers did that to them on purpose."

He nodded. "That sounds like something NASA would do. They want to find out how we'll deal with frustration . . . and the unexpected." He grinned. "After the way you reacted to the cockroaches, I'm guessing you wouldn't pass the astronaut selection tests."

He'd meant to make her smile again. But instead, a frown drew her brows together as she looked down at her bare feet.

Maybe her ribs were hurting.

"How's your injury? Are you feeling it?"

She looked up again. "It's fine. A little painful, but I'll survive."

"I'll get you an ice pack."

"You don't have to—"

"And a cup of tea."

That brought her smile back.

"Tea sounds wonderful. But you don't have to wait on me, Hunter. I can get it myself."

He brushed that off. "Go make yourself comfortable. I'll be back in five minutes."

He was wearing boxers and a T-shirt, so he stopped in his room to pull on a pair of jeans. Then he went down to the kitchen and nuked some water in the microwave.

Airin was sitting up in bed when he came in through her doorway, carrying a mug of lemon mint tea in one hand and an ice pack in the other. She was wearing white cotton pajamas, light enough for a tropical night . . . which meant they were light enough that he could see the contrast between the pale skin of her breasts and the darker skin of her aureoles.

Awesome. Just what he needed to calm his body down.

Still, it was better than that quick, searing glimpse of her naked body. Which reminded him: "Were you going to take a shower when you saw the cockroaches?"

She took the tea from him, setting it down on the nightstand beside her. Then she took the ice pack.

"A bath, actually. I couldn't sleep, and I thought a bath would help."

He should just go. Say good night and get back to his own room.

Instead, he sat down on the edge of the bed.

"Do you still want to take the bath? I could run one for you."

She shook her head. "No way. I'd keep thinking about the cockroaches. I may never go into that bathroom again."

"Yeah, you will," he said as she positioned the ice pack against her ribs and held it in place. "You're not a coward, Airin. You were just surprised."

She frowned a little. "I thought you said I was a coward."

When the hell had he said that?

"What are you talking about?"

"In the bathroom. You said I'd fail the astronaut selection tests."

He remembered her reaction to that offhand joke.

"It's quite a leap to think I was calling you a coward. Which I wasn't, by the way. But why would the idea of failing some NASA thing bother you?"

Airin was quiet for a moment. Through her open windows, moist air flowed in as the wind picked up. It smelled like rain, and as though his thought made it happen, the patter of drops came moments later.

"It didn't bother me, exactly," she said after a long pause. "But I dreamed of being an astronaut once, when I was a little girl. What you said about selection tests reminded me that I'll never be one. That's all." She shrugged. "I'm living with three astronauts now. Three people who know exactly what they're doing with their lives, while I still don't have a clue. I guess I'm jealous."

The smell of rain in Hawaii was like nothing else. It was rich and soft and earthy and green, with the delicate scent of a hundred different flowers mixed in.

That must be why he felt so awake. Because of the rain-washed air blowing in through the windows.

He pulled up his legs and sat cross-legged on the end of Airin's bed, facing her. He rested his elbows on his knees and clasped his hands in his lap as he leaned forward.

"Your dad told you stories about a little girl. She stowed away on a rocket ship and went to Mars."

She smiled at him. "You remember that?"

"Yeah. Tell me more about what you and your dad talked about. Was he always interested in space travel?"

Her eyes went far away for a moment. Then she shifted against the pillows to get comfortable.

"My father was nine years old when Apollo 11 landed on the moon. From that moment on, he wanted to be an astronaut. He joined the navy because he thought that was his best chance. He applied for the Astronaut Candidate Program through the military, and he was chosen."

His eyebrows went up. "He was? Wow. That's a pretty big deal. There are more astronauts now, between NASA's new programs and private companies like your mother's, but back then your dad would have had something like a point five percent chance of being chosen."

"Point six percent, actually." Airin smiled a little. "And yes, it was a big deal."

He frowned. "But he didn't join the program?"

"No."

"Why not? What happened?"

"I happened."

"You mean . . . you were born?"

"Yes. And I know lots of astronauts have wives and kids and all that. But my mother already hated that she'd fallen in love with a fighter pilot, because her father had been an aviator in Iran."

"Your father and your grandfather were both pilots?"

She nodded. "And they were both killed in action—or at least, we assume my grandfather was. My grandmother was never given all the details, but he was lost during the sixties when the Iranian air force joined forces with the CIA to do reconnaissance over the Soviet Union. Several planes crashed or were shot down during that time, but not all of the losses could be reported because of the secrecy of the mission. We still don't know—officially—what happened to my grandfather."

One of his classmates at the Air Force Academy was the son of an airman who'd been declared MIA in Vietnam. Nothing was worse than the uncertainty of not knowing what had happened to a family member.

"How old was your mother when she lost her dad?"

"Only eight. Things got worse after that. The Kurdish separatist movement was escalating, and there was violence. My mother and grandmother came to America as refugees in the seventies, when my mother was a teenager. They lived in Maryland when they first got here, and my mom met my dad when he was at the Naval Academy. Midshipman Frank Delaney."

She set the ice pack on the nightstand and shifted her position so she was sitting cross-legged like him. Her shirt was wet where she'd been icing her ribs and her nipples were pebbled, but by God he was going to ignore that fact if it killed him.

She was smiling at a memory, her brown eyes far away again. "My grandmother liked to tell the story of how she warned my mother not to fall for a pilot. She gave her a big lecture one day, not long after my mom met my dad at a party. Gran said that even as the words came out of her mouth, she could see in my mother's eyes that she was a goner.

That was Gran's favorite part of the story, because she loved the word *goner*. She prided herself on her knowledge of American slang."

"Did she object when your mother wanted to marry your father?"

"Loudly. But she adored my dad from the moment she met him, and he loved her, too. I was glad she passed away before my father was killed. His death would have broken her heart."

"You were telling me why your dad didn't become an astronaut."

"Right. Well, like I said, my mother and grandmother didn't love that he was a fighter pilot. But they made their peace with it, and they were ready to make peace with the astronaut thing, too. Then my mother got pregnant with me, and he changed his mind. We moved to Florida, and he taught at the naval flight school in Pensacola. It was great for the whole family. My grandmother loved the climate. My mother got her third advanced degree at the University of Florida and began her nanowire technology work. A few years later, she started on rocket fuel. My father enjoyed teaching, and both my parents were able to spend a lot of time with me, all things considered. My memories of Pensacola are good ones." She paused. "Really good."

It sounded like a nice life. But in a way, what she was describing was his greatest fear realized. A fighter pilot, no doubt as cocky and in love with flying as they all were, grounded because of emotional attachments. Turned into a no-load because he had too much to lose . . . and people in his life who couldn't bear to lose him.

This was why single men and women made the best astronauts—and fighter pilots. How could you give your focus to your job if you were worried about your spouse and kids at home?

Worrying about a teammate was different. They were like you; they'd signed up for this crazy shit and knew what they were getting into. But a husband or wife? Or kids? They hadn't signed up for it. And having met the spouses and children of pilots over the years, he knew they worried every minute of every day that their loved one was in the air.

And every minute of every day that he wasn't in the air, a pilot was wishing he was.

Or at least he'd always thought so. But maybe Airin's father hadn't felt that way.

Still, he'd died a fighter pilot's death in the end—in the North Arabian Sea, Hunter had learned when he'd looked up the record. So Frank Delaney had found his way back to a mission.

He thought he could guess why.

"When did your dad start flying combat missions again? Was it after 9/11?"

Airin nodded. "I was twelve years old when he was killed." She paused. "I didn't mean to talk about that, though."

Shit. "I'm sorry. I didn't mean to remind you of—"

"No, it's not that. I don't mind talking about any part of my dad's life . . . or death. But it must be after midnight and—"

"You're tired. And your ribs hurt."

She shrugged. "I'm a little tired, but I'm okay. And the ice helped my ribs. But you have an early-morning meeting tomorrow, don't you? And a PT test before that? At, like, five in the morning or something?"

Yeah, he did. But like a college kid willing to sacrifice sleep to spend time with his crush, he'd pretty much forgotten all about his morning commitments.

There was something about talking to Airin that made him want to keep going. And it wasn't just because talking to her meant he could look at her, too.

Although keeping his eyes on her face when he was so conscious of her body had resulted in a special kind of wide-awakeness. That top she wore was no barrier at all. All he'd have to do was lower his gaze a few inches and he'd see her nipples and the soft curve of her breasts with only a whisper of material covering them . . . and the memory of seeing her naked in the bathroom to sharpen the experience.

It was no hardship to look into the rich brown of her eyes, and it felt like he could do that one thing forever. But his awareness of her body—and the need to keep that awareness from Airin—created an electric tension that made him anything but tired.

"Yeah," he said, wondering how long it would take him to fall asleep tonight. "I should probably get to bed. And you need rest, too. We can pick up this conversation tomorrow."

Another gust of rain-damp wind blew through the window, and both he and Airin turned like animals scenting something on the air.

"What is that smell?" Airin asked him. "It's so . . . I don't know. Delicious. Perfect. It makes me want to walk in it."

"I know what you mean." He thought about walking in the gentle Hawaiian rain with Airin, and it was such an appealing idea that it took his breath away.

"You're right," he said abruptly. "It's getting late. I should go." He surged to his feet. "You didn't drink your tea. Do you want a fresh cup? Or anything else? Is there something you need before you go to bed? Anything that's hard for you to do because of your ribs?"

Airin shook her head. "Only my princess routine. And I can do without that until my ribs heal."

He blinked. "Princess routine?"

She smiled. "That's what my dad used to call it. Every night before bed, my grandmother and I would brush our hair together. One hundred strokes. We started when I was a toddler, and I've done it ever since. But with my ribs, all I can manage now is one or two strokes. It's fine, though. I'm thinking about cutting my hair, to be honest. It would be so much easier to take care of."

Cut her hair? He was surprised at how much he hated that idea, even though he knew Airin's hair was none of his goddamn business.

"Let me do it," he heard himself say.

Her eyebrows rose. "You want to brush my hair?"

His fingers curled into his palms at the thought of touching that incredible softness again.

Man, this was a colossal mistake.

"Sure. Why not? It's part of your routine, and routines are important. Pilots are all about routine. Space psychologists talk about the importance of routine on long missions."

"I'm not on a long mission," she pointed out.

"Sure you are. It's called life on Earth." He looked around the room. "Where's your brush?"

She opened the drawer of her nightstand and pulled it out. It was a beautiful thing, the handle made of smooth dark wood and the bristles as black as her hair. It felt good in his hand, solid and functional and satisfying to hold.

Airin didn't say anything else. She moved to make room for him and then turned her back, sitting cross-legged again, her hands clasped in her lap and her spine very straight.

He sat down on the bed behind her.

The waves of her black hair fell to the middle of her back, between her shoulder blades. He reached up, placed the brush against the top of her head, and then moved it down, slowly, to the tips of her hair.

God, that felt good.

There was just enough resistance against the bristles of the brush to give a satisfying feeling of substance and heft to what he was doing, like moving a paddle through water. He did it again, moving the brush to the right, and again to the left.

Then again. And again.

There was something hypnotic about the repetition of this simple action. The scent of her hair was just as he remembered—faintly spicy with an undertone of amber. He remembered her mother's assistant bringing her toiletries from the hotel and the nurse offering to help her shower.

He wished he could thank that nurse. Because of her, Airin smelled the way she had that first night: like everything mysterious and delicious that had ever been.

The scent pulled him in. He was holding himself very still as he brushed, because every cell in his body was tugging him forward, telling him to mold his body to Airin's, to comb his fingers through her hair, to kiss the side of her neck.

But somehow he stayed on task. This should be one of NASA's psych tests—a way to prove you could stay rational and focused in the most extreme circumstances.

"Hunter?"

He froze. Neither of them had said a word since the brush had first touched her hair.

"Yeah?"

"Do you mind if I ask you a question?"

Chapter Thirteen

Airin held herself absolutely still. The two times she'd kissed Hunter had been about unleashing desire, swimming in it, while this was about restraining it. Hiding it. Hanging on by a thread to a kind of self-discipline she'd never needed before.

It would be so easy to turn and kiss him. Her broken ribs wouldn't stop her. With all the adrenaline pumping through her veins, she couldn't even feel them.

But he'd told her today he didn't want a relationship. He'd said nothing was going to happen between them physically. Maybe she could get him to change his mind if she turned right now and pressed her body to his. But what if he didn't change his mind?

She'd already shared so much with him. She'd made herself vulnerable while he kept all his secrets. That, at least, had to change.

The question she'd just asked echoed in the space between them. He'd stopped brushing her hair halfway through a stroke, and for a few heartbeats they stayed like that, all movement arrested.

Then he finished the stroke. "Go ahead," he told her.

"Why don't you like talking about your parents?"

Stillness again. This time he stopped between strokes, so there was no point of physical contact between them. They were joined only by the energy that crackled in the air like a static charge.

"That's a hell of a question," he said finally, the brush moving through her hair again.

All the tiny invisible hairs on her arms were standing straight up. "You know things about me. I want to know things about you. It's only fair," she added.

Another stroke. "You have a way of putting things that's not like anyone else. You say things out loud that other people don't."

Did she? "Well, it's up to you whether you talk to me or not. All I can do is ask questions. You know what my childhood was like. What was yours like?"

Two more strokes, and then he answered. "It was pretty decent, for a while. My brother and I grew up on a ranch in Colorado. It was my dad's ranch, in the family five generations."

"And your mother?"

"She was a singer. Dad saw her at some bar in Colorado Springs and fell head over heels. They got married three weeks later."

"Three weeks? Wow."

"Yeah. In retrospect, not such a great decision. I think my mom was happy for a while, but when I was thirteen she took off."

"Took off? You mean . . . she left?"

"Yep."

"Did she ever come back?"

"No. Caleb and I would get postcards once in a while. She started singing again, traveling to honky-tonk bars in Las Vegas and Mexico and California. I still get postcards sometimes. The last one was six months ago, I think. She was in Bakersfield."

She tried to imagine her own mother abandoning her like that. Just . . . taking off one day, never looking back.

There was a pain behind her breastbone that had nothing to do with her ribs.

"That must have been so hard. On your dad, too. He had to be both mother and father to you and Caleb."

He was still brushing her hair, slowly and carefully. How many strokes was he up to now? Fifty? Sixty?

"Yeah, it was hard on him. Too hard. He killed himself a year later, when I was fourteen."

Oh God.

Why had she started asking him questions?

The ache behind her breastbone spread through her whole body. She wanted to turn around, but not to kiss him. She wanted to look into his eyes and comfort him, but she didn't know how. What could she possibly do? What could she say?

"Hey, Airin?"

She swallowed. "Yes?"

"You don't have to say anything."

Had she spoken aloud? Or did he just know what she was thinking?

"Okay," she whispered.

"You don't have to be sad, either."

The brush still moved through her hair, and the sensation mingled with the pain she was feeling until she was almost overwhelmed.

She closed her eyes. "How can I not be sad?"

"Because I'm not. Not anymore. I've had a lot of years to deal with it. I even saw a shrink when I was at the Air Force Academy. A really good guy."

"What did he tell you?"

"When someone commits suicide, it's like they had a terminal illness that finally killed them."

She thought about it. "And that . . . helped?"

"Yeah. It did. It helped me stop blaming myself."

That made sense. But her heart still ached, and there was a lump in her throat she couldn't swallow past.

"Who took care of you after your father died?"

"My aunt Rosemary. She's an incredible person. She did a great job with me and Caleb, and with the ranch, too. I just saw her at Caleb's wedding. She gave him away."

"Gave him away? But he was the groom."

He chuckled. "Yeah. He and Jane decided they both wanted to be given away. Jane by her parents, and Caleb by Rosemary. It was nice."

It sounded nice. But the lump was still in her throat.

"I'm glad your aunt was there for you. After . . . after everything."

There was a soft stroke on the side of her neck, as though he'd brushed her skin with a fingertip. "Do you wish you hadn't asked me about my childhood?"

She shivered. Everything felt intense—so intense that every word, every movement, every breath of air felt strange and powerful and poignant.

"No," she said. "I don't wish that." She paused. "But I'm sorry if I made you uncomfortable."

"That's not what's making me uncomfortable," he said, his voice low. He stopped brushing. "Okay. One hundred strokes—more or less."

She felt him shift behind her, and she heard the clatter of the brush on her bedside table.

"Good night, Airin."

She turned her head in time to see him disappear through the doorway. "Good night, Hunter."

He was gone. But that one glimpse had been enough to see the erection straining against his jeans.

◆ ◆ ◆

Airin woke up late—after nine in the morning. Her torso was stiff, and she got up slowly, going over to the window.

Last night's rain had left everything fresh and sparkling, and the white and yellow plumeria blossoms looked like velvet in the morning light. There were no vehicles in the driveway—Hunter's truck, Val's Toyota, and Dean's electric car were all gone.

The house was empty. She was alone.

Wow. When was the last time she'd been able to say that? Had she *ever* been able to say it?

Her torso was aching badly. She took some Tylenol and got an ice pack from the freezer, bringing it back to her room so she could lie in bed to ice her ribs.

As soon as she rested back against the pillows, thoughts of Hunter filled her mind.

She ought to be thinking about the day ahead. Her stay here on Oahu was about figuring out what she wanted to do with her life, so she'd made some appointments at the university. Her next step would most likely be a master's degree, but she still wasn't sure what she wanted to study. Medicine was at the top of her list, but there were plenty of other subjects that interested her.

She wanted to explore all the possibilities.

The University of Hawaii probably wasn't where she'd end up, but she relished the idea of exploring a campus in person after years of distance learning, and UH was only a short bus ride away. Val had given her a bus schedule after dinner last night, unaware that this would be the first public transportation Airin had ever taken in her life.

She relished the idea of that, too.

Yet even as she tried to focus on the coming day, going over mental checklists of what she wanted to do, images of Hunter kept intruding.

Thoughts of what he'd told her about his childhood got tangled up with the memory of him brushing her hair, until attraction and affection and concern and admiration were all jumbled together in her mind.

The concern was for what he'd gone through as a boy. The admiration was for the man he'd become. The attraction and affection had been there all along, almost from the first moment she saw him.

And they'd been growing ever since.

Is this what it feels like to fall for someone?

God, she hoped not. Because Hunter had made it very clear he had no intention of falling for her.

Instead of hoping she wasn't falling for him, she had to make sure she didn't. Hunter was an amazing person, and she wanted to know him better, but if she let herself get all starry-eyed over a man who'd never be with her, she was just asking to get her heart broken.

It was time to stop mooning and start figuring out the rest of her life. And in order to do that, she needed coffee.

That simple thing turned out to be more of a challenge than she'd expected. Because when she got down to the kitchen and stared at the coffeemaker on the counter, it occurred to her that she'd never used one before.

She'd never had to.

Thank God Hunter, Val, and Dean weren't here to witness her ignorance. Only the entitled daughter of a billionaire would be baffled by the prospect of making her own coffee, and she didn't want to be seen that way.

Besides, she wouldn't be baffled for long.

Human beings can solve any engineering problem they face, whether it's large or small. When confronted by a machine you don't understand, you just have to be smarter than it is.

Dira had said that to her once. It was mildly irritating that she still heard her mother's voice in her head sometimes, but in this case, the voice was useful.

So. There were three elements involved here, right? Water, coffee grounds, and heat. The coffeemaker heated the water and then forced that water through the coffee grounds, resulting in a delicious morning beverage.

The controls were simple: just On and Off. The water reservoir in the back was easy to identify. When she pulled on the plastic handle above the empty pot, she discovered used coffee grounds in a damp paper nest—the coffee filter.

Okay, good. She could reverse engineer what to do on the front end from what she saw here on the back end. She took out the wet filter and set it on the counter, rinsing out the detachable plastic basket that had held it and setting it on the counter as well.

Next step: finding the coffee and the filters.

She didn't have any luck finding coffee, and she finally checked the trash to see if they'd used the last of it making this morning's pot.

No empty coffee container, but there was an empty box of coffee filters.

Great.

Okay, one problem at a time. Where else would you store coffee, if not in your kitchen cabinets? A memory of her grandmother came to her, and she checked the freezer.

There it was: a bag of coffee. When she set it on the counter and opened it, a delicious scent arose.

Now for something that could approximate a filter. What was its function? To keep the grounds out of the finished product.

All right, then. She just needed something that would accomplish that.

Like paper towels.

She used two, wanting the base to be sturdy enough not to fall apart, and folded them to fit in the basket. Then she measured out coffee until she had an aromatic pile that looked similar in size to the one in the used filter.

She slid the basket into place, rinsed out the coffeepot, and filled it with cold tap water. Then she poured that into the water reservoir, set the pot on the burner underneath the basket, and turned the switch from Off to On.

Then she waited.

A mechanical noise began: the heating elements, she assumed, beginning the process of boiling the water. It sounded like steam. Once the water was hot enough, it would be introduced into the basket, where it would work its way through the coffee grounds. She waited and watched, and after a few minutes a small steady stream of brown fluid began to splash into the pot.

She was making coffee.

It was ridiculous to feel so excited about such a tiny accomplishment. But as she poured out a mugful and added milk and sugar, watching the liquid turn the perfect shade of medium brown, she was grinning. And when she took her first sip, it was the best coffee she'd ever tasted.

Still, she might experiment tomorrow, using more coffee or less water to adjust the strength of the brew.

Whatever she decided to try, she could figure it out.

She figured out the bus, too, and spent the day on the university campus. She'd made her appointments while she was in the hospital, and she'd been cynically unsurprised when busy professors and department heads had agreed to meet with her. They knew who she was—or rather, who her mother was—and Airin was sure they had dollar signs in their eyes as they imagined Dira Delaney's daughter matriculating at their university. Donations, endowments, a new science building funded by and named after her . . . no doubt all of those possibilities had motivated people to find space for her in their schedules.

She wasn't sure what to expect when she went into the meetings. But when she came out of the last one and met Val in the library parking lot—her new housemate had offered her a ride home when they'd bumped into each other at the science center—she had a new and sort of wonderful problem.

"I'm interested in everything," she said when Val asked her how the day had gone.

Val grinned as she pulled out of the parking lot onto University Avenue. "You should be an astronaut. They're interested in everything. Science and exploration, adventure and philosophy, engineering and physics."

Another reminder of the one career she knew she couldn't have. People with medical issues didn't become astronauts.

She was quiet for the next few minutes, looking out at the houses and gardens they were passing. University Avenue became Oahu Avenue, and half a mile later they turned right on Manoa Road, heading deeper into the valley.

Only when they turned onto the network of smaller roads that led to their house did Val speak again.

"Did I upset you somehow? I'm sorry if I did."

Airin shook her head. "You just reminded me of a conversation I had with Hunter last night."

Val accepted that answer without comment, and Airin realized that she was very comfortable in the other woman's presence. It was nice to be around someone who could let some things go.

"Thank you for the ride," she said as Val pulled into their driveway.

"Anytime."

All three of her housemates—Hunter, Val, and Dean—were doing so much for her. She was paying rent, but did that make up for adding another person to the household? It was no small thing to go from three people to four. They'd increased their population by 33.33 percent, and now Val was giving her rides. Was she contributing enough in exchange for what they were giving her?

"Is there anything I can do for you?" she asked as she followed Val through the door into the kitchen.

Val looked confused as she went into the living room and set her laptop case on the coffee table. "You mean around the house? Or in general?"

"Either. Both." She rested her forearms on the granite countertop that separated the kitchen area from the living room, where Val was taking her usual seat on the couch. "I've spent a lot of my life feeling useless. I'd like to start feeling useful."

Val nodded. "I get that. If you're serious, I'll take you up on your offer. I'm always looking for help in the lab." She grinned as she kicked off her flip-flops and tucked her bare feet underneath her. "As far as doing stuff around the house, that can wait until your ribs heal up."

Airin grinned back. "It's a deal. What are you working on? The Mars terrain simulation for Dean's drones?"

"That's more of a side project. What I'd really love help with is my ISRU procedures." She paused. "That's—"

"In-situ resource utilization," Airin finished. "The ability to harness Mars's own natural resources for survival."

Val looked delighted. "Right. Exactly. That'll be the key to creating a self-sustaining community on Mars someday, one that won't depend on endless resupply ships from Earth. I'm developing techniques for extracting water and carbon dioxide from volcanic rock. It's a good analog to Martian regolith, and there's plenty of it here in Hawaii. Would you want to help with those experiments?"

"I'd love to. That sounds amazing."

And it did. Someday, those techniques would be the difference between a mission to visit Mars and a mission to live there.

Even if she couldn't go into space herself, she could find ways to help the people who could. People like Val and Dean.

And Hunter.

Chapter Fourteen

Hunter stayed out late that night—late enough that Airin was already in bed when he got back, which was exactly what he'd been hoping for.

Not that he didn't want to see her. The problem was, he wanted to see her too damn much.

He'd sent a group text to her and Val and Dean earlier. It said simply, Working late tonight. See you all tomorrow.

Val had sent a thumbs-up emoji in reply. Dean and Airin hadn't responded.

Maybe they'd all been together when they got the text, and Val had answered for the group. But now he was wishing he'd texted Airin separately. Because twenty-four hours had gone by since he'd seen her, and he didn't know how she was doing. She'd been planning to spend the day on campus. How had that gone? How was she feeling?

Did she want him to brush her hair tonight?

And there it was. The reason he hadn't texted her separately. The reason he'd stayed out so long, putting in extra hours on Jones's pilot simulation project.

Something about Airin pulled him in deep whenever they were together. He needed to break that cycle before it led to a place they shouldn't go.

There was a light showing under Val's door when he got home, but Dean's room was dark. When he went upstairs, Airin's room was dark, too.

It was hard to tell which was stronger—his relief or his disappointment.

He checked his email before he went to bed, and Caleb had sent a photo of him and Jane on their honeymoon. Their arms were around each other's waists, and they were grinning like fools.

See you in eight months, Caleb had written under the photo.

He and Jane had gotten married when and where they did because of Hunter's biosphere mission. He still hadn't told them what had happened.

He wrote a long email to his brother explaining the last few days and then sat staring at his computer. He was tired and ready for sleep, but something had been nagging at him all day, and now he Googled it.

Wolff-Parkinson-White. The name of Airin's heart condition.

He read for a few minutes. Then he turned off the computer and went to bed.

He didn't see Airin in the morning, and by the afternoon he couldn't take it anymore. Almost forty-eight hours had gone by since the last time they'd spoken, and that had to have been enough to put a little distance between them.

As he drove home in the early evening, a miracle in the sky gave him the perfect reason to talk to her . . . if she was home.

She was.

He pushed open the screen door and saw Val and Airin on the couch. They were facing each other with Val's computer between them, having an animated discussion about something technical.

He crossed to the counter that separated the kitchen from the living room and rested his forearms on it.

Val glanced up. "Hey, Bryce."

"Hey."

In theory he was speaking to both of them, but the only one he really saw was Airin.

She looked eager and alive, interested in whatever Val was showing her. She was wearing shorts, a white T-shirt with green turtles all over it, and sandals. All were brand-new.

She looked up at him with a smile. "Hunter! It feels like I haven't seen you in days. How are you?"

Her mahogany eyes were like a gravity well—deep and inescapable.

"Not bad," he said. "Jones is doing great in the biosphere, so the mission directors aren't as pissed at me as they were a few days ago. They're still pissed enough to take it out of my hide in work hours, though. They've got me on the hook for more simulations than I ever wanted to do in my life."

Val shook her head at him. "Welcome to the world of the backup crew. Airin might have some sympathy for you, but Dean and I don't."

"Fair enough. How about I buy dinner tonight? Chinese takeout? I'm willing to do whatever it takes to get on your good side."

"I won't say no. How's eight o'clock? Dean won't be back until then, and I'd like to finish the project I'm working on."

"Sure. Hey, Airin? What are you doing right now?"

"Val's getting me up to speed on her research projects. I'm going to be helping her out for the next month."

Val had mentioned that when he'd run into her at the gym. "I heard. I think that's great. But aren't you focused on figuring out your next steps? Where you want to go to grad school, what you want to study?"

"That's not a full-time job. And whatever I end up pursuing, I've decided I want to be part of the space program. I'll never be an astronaut myself, but I can support the people who are. Helping Val is a good start."

That reminded him of what he'd read last night and what he'd been thinking about today. But he could get to that later. "Can you guys take a break? There's something I want to show you."

"Airin's a free agent, but I've got some more work to do. Will it take long?" Val asked.

"Nope."

Val closed her laptop, and the two of them came toward him. He held the screen door open, and Airin gasped as they stepped outside.

The setting sun was behind them. In front of them, glowing like the heart of a prism against the rain on the far side of the valley, was a double rainbow.

Hawaii was famous for its rainbows. He'd probably seen a hundred since he'd moved here. But this one . . . this one was something else.

Both rainbows were complete arches, and both were perfect. They seemed close enough to touch, and the colors were so real and so vivid it felt like they were their own element, something you could dive through like water.

After a minute, Val sighed. "Wow, that's beautiful. I'm going back to work, but I'm glad you brought us out here. Thanks, Bryce."

"Sure."

Airin hadn't said a word yet. They stood in silence for another minute, just looking at the sky, before she spoke.

"Can we walk that way? Toward it, I mean?"

"Yeah," he said, and they started down the driveway to the road. When they turned left at the cross street, the rainbow was right in front of them.

It was like walking in a dream.

"Why isn't everyone outside staring?" Airin asked. "There should be a crowd."

He chuckled. "People who live here get used to it. Although I have to say, this is one of the most gorgeous rainbows I've ever seen. There, see?" He pointed at an elderly Japanese man standing in his garden, leaning on a rake as he stared at the Technicolor marvel in the sky. "Even a *kama'aina* thinks this one is special."

"*Kama'aina*?"

"Local."

Five more minutes of walking brought them to the end of the street, with a choice to turn left or right. Instead, he and Airin reached a mutual, unspoken decision to stop and stare.

Eventually, the conditions in the sky changed. Behind them, the sun was sinking behind the mountains; in front of them, the rain was coming to an end. The rainbow began to fade.

Airin took a deep breath and let it out slowly. He did the same, taking in a cool wash of air that seemed to fill every corner of his lungs.

They turned to walk back toward the house. The sun was almost hidden behind the mountains, but the air around them was suffused with gold, so thick and luscious it was like walking through honey.

He bumped Airin's shoulder gently with his. "Tell me some more about your dad. Was he always interested in space?"

"Always," she said after a moment. "He was six foot one, and he was glad NASA had changed their height requirements for astronauts. Back in the Mercury and Gemini days, you had to be between five foot five and five foot eleven to fit inside the capsule." She smiled up at him. "You must be happy NASA makes their seats adjustable now and that they paid Russia to modify the Soyuz for heights up to six two. You're just barely under that limit."

He grinned down at her. "Yeah. If I'd been born a generation earlier, I'd be out of luck. The shorties got all the cool missions back then. Yuri Gagarin, the first man in space, was only five two."

She nodded. "My dad told me stories about him. But his favorite astronaut was Valentina Tereshkova, the first woman in space. He also admired Sally Ride, the first American woman in space, and Anna Lee Fisher. She was the first mother in space."

"He was big on firsts, huh?"

She drifted a little closer to him, just a couple of inches, but it was enough to bring her arm into contact with his for a moment. The fleeting touch gave him goose bumps.

"He thought I could be the first woman on Mars. Maybe even the first human."

"That's a pretty big expectation to put on a little girl."

"It wasn't an expectation. It was more like a wish. A belief in what was possible."

The last ray of the setting sun broke through a cloud, making them blink. They turned their heads at the same time and found themselves looking at each other.

"I bet you're big on firsts, too," Airin said. "Aren't you? All the astronauts I've ever met are, especially the pilots. I bet you want to be the first man on Mars. Don't deny it."

She turned her head away, looking at the road ahead of them again, and he did the same.

"Hell yeah, I want to be first. It's the only thing they can't take away from you."

"What do you mean?"

"However fast you go, someone will always go faster. However high, however far . . . someone else will go higher and farther. But if you're the first person to do something, that's it. You'll always be the first person who did that thing."

There was a short silence. Then Airin glanced up at him again.

"What?" he asked after a moment.

She was looking thoughtful. "I was just wondering."

"Wondering what?"

"If what you just said has anything to do with your parents. I mean, being first. You said it's the only thing they can't take away from you. So . . . it's something permanent. A kind of immortality."

He shook his head. "Damn. You're going to psychoanalyze me now, aren't you? I knew I shouldn't have told you all my sad stories."

He spoke lightly, but Airin answered seriously.

"I'm glad you told me. You knew all my sad stories, and I didn't know any of yours. It was an imbalance."

An imbalance.

There was another imbalance between them, one she didn't know about. His arrangement with Dira. Information about Airin in exchange for his heart's desire.

He wished he hadn't thought the phrase *heart's desire*. Because looking down at Airin, the words took on a new, terrifying meaning.

He forced himself to imagine how her expression would change if she knew that in a few hours, he'd send an email to her mother. He'd tell Dira how Airin was spending her time, how her ribs were healing, how happy she seemed.

"But anyway," Airin went on, "I know the chance to be first isn't the only reason you want to be part of the Mars mission."

It took him a moment to refocus on the conversation. "How do you know? Maybe I'm just a glory hound."

She shook her head. "You told me that night on the beach why you want to travel into space. And people who are in it for the glory get weeded out pretty fast. You know that. There's too much stress and boredom and pain-in-the-ass stuff to put up with if your motives are that shallow."

"I hope you're not accusing me of being deep. No one's ever done that to me before."

She was starting to answer when he grabbed her hand. There was a little pile of dog poop on the sidewalk, and he tugged her to the side.

"Watch your feet," he said.

"Thanks."

Now they were walking hand in hand, like they had that night in Waikiki. Like kids or sweethearts or an old married couple. Her hand felt small and soft and warm in his, and he should really let it go.

But he didn't.

"So why did you and your dad talk about going to Mars?" he asked. "If it wasn't for the glory."

"For my dad, it was about curiosity. He said the urge to travel is built into our DNA and that the next phase of exploration is into space. It's humanity's next call to adventure, he said, and we have to answer it."

"What about your mother?"

"My mother?"

"Yeah. She wants to go to Mars, too, right? What's her motivation? The same as your dad's?"

"No. I mean, she liked to hear my dad talk about it. She always said he was the romantic in the family. But for her, it's not about exploring for the sake of exploring. She sees going to Mars as a kind of insurance policy for the human race."

"An insurance policy?"

"Yes. She believes the best way to avoid the possibility of human extinction is for us to become a spacefaring race. She says the sooner we establish a self-sustaining community on Mars, the sooner we increase our odds of surviving a disaster on Earth—something immediate like an asteroid or nuclear war, or something gradual like climate change."

"That's kind of an apocalyptic vision, isn't it? I mean, it's not exactly the inspirational stuff of her space talks."

"That's why she doesn't emphasize that part of it when she gives speeches. She's more long-term then, more aspirational. She doesn't talk about species-ending disasters, whether natural or manmade, as much as the reality is that we can't stay on Earth forever. I mean, our sun will die eventually."

"In five billion years? That's a pretty long time from now."

"But Earth will be uninhabitable long before that. In a billion years the sun will be hot enough to boil our oceans. My mother's point is, if we evolve into a spacefaring species, we have a way to make sure humanity can survive anything, including the loss of Earth. Whenever that happens."

He remembered what she'd said about his parents. "So . . . immortality, then."

"Sort of. The only kind we can ever hope for—the kind that goes beyond our own generation. My dad used to talk about that, too. The idea of starting something you won't live to see completed. It used to be that way when people built cathedrals. Stonemasons and other craftsmen would begin the work, knowing that their grandchildren or even their great-grandchildren would see it finished, while they never would. My dad identified with that. He loved the idea of me going into space someday, even if he wasn't there to see it."

He was quiet for a moment. "So both your parents had the same vision. A future for humanity. But your dad saw it like a romantic, and your mom sees it like a scientist."

She smiled at that. "Basically."

"Which one are you?" he asked. "Scientist or romantic?"

The question seemed to take her by surprise.

Although it was pretty straightforward, really. The kind of thing you ought to be able to answer right away. How do you look at the world? What kind of person are you?

"I don't know," she said after a long pause. "What about you?"

He shrugged. "I'm not either. I'm a pragmatist."

"A pragmatist with a soul," she corrected.

He squeezed her hand. "Yeah? That's the second time on this walk you've called me deep. No one's ever accused me of having a soul before." He thought for a moment. "What if I ask the question another way?"

"What do you mean?"

"Which one of your parents are you more like? Your mother or your father?"

"My father." She paused. "But that doesn't necessarily make me a romantic. My father was a pilot and a mechanical engineer, too."

"Why did you want to go into space? Was it because of your dad, or your mom? Or did you have your own reasons?"

"I always wanted to go, and not just because of my parents. I used to lie awake at night wondering about Mars. I thought about the things my dad was interested in—the exploring, the achievement of getting there, all that. And the things my mom cares about, too. The science of it, and the idea of guaranteeing humanity a place in the universe. But the question I was obsessed with was different."

"What was it?"

"Life. Is there life on Mars today, buried deep where there's liquid water? Was there ever life there? Did it leave behind evidence that we could study? It wasn't the idea of humanity spreading through the universe that inspired me. It was the idea of encountering another species. Think of the strangeness of that. The mystery. That's the kind of unknown I was interested in."

"Was?"

She looked up at him. "What do you mean?"

"You talk like that interest is in your past. Is it?"

She shrugged. "I'll never go to Mars. I've known that for years. I experienced my first tachycardia when I was nine, and I was diagnosed with Wolff-Parkinson-White not long after. Any dreams I had of going into space ended then. I was in and out of hospitals for years. My mother was terrified I would die, and she kept me home as much as she could, in as antiseptic an environment as she could create. If she could have made me the girl in the plastic bubble, she would have. The idea of going to Mars or being an astronaut or even just having a normal life was out of the question. My dad stopped talking about it, and he and my mom mostly focused on my health. They researched all these diets and exercise programs, and I ended up being the healthiest kid you ever met . . . except for the fact that the electric pathways in my heart were messed up."

"I read up on Wolff-Parkinson-White," he said.

She looked up at him. "You did?"

"Yeah. I wanted to know what you'd been up against as a kid. It seems like your mom went way overboard. Lots of people with WPW do just fine. They don't all get homeschooled, and some can participate in sports."

"Sure. Some people with WPW never even show symptoms. But my condition was on the severe end of the spectrum. I had multiple abnormal pathways in my heart, which made it more challenging for the doctors to ablate all of them. I had episodes of tachycardia pretty frequently, and I fainted a lot, which tended to freak people out. Then I'd get freaked out because they were freaked out, and . . . well, you get the idea. Finally my mom said she needed to control my environment more or she'd go crazy. So we switched to homeschooling."

"Did you mind?"

"It was fine for a few years. I kind of liked it, really. I still saw my friends, and I spent more time with my parents than I ever had before. They were still busy, and I had tutors for most subjects, but my dad coached me in math and science, and he made it fun. My mom pitched in, too. I had kind of an amazing education, to be honest." She sighed. "But then my dad deployed. After he was killed, my mom got worse. More overprotective, I mean. I was in high school then, and I threw myself into what I was studying—and into my own world, I guess. I met people online and formed communities the way you do, with people you have weird things in common with."

He shifted his hand, threading their fingers together. "What kinds of things?"

"I joined an online community for people who wrote *Buffy the Vampire Slayer* fan fiction. Another one about net neutrality. One for fractals, one for people interested in dark matter, one for Greek mythology. That kind of thing."

"Huh. Okay. But, Airin . . . you said you were training and eating well, right?"

"Yes."

"And you said your last surgery was a complete success."

"It was."

"Well . . . what did the doctor say about your heart afterward?"

She hesitated, obviously unsure about where he was going with this.

"He said I had one of the healthiest hearts he'd ever seen . . . considering. I passed all kinds of exercise and stress tests with flying colors. He said I was fit enough to run a 10K or climb a mountain."

He stopped walking. "So," he said.

Airin stopped, too, turning to look at him. They were only a few houses away from their place.

"What?" she asked.

"The issue with WPW is abnormal electric pathways in the heart, right? And once that problem is solved, that's it. Complete recovery. So why couldn't you be an astronaut if you wanted to? What's holding you back if it's still something you're interested in?"

She stared at him. Then she pulled her hand away from his and took a step back.

"Don't be stupid."

Her cheeks were red, and she looked almost angry.

"Why is that stupid?" he asked. "Things have changed since John Glenn and Alan Shepard went through NASA's crazy testing program."

She folded her arms. "Come on, Hunter. You know standards are still strict. They want the healthiest people they can find, people who can endure the rigors of space travel. They turn people down if they've ever had kidney stones. Even one."

"You know why that is. In micro-g, calcium is leached out of your bones. That increases the risk of kidney stones. Those suck enough on

Earth, but in space they could be fatal. Other things are a down-check, too. Some respiratory issues, for instance. But I broke my arm once and my collarbone twice and they didn't turn me down."

She turned away slightly, her body language defensive. "You know it's not the same. Once a bone is healed, it's no more or less likely to break than any other part of your body."

"Well, you said your heart was recovered completely. You said—"

"Stop it."

It was the second time she'd snapped at him.

"I didn't mean to piss you off," he said after a moment.

She chewed on her bottom lip for a moment, frowning down at the sidewalk. Then she looked up again.

"You didn't. I mean . . . not really. It's just that with a hundred thousand people wanting to go into space, you know they can find plenty of candidates who've never had a heart condition. The selection committees are risk averse, Hunter. You know they are. Why would they introduce any element of uncertainty into their program when there are already so many things they can't control?"

"So you've thought about it, then."

She stared at him for a moment, then turned away and started walking. "I don't want to talk about this."

He fell into step beside her. "Okay. Sorry."

He didn't say anything else, just walked at her side until they reached the house. He'd pushed her enough for tonight.

He missed the feel of her hand in his. He'd sacrificed the sweetness that had been building between them since he'd showed her the rainbow, and he didn't know if it had been the right thing to do. Had bringing up her old dream helped her or hurt her?

In one way, though, it had definitely been a good thing. That sweetness could be dangerous to both of them. Addictive. Disorienting. The kind of thing that led to bad decisions and car crashes on the Pali Highway.

The kind of thing that changed lives.

They crossed the front yard and climbed the three steps that led up to the front door. He held it open for her, and Airin walked through.

She crossed to the foot of the stairs and turned to face him. "Thank you for showing me the rainbow. It was a lovely walk."

She sounded polite, almost formal. Once again he missed the intimacy they fell into so easily, and once again he told himself it was better to avoid those moments. "You're welcome. Is there anything in particular you want for Chinese food, or should I just get a bunch of stuff?"

"A bunch of stuff sounds good."

She smiled a little stiffly, and then she turned away.

Chapter Fifteen

Airin replayed that last conversation as she climbed the stairs. She'd sounded like an eight-year-old thanking an adult for a birthday present.

Thank you for showing me the rainbow. It was a lovely walk.

Going into her room, she could feel the tension in her muscles. She decided that this time, even if there were cockroaches in the tub, she was going to run herself a hot bath. Her shoulders were up around her ears, her ribs were aching, and she felt discombobulated.

Her father had used that word once when she was little, and she'd loved the way it sounded. She'd asked him what it meant, and he told her to look it up, which had been his standard response to a request for a definition.

Confused or disconcerted, the dictionary had informed her.

She'd looked up *disconcerted.*

Perturbed.

She'd looked up *perturbed.*

Disturbed; confused; made uneasy or anxious.

"I feel uneasy and anxious," she told her reflection in the bathroom mirror a few minutes later as the hot water splashed into the stoppered tub.

Astronaut candidates were often deliberately put into situations designed to make them uneasy or anxious. The ones who advanced to the next round of training were the ones who kept going in spite of it. The ones who could function while discombobulated.

A year and a half ago, when she was lying in the prep room before her last surgery, the thought had come to her that dealing with a heart condition was excellent preparation for a life in space. You had to cope with a lack of privacy, with being confined and restricted, with spending time indoors surrounded by metal and plastic and the omnipresence of machinery. You had to cope with fear and boredom, too—an astronaut's constant companions in space.

The tub was full. She stepped out of her clothes and into the water, and God, it felt good. Of course heat wasn't really the best thing for her type of injury—she'd make up for it by icing afterward—but that was counterbalanced by the good it was doing the rest of her.

She leaned her head back on the lip of the tub, closed her eyes, and sighed.

That was another problem being in a hospital shared with being in space. Most of the ways people had developed to de-stress weren't available. You couldn't take hot baths, you couldn't meet someone for coffee, you couldn't shop, you couldn't have pets, you couldn't down a fifth of vodka as a last resort.

But putting up with the confinement and the lack of privacy and a narrow world of metal and plastic, putting up with the fear and the boredom and the lack of de-stressing opportunities, would be worth it for the larger goal of going into space.

Especially going to Mars.

Enduring seven months of hardship and restriction in order to reach another world would be a million times better than enduring them for the dubious goal of saving one human life.

Even if that life was her own.

She opened her eyes.

She'd thought she'd given up on the old dream years ago. What was more pathetic than hanging on to a wish that would never come true?

And yet . . .

She'd studied Russian on her own as a teenager. She'd never told her mother or her tutors or anyone else. It was something she'd done just for herself.

And when she'd trained in the exercise room her mother had built for her or swam in the Olympic-length pool, she'd been aware of how many astronauts were distance runners or distance swimmers. The will-power and discipline needed to run a marathon was a lot like the will-power and discipline needed to become an astronaut.

She couldn't get a pilot's license, but she'd looked at the ground-school training videos online. And after the doctors had pronounced her fully recovered, she'd had them fill out the medical certificate she'd need to begin flight training.

But she'd never mentioned it to her mother, and she'd never followed up on it.

What do you want to do with your life? she'd been asking herself.

And all along, she'd known the answer.

How could she have been so blind?

She wanted to see things no human being had ever seen before. She wanted to walk on an alien world. Most of all, she wanted to be involved with something that was bigger than she was, bigger than any one person.

Traveling to Mars would be a mission for the entire human race. Even if you died trying to get there or trying to survive there, your struggle and your efforts would teach the crew that came after you. They would build on what you had done, and the next generation would build on that. And on and on, until they finally made it work.

Until they had a self-sustaining community on Mars. A community of people free to explore, to innovate, to learn how to survive on a world they weren't born for. Free to look for signs of alien life. Free to begin a process that would lead, someday, beyond the solar system.

She sat up in the tub, pulled out the stopper, and stepped out onto the mat as the water drained. She toweled off quickly and incompletely, leaving her hair still dripping down her back, and put on the robe she'd hung on the back of the door.

It was a beautiful robe, a birthday gift from one of her mother's assistants a few years back. It was cream-colored chenille, like something you'd find in a spa, and while its cozy absorptiveness made it the perfect post-bath garment, it only occurred to her after she was standing in Hunter's doorway that it wasn't exactly a dignified thing to wear for a conversation.

But it was too late to think about that now.

Hunter was at his desk, running what looked like a flight simulator program on his computer. He paused the program when he heard her behind him and turned his chair around, taking her damp appearance in stride.

"Hey," he said.

She took a deep breath.

"Did you know the first submariners underestimated how much they would miss the natural world, stuck in a tin can for months at a time? They had to come up with ways to address it. They gave crew members time to listen to whale songs and other ocean noises at the sonar station. They gave them periscope time so they could look at clouds and see birds, and so they could retain their distance-vision muscles. Those get screwed up in a submarine, where the farthest away you ever look is a few yards."

Hunter looked at her for a moment. Then he leaned back in his chair and clasped his hands behind his head. The movement made his triceps look particularly well defined, but she refused to be distracted by that.

"I sense you're going somewhere with this," he said.

"Astronauts say the ability to see Earth's beauty is one of the best things about space travel. But the astronauts who go to Mars and the colonists who try to live there won't have that. It'll be the first time in history that human beings will see Mother Earth reduced to insignificance in the sky. It'll get smaller and smaller until it's the size of any other star, just another dot in the heavens. Scientists don't know how humans will respond to that. They call it Earth-out-of-view syndrome, and they don't know what the effects will be."

Hunter nodded slowly. "Okay. And?"

"You love Hawaii, don't you? I can see it in the way you look at the ocean. At the valley we're living in. At the sky. At the rain." She gestured toward the window. "The surface of Mars is as different from Hawaii as it's possible to be. Cold, dry, barren. No liquid water. No plants. No animals. No soft air against your cheek. No scent of flowers, no sound of raindrops."

He nodded again. "Is there a question coming?"

"Are you sure going to Mars is something you really want to do?"

He unclasped his hands from behind his head and leaned forward, resting his elbows on his knees as he grinned at her.

"Yeah."

She wasn't really surprised by his answer. She'd seen his commitment before now. But then, it wasn't really him she was questioning.

"Just like that? Can you really be so sure?"

"Yeah."

She leaned against the door frame. For a minute, maybe longer, they just looked at each other.

Then she took a deep breath.

"I want to go, too."

Those hazel eyes were locked on hers. "I know," he said.

Of course he did. Hunter was a flyboy, an astronaut, a human being willing to take unimaginable risks to go into thin air, into space, into places where people don't belong. He knew exactly what that kind of insanity looked like in someone else.

"But I also know I won't be going," she said. "That's why I don't like to think about it. To talk about it."

"I understand," he said, and she could tell he really did. "But I don't agree. You know that luck and desire play as big a role in getting chosen as any specific skill set. We'd all love to believe it's a completely logical and straightforward process, but it's not."

"So you're saying I might somehow get into space, but if so, it would be because logic and straightforwardness went out the window."

He grinned again. "Exactly. But look at Apollo 13. Nothing those guys expected to happen happened. That's life. And you've got something going for you that most people in space programs don't have."

"Really? What's that?"

"Nepotism."

Did he actually believe that was an advantage? The thought of sharing any of this with her mother made her slump against the door frame. But slumping hurt her ribs, so she stood up straight again.

"That's just one more thing working against me. My mother would never let me be part of her Mars mission, and the other private companies would think I was a spy or something if I applied to their programs. And NASA would never pass me because of my medical history."

"I don't think any of that is necessarily true. But you don't have to worry about it."

She stared at him. "I don't have to *worry* about it?"

"Nope. Because worrying about it won't change a damn thing. You're going to behave like any other aspiring astronaut. You're going to get an advanced degree in something you enjoy that would also be useful on a manned mission to Mars. You're going to stay in peak physical condition. In addition to your chosen field, you're going to study planetary science and rocket design schematics and a hundred other things. You're going to go through survival training and weightless training and g-force training and any other hellish scenario you can think of. Along the way you'll apply to every program looking for candidates to go to Mars. You'll deal with one problem at a time, like any good explorer does. And when you get your call to adventure, you'll be ready."

A strange feeling was flooding through her. As Hunter talked, what he was saying seemed almost . . . possible. Inevitable, even. As though all she had to do was put one foot in front of the other and eventually she'd end up on Mars.

The odds were against her. Astronomically so, in fact. They were for everyone who wanted to go into space. The question was, would she enjoy the journey even if she never reached her destination?

The answer was yes.

She started to smile, and Hunter was smiling back at her.

Then she noticed, suddenly, that her hair had begun to drip.

"I'm so sorry," she said, backing out of his room and into the hallway. "I got water on your floor. I'll get a towel and—"

"Come back in here," Hunter said. "And close the door."

She obeyed almost without thinking, crossing his threshold again as he rose to his feet and came toward her.

Something about the look in his eyes made her cinch her robe a little tighter at the waist and grab hold of the lapels with one hand. She leaned back against the door she'd just closed.

"What's wrong?" she asked, her heart pounding.

He stopped less than a foot away from her. "Nothing."

She swallowed. "Something is. You're looking at me like . . ." She stopped.

Her cheeks were hot, her pulse crazy. It felt like she would never get used to how big Hunter was, how broad his shoulders were. It felt like there was no end to his strength, as though he were a stone wall or a mountain.

"Your hair is wet," he said, his voice low and rough.

He reached out and touched it, running his palm down one damp strand, and when he pulled his hand back again, there was a droplet of water on his skin between his thumb and his index finger.

"I know." Her voice was trembling, and she cleared her throat. "I told you I'm dripping on your floor. I was going to get a towel, but you . . . you said to come back in here."

He stepped a little closer, and she didn't have enough air to breathe.

God, his eyes were intense.

No one had ever looked at her like this. Like something inside her made him alive, somehow.

"Airin." His voice was soft now, almost a whisper. "You're so beautiful. So beautiful and so brave."

Her heart was going to fly right out of her body.

"I'm not brave. If you only knew how scared I—"

But she didn't get a chance to finish that sentence. He put his hands flat on the back of the door, caging her between his powerful arms.

Then he leaned in and kissed her.

His arms weren't touching her. His chest wasn't touching her. Only his mouth was on her mouth, and she knew that even in the grip of the intensity she'd seen in his eyes he was worried about her, afraid of hurting her ribs.

He tasted so good. Like a flavor she'd experienced once and would never forget, a flavor she could spend the rest of her life chasing.

His tongue stroked against hers like he had all the time in the world, and she was melting like chocolate in the sun. Her bones were turning to water, and it was sheer survival instinct that made her reach up and grab fistfuls of his T-shirt in her hands.

But the quick, desperate movement made her yelp in sudden pain, and before she could tell him *It's fine, keep going, don't stop,* he'd jerked his head away and was staring down at her like he'd driven a knife through her heart.

"Shit. I'm so sorry, Airin. Are you okay?"

Now she could say it. "I'm fine. Don't stop."

Her breath was short and shallow. Her hands gripped his shirt as though glued there by some electromagnetic force.

He covered her hands with his and slowly, inexorably, broke the connection between them.

"Are your ribs okay?"

"My ribs are fine. Kiss me again."

She could tell he wasn't going to. He looked guilty and regretful, even though his eyes were still intense and his face looked as flushed as hers felt.

And then his phone rang.

He pulled it out of his pocket. It was a blocked number calling, and after staring at it for a second, he hit Decline.

He slid the phone back into his pocket and looked at her.

"This can't happen," he said.

The frustration that filled her felt like anger. *"Why?"*

"There are a lot of reasons. You know that."

"No. I don't. Tell me what they are."

He looked away for a moment. His jaw muscles were tight, and more than she'd ever wanted anything, she wanted to know what another human being was thinking.

He met her eyes again, his expression resolute. "The most important reason is that I don't want it to."

Airin had been collecting new experiences ever since she got to Hawaii. Now she had another to add to the list.

Rejection.

It actually hurt. Physically. Like she'd been slapped in the face and punched in the gut.

One minute he was calling her beautiful and brave and kissing her like it was the most important thing he'd ever do. The next he was standing there saying it would never happen again, because he didn't want it to.

She wanted to say something to hurt him as much as he'd hurt her. But how could she? He'd probably been with hundreds of women. He knew how to protect himself from emotional pain.

She didn't know how to do that. She really was as naive as Hunter had said she was.

Dean's voice came from downstairs. "Food's here!"

She took a deep breath and let it out slowly.

"Food's here," she said.

Then she turned, opened the door, and walked out.

◆ ◆ ◆

Hunter had been starving half an hour ago, but now the thought of eating made him nauseated.

He closed the door Airin had just walked through, turned his back to it, and slid down until he was sitting on the floor. Then he pulled out his phone and called Dira back.

"It's two in the morning your time," he said tersely. "Why are you calling?"

"I'm in London right now. It's seven in the morning here. And I called because I haven't received your daily report yet. Is Airin all right?"

He leaned his head back against the door and closed his eyes. "Airin's fine. What did you think had happened to her?"

He heard Dira sigh. "I don't know. I worry. I swear to goodness, if I had to do it all over again, I don't know if I would have a child at all."

For a moment he let himself imagine a world without Airin in it. A world where he'd never met her, never crashed on the Pali Highway, never missed the biosphere mission.

He'd be there with his crew right now. His life would be on track.

And he wouldn't have the image of those chocolate-brown eyes haunting his every goddamn waking moment.

"She wants to be an astronaut."

There was a moment of silence.

"What are you talking about?" Dira finally asked.

"Airin wants to be an astronaut."

"She hasn't mentioned such a thing since she was a little girl. She knows it's impossible."

"It's not impossible. And I think you should help her."

Another silence, this one longer.

"It's out of the question," she said, her voice flat. "As long as I'm alive, I'll do everything in my power to keep Airin from going into space."

He got to his feet and walked over to his window, shifting the phone from his right hand to his left. "That seems a little extreme. Why not help her do what she wants to do?"

Dira's voice was clipped. "When I met Airin's father, he was already a pilot. There was nothing I could do about it. It was part of who he was." She paused. "I lost my husband to your godforsaken profession, but I'm damned if I'll lose my daughter the same way."

He leaned against the window frame, looking out at the night. After the rain earlier the sky had cleared, and he could see the Milky Way over the eastern wall of the valley.

The Hawaiians called it Hokunohoaupuni. Reigning star.

"She doesn't want to be a pilot. She wants to be an astronaut. An explorer."

"She wants to be in the company of lunatics willing to sit on eight million pounds of explosive rocket fuel for the privilege of subjecting their bodies to the stresses of high-g, micro-g, and solar radiation."

"Lunatics like me."

"Exactly. You of all people should understand this, Hunter. Would you want someone you loved to go into space?"

He shied away from that question.

"But it's what she wants. You're her parent. Shouldn't you be doing everything you can to help her achieve her goals?"

Dira huffed out an irritated breath. "Airin's body has already been subjected to enough for one lifetime. She's staying on Earth."

He thought about how Airin talked about her medical history and the way it had changed her.

"What she's gone through has made her stronger. Physically, mentally, emotionally. You know it has. Her heart is probably stronger than mine."

Silence.

Then she said, "Do you know one of the reasons NASA has resisted the idea of sending couples on long-haul trips?"

"Because the headline First Divorce in Space would be bad publicity?"

Dira didn't laugh. "Because they don't like the idea of informing families of a double loss. I'm going to spare myself the possibility of a double loss, Hunter. I couldn't control Airin developing Wolff-Parkinson-White or the course of treatments that followed. But I can control this. I have a lot of pull in the world of private space programs, and I'd be willing to use every bit of it to keep my daughter on this planet."

"NASA might—"

"NASA won't. Even if they were willing to overlook her medical history, I have contracts with them and a certain amount of influence. It's not happening."

Mars wasn't visible in the sky right now. But it was out there, the Red Planet, calling to him with the same pull it called Airin.

"I think you're making a mistake. I saw the speech you gave to the United Nations two years ago. You said the hope of all mankind lies in reaching for the stars. Don't you want your own daughter to be part of that? Isn't space travel your dream for humanity?"

"No."

Maybe he hadn't heard her right.

"But—"

"It was my husband's dream. After he died, I did everything I could to make it happen. I'm still doing that. I will always do that. But my own dream was to find more sustainable ways to manage our energy use here on Earth. It just so happens that my work has also had an impact on the space program."

"Your husband's dream," he repeated.

Damn. What was it like to spend your life making someone else's dream come true?

"Yes. Frank lived and breathed piloting and space travel and the possibility of a manned mission to Mars." She paused. "My daughter is named for her grandmother, but there's another reason behind the choice. Frank loved my mother's name because it sounds like Ares."

"The Greek version of Mars."

"Exactly."

"Frank wanted his daughter to be a god of war?"

For the first time since he'd met her, he heard Dira laugh. More like a dry chuckle, really, but it was something.

"Not exactly. But he believed her generation would be the first with a real chance of setting foot on the Red Planet."

"He was right."

"He was right about the timing. But let me say this again. As long as I have anything to say about it, my daughter will never go into space." She paused. "You're a flyboy, Hunter. You know how dangerous your job is, and you've already factored in those risks. But Airin isn't like you. Do you honestly want her to risk her life? To die in one of the horrible ways that spaceflight can kill a person?"

She is like me.

She wasn't a pilot, but she had the heart and mind of an explorer. He knew it, just as surely as he knew her mother would never accept that fact.

But one thing Dira had said was true.

"No. I don't want her to die."

"We're on the same page, then. And she's in good spirits? Her ribs are healing? She's not in pain?"

He remembered the look on her face just before she'd left his room, and he winced.

"No."

"Good. Until next time, then."

She disconnected the call.

His appetite was starting to come back. Chinese food, his favorite kind of takeout, was waiting for him downstairs. But he stayed where he was a few minutes longer, staring out at the Milky Way and remembering what it felt like to kiss the most beautiful woman he'd ever known.

Chapter Sixteen

Airin managed to avoid Hunter the next morning, and she threw herself into work with Val for the rest of the day. She worked for so long in the lab that her ribs ached when she got home.

A bath would help. A hot bubble bath she could soak in for . . .

There was a cockroach in the bathroom. Not in the tub this time—on the wall near the window. It was motionless except for its obscenely long, slowly waving antennae.

No bath, was her first thought. *I don't need a bath.*

But after a moment she went to the hall closet where they kept their cleaning supplies. There was a duster there with a long plastic handle, and she took it back into the bathroom with her.

Standing as far from the cockroach as she could, she used the handle of the duster to slowly raise the window screen. Then she turned it around so the duster end—some kind of synthetic material, bright yellow and fluffy—was extended.

She took a deep breath. Then, moving as quickly and decisively as she could, she swept the cockroach out the open window.

It worked. The thing was gone. She lunged forward to close the screen after it and stood panting, her heart pounding, the duster still clutched in her hand.

Not exactly a dragon, maybe, but a victory nonetheless. It felt like she'd really earned her bath this time.

The bath felt wonderful, and so did she. She'd done a good day's work, she'd triumphed over a cockroach, and best of all, there'd been long stretches of the day when she hadn't thought about Hunter at all.

After the bath she stood at her bedroom window, braiding her wet hair. It was sunset, and her view was drenched in gold. The light made everything in it, trees and grass and houses and cars, seem as rich and crystalline as the inside of a geode.

She finished her braid and leaned against the windowsill. The light would fade soon, and she wanted to stay here until it did, drinking in every last golden droplet.

And then, like a hero out of an old epic, Hunter came into view. He was shirtless, jogging in a pair of blue running shorts, and as he came up the driveway, she could see the sheen of sweat on his tanned skin.

Great.

He did some stretches in the front yard, cooling down from the run, and then some push-ups. He performed them effortlessly, as straight and sturdy as a plank of wood, only his arms moving him up and down. His muscles were like bands of iron beneath warm, glowing skin.

His body was like poetry. Dirty, sexy poetry.

When he finished his last push-up, he rolled onto his back, looking up at the sky. After a moment his head turned toward the house, and she sprang back from the window, terrified he'd catch her watching him.

That image of Hunter, shirtless in the golden light, was still with her at dinner an hour later. Dean had made mahi-mahi and vegetables, and the four of them were eating at the countertop between the living room and kitchen.

She and Val were on the living room side, across from the two men. Val and Dean were leaning in, talking and laughing, while she and Hunter were quieter, concentrating on their food.

She didn't look at Hunter, but she was aware of him the way you were aware of a fireplace on a cold day. About midway through the meal, she glanced up and found him looking at her, his hazel eyes inscrutable.

Heat flamed in her cheeks, and she looked down at her plate. She didn't look up again until the meal was over.

She volunteered to wash the dishes, and Hunter cleared the table, bringing the plates and silverware to her as she filled the sink with soapy water.

"How are your ribs?" he asked. "You look a little tired. Did you work too hard today?"

She shook her head, wishing she could talk to him like she had yesterday or like that night on Waikiki Beach. Something precious had been lost, and she didn't know how to recover it.

And the only thing she'd done wrong was to kiss him back when he'd kissed her.

Maybe if Hunter stayed in the kitchen long enough she could figure out how to talk to him again. But the memory of last night's humiliation was still raw, and she didn't want to feel that way again.

God, she was bad at this stuff. By the time most women were twenty-four, they'd figured out how to deal with the awkward emotions of attraction and rejection and everything in between. But she was new to this, and everything felt shaky and uncertain, like walking on a frozen lake with **BEWARE OF THIN ICE** signs everywhere and pockets of danger she couldn't see.

Hunter handed her the baking dish the fish had cooked in, and when she took it her hand brushed his. The contact sent a ripple of tension through her whole body, her stomach muscles tightening and her fingers gripping the ceramic dish. Her cheeks were hot, and all she could think of was his mouth on hers last night.

She couldn't meet his eyes.

He cleared his throat. "I'm going to head upstairs. Good night, Airin."

She didn't trust herself to answer, so she just nodded, feeling rather than seeing Hunter leave the kitchen.

Later that night she lay on her back, staring up at the ceiling fan. She was propped up at a thirty-degree angle by her pillows, which the doctor had told her would help ease the discomfort of her injury.

But there was one thing they hadn't advised her on. How to masturbate successfully after you'd cracked a couple of ribs.

She might have been able to do it if she'd ever masturbated successfully before. If she knew what she was doing, she could have found a workaround as she had for other tasks. But for her, the act of self-pleasure was still a frustrating, way-too-lengthy experimental procedure that never led where she wanted it to.

So all she could do was lie in bed staring up at the ceiling, wanting something she couldn't have. Longing for a release she couldn't even imagine because she'd never experienced it.

She tried to relax. She breathed in through her nose and out through her mouth. She thought about nonsexual things—bad TV shows, the food she'd eaten in the hospital, the cockroach she'd seen earlier and the two she'd seen that first night.

But even that didn't cool the fever in her body. Instead of killing the ardor that ripped through her, it went the other way around. Lust colored even the most unpleasant memories, so she found herself wondering how cockroaches mated.

Cockroach copulation. God, what is wrong with me?

But the cockroaches, like bad TV and hospital food, didn't grip her imagination for long.

The need that made her panties damp and her lower belly ache was more powerful than her mind's ability to quell it. All she could do was want and need and lie there staring at the ceiling fan. Meanwhile, she practically vibrated with an urgency that felt more powerful than the four fundamental interactions of nature.

Gravity. Electromagnetism. Strong and weak nuclear forces.

Even physics was turning sexual in her mind.

Friction. Weight. Rhythm. Heat.

A misty rain had begun to fall outside, and the soft sensuality of the Hawaiian breeze wasn't helping. It made her feel restless, mind and heart and body and soul.

This was why prehistoric fish had grown legs and crawled out of the ocean. This was why people risked death sailing the ocean and climbing mountains and hurtling themselves into space.

Because they were restless.

This molten lust felt part and parcel of that somehow. She longed for the unknown, for the incursion of masculinity into her body.

Except it wasn't as nonspecific as that. It was Hunter she wanted, Hunter she needed.

He'd felt the same way last night. She'd seen it in his eyes. But tonight, she hadn't been able to read him at all. Whatever he'd been feeling and thinking had been hidden.

It wasn't fair that she blushed and he didn't. It wasn't fair that he'd had relationships before and she hadn't.

What would happen if she went across the hall right now? If she took her hairbrush and knocked on his door and asked him for help with her one hundred strokes?

Nothing would happen. Not unless he wanted it to.

He made all the decisions. He was the one who'd kissed her, and he was the one who'd put on the brakes.

She'd had enough of waiting on other people's decisions to last a lifetime. Other people had always determined what would happen to her—her mother, her doctors. She didn't want to feel that way anymore. She didn't want to wait breathlessly for Hunter to look at her like he had last night, hoping against hope that he'd slip the leash of his self-control.

She had self-control, too. She had the power to focus on her mission: working with Val and figuring out a path to becoming an astronaut.

Hunter had helped her realize her old dream hadn't died, and she was grateful to him for that. But she needed to keep her distance from him for a while. Holding out hope for another kiss, for evidence he was still attracted to her, could only bring heartbreak.

She needed to keep her heart safe. It had been through enough.

The patter of raindrops outside her window stopped. The sweetness of plumeria drifted in her window on a softer, drier breeze.

In through the nose, out through the mouth.

And eventually she fell asleep.

◆ ◆ ◆

After a few days, Hunter knew Airin was avoiding him. He couldn't blame her, but he wished like hell it didn't have to be this way.

If only he hadn't kissed her after the rainbow walk.

If only he'd kissed her again.

If only he hadn't made this goddamn bargain with Dira.

His email tonight was pretty short. Just: Airin seems good. Her ribs are healing. She's eating well. She's enjoying her work with Val in the lab.

He hesitated before hitting Send. Then, instead, he moved his cursor above his sign-off and added, Is Airin in touch with you at all? If you're getting this information from her, you don't need me. We can dissolve our agreement, and you won't owe me anything.

Send.

He answered an email from his aunt Rosemary and one from Caleb while he waited for Dira's response. It came twenty minutes later.

> Airin is hardly talking to me. A few texts to say she's doing well and hopes I am, too. If it weren't for you, I wouldn't know anything. We need to continue our arrangement.

She'd sent an attachment with the email—a prospectus detailing a proposed timeline for the DelAres mission to Mars.

He read it. Then he put his elbows on the desk and his head in his hands.

If she stayed on track, Dira really would beat NASA to Mars. Maybe not by five years, but by three at least.

He wanted a place on that crew. And, apparently, he was willing to talk to Dira behind Airin's back to get it.

But maybe there was a way to balance the scales. He could help Airin get what *she* wanted.

In spite of the biosphere misfire, his working relationships at NASA were still good. He could start sounding people out about Airin's situation, see what might be possible for someone with her medical history.

One way or another, he would do whatever he could to help Airin reach her dreams. In the end, that would be a lot more lasting than a relationship.

Romance was temporary. But becoming an astronaut, going into space—those were things no one could take away from you. That's what counted. Not short-term gratification or emotional comfort, but dreams, goals, missions.

Things that lasted.

Chapter Seventeen

Hunter kept himself busy during the next few weeks. Airin was still avoiding him, and he let her keep her distance. He saw her at least a once a day, usually at breakfast or dinner, and he always asked how she was doing, how she was feeling, how her work with Val was going. Enough information to satisfy Dira, if not enough to satisfy him.

NASA was working him hard, which he appreciated. His various assignments gave him something to focus on besides Airin. During his fifth week as Jones's replacement, they had him in the university simulator at least six hours a day, testing out flight scenarios for the long journey to Mars and what promised to be a hellishly difficult landing procedure.

"We're fifteen years away from this mission," he commented after a particularly long session, during which they'd killed him about forty different ways.

"And?" the project engineer asked, scribbling something down on a clipboard as Hunter emerged from the cockpit and stretched.

"And you're acting like we're heading for Mars in six weeks. They didn't sim this much for the Apollo missions."

Janelle glared at him over her glasses. "There's one big difference between a flight to the moon and a flight to Mars. A twenty-six-minute difference, to be precise."

There was virtually no communications delay between Earth and the moon. That meant if an emergency happened, the pilots in the spacecraft could communicate instantaneously with mission control. You might only be up there with two or three other people, but you had the resources of a thousand people—some of them the smartest on the planet—down there on the ground, working out problems on your behalf.

On a journey to Mars, you wouldn't have that help. It could take between three and twenty-two minutes for signals to travel between Earth and Mars, meaning that six minutes was the bare minimum to get a reply from the other end after you asked a question. In the simulator right now, dealing with landing scenarios, they were working with a thirteen-minute delay each way. If something blew up on the spacecraft—literally or figuratively—the crew wouldn't hear back from mission control for twenty-six minutes.

Crises tended to develop a lot more rapidly than that.

"That's why simulations are so much more important with a Mars mission," Janelle went on. "The name of the game for a Mars crew is—"

"Autonomy." Hunter, like everyone else on the Mars teams, had heard that word a lot.

"Exactly." She pointed at him. "You're lucky, you know. Ten or twenty years ago, you wouldn't have been such a hot property. While our missions were all low-Earth orbit or to the International Space Station, the selection folks weren't as focused on independence and risk taking and creative problem solving. But now that we're going to Mars, cowboys like you are back in style."

He grinned. "Cowboys are always in style. And rugged individualists make great explorers."

"The challenge is balancing independence with teamwork."

"Those qualities aren't mutually exclusive. I'm all about teamwork. And that's what they're studying in the biosphere, right? How different personality types work together? I'm sure NASA will figure it out."

Janelle nodded thoughtfully. "I'm starting to hear some interesting things about the biosphere project."

"Yeah? I thought the first report wasn't due out till next week."

"I've seen some of the preliminary data, and one thing stands out. All eight subjects are coping well with the isolation and close quarters and other restrictions, but the two couples are exceeding expectations. They're operating with higher levels of emotional resilience and productivity."

He remembered his conversation with Dira. "NASA will never send couples into space."

"I used to think so, too. But a mission to Mars is different from anything NASA has planned before, and they wouldn't have included couples in the biosphere study if they weren't interested in how they'd perform." She glanced at her watch. "Okay, break's over. Time to let me kill you again."

"That was just a break? I thought we were done for the day. Did I mention we've got fifteen years to get ready for this mission?"

"If we're going to produce an autonomous crew in that time, we have to start training now. Fortune favors the prepared." She gestured with her clipboard toward the simulator. "Anyway, you're just cranky because we're working your ass off instead of Jones's. Stop complaining and let's tackle the next scenario."

"Whatever you say, ma'am. Like I said, I'm all about teamwork."

An hour later, they finally finished for the night. As Hunter was driving home, he found himself thinking about the conversation with Janelle.

Would NASA really consider sending couples to Mars?

He hoped not. Adding built-in emotional baggage to a mission was a bad idea.

But for some reason, he kept picturing two astronauts in pilot couches, side by side, their helmets titled toward each other as they looked at telemetry data. One of the astronauts was him. The other one . . .

He shied away from identifying the second astronaut. Another image filled his mind's eye instead: Airin as he'd seen her that morning. Her ribs had been declared fully healed by her doctor, and she and Val had been headed to the ocean for Airin's first long swim since her injury. She'd been wearing a red bikini under a white cover-up that covered absolutely nothing up, and he'd wanted to follow her so bad he'd been like a dog lunging against his leash.

When he arrived at the house a few minutes later, Val was in her favorite spot on the living room couch, but Airin was out.

"How was the swim?" he asked, dropping his bag on the floor and going over to the refrigerator.

Val looked up from her laptop. "What?"

He grabbed a container of yogurt. "Your swim. This morning. How did Airin do?"

"She did great. She's a monster in the water. Not faster than me, of course."

"Of course."

"But still good."

He took his yogurt into the living room and sat down on the chair across from Val. "How is she doing otherwise? Did you guys do more work on carbon dioxide extraction today?"

Val studied him for a second. Then she closed her laptop with a slow, deliberate motion and set it down on the coffee table.

Shit. Val never closed her laptop, no matter how gripping a conversation or TV show or anything else going on around her might be.

She leaned back and folded her arms.

"For a month now I've been pretty patient with your questions. 'How is Airin doing?' 'What is she thinking?' 'How is she feeling?' 'What do you talk about?' 'How are her ribs?' 'Is she working too hard?'"

"I—"

She spoke right past him. "I haven't asked why you can't ask her yourself, considering that you live in the same damn house. I haven't asked why you're avoiding her, either. The reason I haven't asked is because it's none of my business. Just like it's none of my business that Airin does the exact same thing."

"She does?"

"Yes, she does. She goes out of her way to avoid you, and then she asks me how you're doing. Just like you do."

He hadn't been expecting that.

"She asks how I'm doing?"

Val didn't answer. She just looked at him, her arms still folded.

He took it for about ten seconds. Then: "Okay, get it off your chest. What?"

"It's time for you to work this out. You're supposed to be a crew commander. Airin's not part of our crew, exactly, but she's part of our household. You need to handle this interpersonal shit, whatever it is. I can't be your go-between anymore."

As much as he hated to admit it, Val was right.

But this was different from any "interpersonal shit" he'd dealt with before. He'd never met a teamwork situation he couldn't handle, which was one of the reasons he'd advanced in his chosen profession. "Plays well with others" was a critical skill in the military, just as it had always been one of the "desirable astronaut attributes."

As Val had pointed out, Airin was a de facto part of his crew. She was working with Val. She was part of a shared living arrangement with other crew members. Functionally, the role she played in his life was as a colleague.

But he'd never felt about a crew member the way he felt about Airin.

He'd thought that avoiding her would weaken the attraction. He'd thought burying himself in work would distract him from it. And he'd thought that Val could be a kind of buffer. As she'd called herself, a go-between.

He thought about the body rescue hooks you find in any electrical safety area. The hook is nonconductive, and it's used to save someone being shocked by an object they can't release—because the electricity is contracting their hand muscles. If a would-be rescuer tries to pull the victim away, his muscles contract, too.

It felt like contact with Airin carried those same risks.

"You were my body rescue hook," he muttered.

Val had worked in plenty of electrical safety areas, and she knew exactly what he meant.

"It's like that, huh?"

He shrugged. And then the worst thing of all happened: pity came into her eyes.

"I'm sorry, Hunter. That's messy. But you still have to fix it. You don't think something like this could happen on a long-haul mission to Mars? May as well figure out how to deal with it now. Think of it as an analog simulation."

He supposed she was right. But the truth was, he was getting pretty damn tired of thinking about everything in his life as an analog simulation.

The front door opened behind him, and when he turned his head, he saw Airin standing in the kitchen.

"Hey," she said, looking at the two of them.

"Hey," Val said.

Airin's gaze fell on the container of yogurt he'd forgotten he was holding. "Is that the last yogurt?"

"Yeah." He paused. "You want it?"

"No, you can have it."

"No, that's okay, you can—"

"Oh, for God's sake." Val leaned forward and grabbed the yogurt from him. "This one's mine. Why don't the two of you walk down to the market and buy some more?"

He and Airin looked at each other.

"What do you say?" he asked after a moment. "Are you up for a walk?"

She looked uncertain, and he was suddenly determined that she would go with him.

He surged to his feet and went over to her. He took her bag, dropped it on the kitchen floor beside his, and grabbed her hand.

"Let's go."

Once they were outside, Airin tugged at his hand, and he released her immediately. But she didn't turn around and go back inside, so he took that as a win.

They started their walk without saying anything.

It was twilight, and the gray sky and growing shadows made everything feel vague and elusive and mysterious. Evening birdsong filled the air, along with the occasional car driving by, but behind all that was the waiting silence of night.

Airin was wearing a pair of khaki shorts, a blue NASA T-shirt, and a pair of flip-flops. Her hair was loose, rippling in coal-black waves down her back, and the memory of touching it was like phantom silk against his fingertips.

Airin had expanded her wardrobe quite a bit in the last month. It now included T-shirts and tank tops, jeans and shorts, sandals and flip-flops. It was a Hawaiian wardrobe, but even though her clothes matched her environment, Airin still stood out.

Whether she was wearing a silk dress or a T-shirt and cutoffs, Airin managed to be elegant. She was elegant like his favorite vintage airplane, the de Havilland Dragon Rapide of the 1930s. It was named for its dragonfly shape, created by two sets of wings, a long, graceful fuselage, and the connected cockpit windows that looked like dragonfly eyes.

But Airin's elegance wasn't only in her design. There was a sense of strength and speed and toughness to her, too, like the SR-71 Blackbird. The Blackbirds had been made of titanium and steel, and they could withstand sustained cruise speeds above Mach 3. They could outrun any enemy aircraft or missile, and though some had been destroyed in accidents, none had ever been lost to enemy fire.

They looked pretty damn cool, too. They'd been painted a dark blue, almost black, with touches of red here and there.

He could probably come up with a few more planes Airin reminded him of, but maybe he should actually talk to her instead. The only problem was, he couldn't come up with a single icebreaker.

Then, thank God, Airin came up with one.

"I've decided what my field of study is going to be," she said.

"Yeah? What?"

"Aerospace medicine."

"Really? I would've thought you'd avoid anything to do with medicine because of your history."

She glanced up at him with a quick smile, and he felt the electric pull he'd been trying so hard to overcome. It was the first time she'd smiled at him in weeks.

"I know what you mean. But I thought about what you said that night . . ."

She faltered suddenly. The words *the night we kissed* hung in the air, and he hoped she'd go right past them so they wouldn't have to talk about it.

She did.

"What you said about, you know, studying something I'd enjoy that would also be useful in space. It's hard to be poked and prodded and operated on when no one's telling you what's happening. It makes you feel out of control. That's one of the issues astronauts deal with in space already, and I thought it would be helpful to have a flight surgeon on board who understands that. So I'm going to focus on space psychology as well as space medicine. Even if I never make it to Mars, I'll be able to help the people who do." She paused. "I'm also going to study electrical engineering. It's a useful field of knowledge on its own, and it also ties into medicine. The body has its own electrical systems, and doctors are starting to look at human physiology the way engineers do. I thought it might be good to have a crew member who can find engineering solutions *and* emotional solutions to a problem. Someone who can speak both languages."

"That makes sense," he said—and it did. As someone who only spoke one of those languages, he could probably use a translator now and again. "That's going to be a hell of a lot of work, though."

"I'm not afraid of hard work. I like hard work."

"I get that. I like to work hard, too."

She glanced up at him again. "But what are you working for?"

"What do you mean?"

She hesitated, but only for a moment. "I get the feeling that all your hard work serves a double purpose. It's to achieve a goal, but it can also help you run away from something."

He stared down at her for a second before turning his gaze back to the sidewalk stretching before them. They were at the midpoint of their journey: as far to their destination as it would be to go back home.

"If I am, why would I tell you about it? Or anyone?"

His tone was mildly aggressive—hopefully enough to shake her off this topic.

She didn't seem shaken. "I was just asking a question. You made me think a lot about my own goals. What I want and why I want it. I wondered if you've ever asked yourself the same questions, or if you're just on autopilot now. A path you started on years ago that you haven't really questioned since."

He felt irritation rising. "What are you getting at?"

"It just occurred to me that your mom and your dad both left you, in different ways. If you go to Mars, you'd be the one leaving. You'd be leaving the whole world behind."

The air in his lungs felt thick and strange, like air from another planet.

"I guess you're getting a head start on the psychology thing. What are you saying, exactly? That I'm messed up?"

"Of course not. You're one of the least messed up people I've ever met—especially considering what you went through as a kid. But I do think you avoid some experiences, and I wondered if you ever thought about why."

His jaw felt tight. "What, because I don't want to be in a relationship? There are good reasons for that, and they don't have anything to do with my childhood."

Airin didn't say anything for a moment. Then: "I shouldn't have said anything. Forget I brought it up."

That pissed him off even more.

"So all this time you haven't been talking to me, you've been studying me instead? Nice."

Airin stopped walking, which meant he had to stop walking, too.

She turned to face him. Even in a T-shirt and flip-flops she managed to look fierce, her stance wide and firm, her hands on her hips.

"You make it sound like this last month was my fault. Like we're not talking anymore because of something I did. But *you're* the one who rejected *me*. You kissed me, and then you said nothing was going to happen between us. And yes, I've been avoiding you, but it's not like you objected. You've been avoiding me, too. We sleep across the hall from each other, and I hardly ever see you."

It was true. Although if Airin thought out of sight meant out of mind, she was wrong. He thought about her every damn night, and a lot of those nights ended with him spilling into his hand as he imagined going into her room and sliding into her bed.

"You're right," he said after a moment. "I have been avoiding you. The truth is, I want to fuck you. I want to fuck you, and I know it's a bad idea, and it just seemed easier not to spend time with you. Because whenever I do, that's all I can think about."

She stood absolutely still, staring at him with wide eyes. As he waited for her to respond, it occurred to him that using that word—*fuck*—was another kind of aggression. Another attempt to scare her off, to warn her away.

A word that crude was miles away from the elegance and grace that seemed to form the core of her being.

You and I don't belong together, a word like that said. *You and I don't fit.*

"I think about you in bed at night," she whispered.

Shit.

"Don't tell me that, Airin. Jesus. Now I'm going to have that image in my head."

She took a half step toward him, and the scent of her hair came to him on the breeze. "You said you didn't want anything to happen between us, but you didn't tell me why. Tell me now, Hunter."

Because I'm reporting on you to your mother.

That was the most obvious reason, and it was the one he couldn't tell her. But there was another reason.

"Because even if I did want a relationship, I suck at them. And you deserve more than someone who'll hump you and dump you. Especially for your first time." A sudden thought occurred to him. "If it still would be your first time. I mean . . . I don't want to assume . . ."

One corner of her mouth quirked up. "You think I had sex with someone in the last month? I know we've been avoiding each other, but I'm pretty sure you would've noticed if I had a guy in my room."

He shrugged. "Hell, what do I know? We made out on Waikiki Beach. Maybe you went to the guy's house. Maybe you got a hotel room."

Now both corners of her mouth were up. "Nope. I'm still a virgin."

Then her smile faded, and her eyes searched his in the twilight.

"I'm still a virgin, and I'd like not to be one. I'm not asking you to marry me, Hunter. But maybe you could show me what I've been missing."

His hands curled into fists. What the hell was she doing, offering him everything he wanted like this?

I'm reporting on you to your mother.

You deserve more than a roll in the hay.

They were both good reasons. But as he stood there staring at Airin, the woman he fantasized about every damn night, he knew there was another, deeper reason to resist his pull to her.

I'm afraid.

It was another thing he could never tell her.

Afraid of what? she'd ask.

And that was a question he didn't know the answer to. A question he didn't *want* to know the answer to.

He didn't want to lie to her, but he couldn't tell her the whole truth, either—because he didn't know what it was himself.

So he settled for telling her part of the truth.

"I can't," he said.

She looked frustrated, and boy could he sympathize.

"Why not?"

"I just can't."

She looked at him for a moment longer. Then she sighed, deep and long, and started to walk again.

He fell into step beside her.

"We're still going to the store?" he asked.

"I see no reason to abort our mission," she said. "Besides, I'm hungry and I want yogurt."

He felt his muscles starting to relax. "Okay."

They walked in silence for a few minutes, but it wasn't an awkward silence. Somehow, even though neither of them had gotten the answers they wanted, they'd moved past where they'd been to a better place.

"I missed you," he said suddenly, bumping her shoulder with his arm.

"I missed you, too," she said. "I've been wanting to ask you something, but things have been weird between us, and I didn't know if you'd say yes. It's a work-related favor."

"I'll do it," he said. "Whatever you need." He paused. "Which is what, exactly?"

They'd reached the market, and as they paused outside the door she grinned up at him.

She had the most beautiful smile he'd ever seen.

"Just remember you've already agreed to do it."

"Agreed to do what?"

"Come with me on a parabolic flight."

There was a swooping sensation in his stomach, like when your foot tries to land on a step that isn't there.

A parabolic flight. His Achilles' heel.

He sighed. "Is there any chance, any chance at all, that you'd accept a substitute for that favor?"

She looked thoughtful. "I guess you could sleep with me. But that wouldn't really be work related, would it?"

He knew she wasn't serious. But the truth was, those two things—the idea of sleeping with Airin and the idea of a parabolic flight—were alike in one way.

They combined temptation with dread.

Parabolic flights were NASA's way of creating weightlessness on Earth. They were used to train astronauts to maneuver in free fall and to test equipment before it went into space. High school and college students competed for opportunities to conduct zero-g experiments, and scientists took advantage of the opportunity, too.

It was a pretty simple operation. A jet plane followed a parabolic flight path—up and down, up and down—to create periods of weightlessness followed by periods of hypergravity, when your weight was nearly double what it usually was.

The first few parabolas were always great. In fact, the taste of free fall during the twenty-second intervals could be addictive. That's where the temptation came in.

But then came the fourth parabola, and the fifth, and . . .

There was a reason those planes were nicknamed vomit comets.

He wasn't afraid of the flight itself. He was a pilot; he trusted the technology and the process. What he was afraid of was the physical weakness it revealed in him. A weakness that, as a pilot and astronaut, he'd never expected to have.

He was susceptible to zero-g motion sickness.

You adapt when you're actually in space, astronauts who'd logged time on the ISS and in low-Earth orbit had told him. *You just have to be up there long enough for your vestibular system to get used to free fall.*

He'd adapted to everything else the military and the space program had thrown at him, and he was sure he'd eventually adapt to this, too. But in the meantime, parabolic flights were the bane of his existence.

Airin was studying him with her eyebrows up. "Val was right. She told me you hate parabolic flights, but I didn't believe it. I was sure you couldn't be afraid of anything flight related."

"There's a difference between hating something and being afraid of it," he practically growled, realizing as soon as the words were out of his mouth that he'd tacitly admitted to the first thing.

Airin smiled. "Great. Then you'll come with me? It won't be on a NASA flight, because I'm not in training and I don't have a micro-g experiment I want to conduct or anything. I'm going on one of the commercial zero-g flights."

"Seriously? Those things cost five thousand dollars per passenger. For a ninety-minute flight that includes about seven total minutes of weightlessness."

"Seven minutes is plenty. That's about what Alan Shepard experienced on America's first spaceflight, so it's good enough for me. But yes, it's pricey. I don't know if I ever truly appreciated being rich until I started doing research on these flights."

"Your ribs have only just healed up. Are you sure you can—"

"The day before Chuck Yeager broke the sound barrier, he cracked two ribs when he was thrown from a horse. He didn't tell anyone in case they scrapped his flight. He had to rig up something with his flight engineer so he could close the cockpit door." She paused. "My ribs are fine, Hunter. The doctor cleared me."

"Okay, but—"

"So will you come? I bought two tickets because I want to go with someone—ideally, someone who's experienced it before. Val and Dean can't spare the time for a trip to California, but Val said you've got a few days of vacation coming up."

"Yeah, I do. But I wasn't planning to spend it going to California for a parabolic flight. I was planning to spend it living the life of a beach bum on Kauai."

She clasped her hands in front of her. "Please, Hunter. Please?"

He imagined Dira's reaction to the news of her daughter's latest adventure. Man, she'd loathe the very idea of it.

The thought of being the one to tell her almost made up for going on a parabolic flight himself.

Almost.

He sighed. "Yeah, all right. I guess I can spend my vacation on the vomit comet."

Airin turned to go inside the store, but he reached out and took her by the shoulder.

"I'm sorry," he said.

The words contained more than he'd meant them to. He'd meant to apologize for the awkwardness of the last few weeks, and that was probably what Airin heard. But he knew he was also sorry for other things.

I'm sorry I kissed you. I'm sorry I stopped kissing you. I'm sorry I'm not kissing you right now, because that's all I want to do.

"That's okay," she said, and he could tell she was responding to the first, most obvious thing. "I'm sorry, too."

"You don't have anything to be sorry for."

She smiled up at him. "I know. But it seemed like the polite thing to say."

As the two of them went into the store, he knew things were good again. The awkwardness between them was gone, and they could move into the dynamic they should have been in all along.

Friendship.

It was the best result he could have hoped for. It was the best thing for both of them.

And maybe if he repeated that often enough to himself, he'd start to believe it.

Chapter Eighteen

Airin's heart was pounding. They were seated in the zero-g plane, which looked like any other passenger jet from the outside. Inside, though, it was a different story. The only seats were in the back, about ten rows in the rear of the aircraft. The front part had been gutted and was padded on the floors, walls, and ceiling like an insane asylum.

Not exactly a reassuring image.

Also not reassuring: the antinausea injection she and Hunter had been given an hour before the flight had taken off.

"It doesn't help," Hunter had muttered.

"What?"

"The shot. It doesn't help. About two-thirds of the people who go up in this thing will still puke." He'd paused. "Or maybe it does help. Maybe without it, a hundred percent of people would puke."

It was then she'd started wondering if she should have picked someone else to go on this flight with her.

Hunter's pessimistic attitude was a direct contradiction to the palpable excitement of all the other passengers. Their eagerness had hardly been dimmed by the lengthy preflight discussion of sick bags—where they were and how to use them in zero-g—as well as techniques to minimize nausea. They'd nodded cheerfully at all the suggestions and continued radiating enthusiasm.

Of course none of them had ever done this before, and Hunter had.

That, too, was not reassuring.

The takeoff was normal. So were the first thirty minutes of their flight, which took them to their designated flying zone. Then they were given a ten-minute warning to unbuckle from their seats and lie down (if they chose) as they waited for their first parabola.

Lying down during the hypergravity part of the parabola—the beginning of the climb, when they'd experience about twice their normal weight—was one of the techniques that had been recommended to avoid motion sickness.

She'd been trying to kid Hunter into a better mood since they'd met in the lobby of their hotel that morning. But he'd stayed glum, and as they'd taken off from the tarmac—the moment she realized it was too late to get off the plane—she'd wondered if going on this trip alone might have been better than bringing along such a determined Eeyore.

Because now she was getting nervous. And as she looked around at the other passengers beginning to unbuckle and move toward the padded part of the jet, she could see they were nervous, too.

"Think of it as an intense roller coaster," Val had said when Airin had asked her what parabolic flights were like. Then she'd added: "A *really* intense roller coaster."

But Airin hadn't been on a roller coaster since she was eight years old, and that was just a kiddie coaster. She hadn't done much of anything since that first episode of tachycardia so long ago. She'd read about other people doing things, and she'd dreamed about doing things herself someday, but all from the safety of her mother's mansion.

How many times during those years had she longed for real experiences? Real adventures? And now here she was, about to subject her body to what astronauts went through in space.

It was an experience the human body often rejected. Hunter had reacted to zero-g with intense nausea, as did many astronauts at first. Human beings weren't meant to be weightless. It was disorienting, destabilizing.

Like everything else about space travel, it was unnatural.

She was supposed to be undoing her seat belt and moving to the open padded part of the plane. Instead she glanced over at Hunter, expecting him to look unhappy. He'd spent the morning grousing, after all.

But oddly enough, out of all the formerly enthusiastic and now subdued people on the plane, he was the only one smiling.

He squeezed her hand. "How are you doing, angel? You look tense."

She swallowed. "I am. I can't remember why I thought it was a good idea to do this. What if—"

"Don't bother with what-ifs. You're about to find out for yourself, which is why you're doing this. And it was a great idea, because you want to go into space, and even if you never get there, you're interested in studying aerospace medicine. Right?"

She nodded. His voice, so matter-of-fact, was starting to calm her down.

"So don't you think it would be helpful to know what astronauts experience in zero-g?"

"Yes. Yes, I do."

"Okay then." He reached over and unbuckled her belt, and then he grabbed her hand and pulled her to her feet. "Let's do this."

They found open space on the floor and lay down on the mats, which were deep and soft. The noise of the jet engines was loud, but she barely noticed it. She was too busy trying to control her crazy heartbeat and keep her breathing steady and even.

Hunter had told her not to indulge in what-ifs. But the big one was still there, looming large.

What if something goes wrong with my heart?

Before she'd booked the flight, she'd called her doctor in Massachusetts to ask him what he thought and if he foresaw any problems for her—and so he could sign off on the medical form the zero-g flight company had sent her.

He'd told her to go ahead and have a blast.

Nonetheless, she couldn't shake the fear that something would go wrong. Either the extra g-force or the weightlessness would stress her heart in unanticipated ways and she'd end up in the hospital again, helpless and hooked up to monitors, her world reduced to EKGs and hospital beds and endless trials of medicines and surgical treatments.

Hunter moved closer to her and took her hand. "Take it easy, angel. You're looking green around the gills, and the fun hasn't even started yet."

She shifted closer to him, squeezing his hand as she stared up at the ceiling. There was a monitor up there, telling them what was going on.

One minute to hypergravity. That meant they'd be starting the climb into their first parabola, which would subject them to twice their normal weight before their twenty seconds of zero-g began. She turned her head and looked at Hunter, and he looked back at her.

"You'd better decide now if you want to keep looking at me for the next thirty seconds, because once you feel yourself getting heavier you shouldn't move your head."

"I know," she said, her voice shaking. "Keeping your head still helps prevent nausea."

"That's the idea," he said, the rumble of his voice lower than the rumble of the engines. "So do you want to look at me, or do you want to look up at the ceiling?"

"You."

"Okay."

So she looked at him as the plane began its climb. His eyes weren't grumpy now, the way they'd been that morning. They were warm and comforting, and they held hers with absolute confidence that everything would be okay.

A voice came over the loudspeaker. "Okay, everybody, get ready! Zero-g coming up in ten seconds!"

Her heart rate kicked up another notch, and she squeezed Hunter's hand so hard it must have hurt him.

And then, just like that, she floated up into the air.

She was still holding Hunter's hand. But except for that, she was . . . untethered. Released from something she'd taken for granted from the moment she was born.

Gravity.

She hadn't realized how heavy her arms had always been, hanging off her shoulders like dead wood. Every bone and muscle and cell in her body had been pulled down all these years. Even her hair had been a burden to her scalp, the weight of it tending earthward like everything else.

And now all that weight was gone. Just gone.

Her hair was floating. Her body was floating. Her organs were floating in her body.

Even her heart.

Hunter was grinning, and she realized that she was grinning, too. She grabbed his other hand, and then they were facing each other and she was laughing, drunk with the euphoria of this extraordinary freedom . . . freedom from a burden she hadn't known she was carrying.

"Feet down!"

That, they'd been told, was the warning that gravity would soon return—in case any intrepid zero-g cowboys had flipped over.

Had it really been twenty seconds already?

She and Hunter positioned their feet toward the floor, still grinning like fools. The return of gravity was gentle, giving them time to lie down before the g-force increased.

There wasn't even a question of where they would look this time. They kept their eyes on each other, waiting for the hypergravity to give way to another bout of weightlessness.

Up they floated again. This was how it felt to be a spirit . . . or an angel.

"I want to do a flip," she said, and Hunter laughed.

"Okay," he said. "Show me what you've got."

He grabbed onto one of the straps affixed to the wall so she could brace herself against him, and she did it—a somersault in the air. Then she used his shoulders as leverage to swing her feet up to the ceiling so she could hang there with her eyes on his but upside down, their faces and their grins inverted.

"Feet down!"

By the time they hit the fourth parabola, a few of their fellow passengers were throwing up. One guy had to go back to the seats and belt in, and he sat there clutching a white sickness bag in front of his face and trying not to move his head more than he could help. A few others were pretty sick as well, huddled with their vomit bags, and she wondered during the next hypergravity interval if Hunter would soon be joining their ranks.

But he didn't. He seemed as enthusiastic as she and the other passengers were—the ones lucky enough not to get sick. It was like being in a bouncy house with a dozen eight-year-olds, only a million times better.

It was like every dream of flying she'd ever had.

They'd been warned not to stray too far (intentionally, anyway) from their original spots, not to try to swim or zoom around the cabin, since it would be all too easy to kick another weightless adventurer in the face. But on their last parabola, she knew she'd never forgive herself if she didn't break that rule.

Just before gravity released them, she said to Hunter, "We're going to be Superman and Supergirl."

He blinked. "What?"

"Just follow my lead."

When they floated up from the floor for the last time, she oriented herself so that she was crouching sideways with her feet against the wall of the cabin. Hunter followed her example, and she guessed he knew now what was coming next.

They pushed off gently, and then they were flying, their hands still clasped and their free arms outstretched like airborne superheroes, until they reached the opposite wall.

She'd felt a lot of different things in her twenty-four years. But never, not once, had she felt cool.

She turned to Hunter and grabbed his other wrist, and they spent their last few seconds of free fall facing each other with both hands clasped.

"We are *so cool*," she told him.

He grinned, his eyes never leaving hers.

"Yeah, we are."

◆ ◆ ◆

During the flight back and the celebration afterward for weightless "graduates," she couldn't stop talking. Neither could the other passengers. They were giddy, exhilarated, jubilant, and they regaled one another with the experience they'd just shared until the party at the airplane hangar broke up. Then they shook hands and even hugged like old friends, despite the fact that they'd been strangers just two hours ago.

But as she and Hunter settled into their rental car—he'd wanted a Mustang convertible even though the drive from the airport to their hotel was only half an hour—they didn't say anything for miles.

The dry air of Los Angeles was very different from the soft, lush air of Hawaii, but it blew her hair behind her as they drove with the top down, and she was glad Hunter had chosen this car.

She wasn't ready to let go of the sensation of freedom.

"You didn't get sick," was the first thing she said after several minutes on the road. It was loud enough that she had to raise her voice, and he had to raise his to answer.

"I know," he said. "I didn't even think about it until we landed. I guess the secret is to go with someone you care about more than yourself."

The words seemed to reverberate in the air around them. A beat went by, and then Hunter said, "Shit. You know what I mean. Someone you're worried about more than yourself. It was your first time, and I wanted to be sure you were okay. I guess that distracted me enough that I didn't feel sick. You know?"

"I know," she said.

But as silence fell between them, a new kind of euphoria was spreading through her.

"What about you?" he asked after a moment. "You're a natural. You were born to go into space, Airin Delaney. You have a stomach of iron."

"I guess I have to have something of iron to make up for my shitty heart."

"Your heart isn't shitty. Your heart is strong. Just like the rest of you."

The compliment felt overwhelming.

"Thanks," she said.

"You're welcome."

It was seven o'clock when they got back to the hotel. As they walked through the lobby Hunter asked, "Do you want to grab some dinner? There are a couple of restaurants in the building to choose from, or we could go out someplace."

She shook her head. They'd reached the elevator bank, and she reached out and pushed the Up button.

"I think I'm just going to get room service. I want to take some notes on the day, capture my thoughts and impressions while they're still fresh in my mind. Is that okay?"

"Of course. Yeah."

The elevator doors opened, and they stepped inside.

"That's absolutely okay," he continued as they rode up to their floor. "I'll see you tomorrow morning, then."

There was a note of relief behind his words, and she smiled to herself as they walked to their rooms. They were across the hall from each other, just like at home, and after their respective key cards had unlocked their doors, they looked at each other.

"So . . . good night, then," Hunter said.

"Good night."

He turned to go into his room and then turned back again. "It was quite a day."

"It sure was."

"Are you sorry it's over?"

"It's not over yet," she said, and he looked confused for a moment before nodding.

"You're going to be making notes. I guess you'll be reliving the experience, right? So . . . yeah. I'll see you tomorrow. Sleep well."

He went inside. She stood looking at his closed door for a moment, thinking about the plan she'd conceived in the car and wondering if she really had the guts to carry it out. Then she went into her own room.

It was a typical airport-area hotel: devoid of personality and with more beige than any human being needed, but more than adequate for a traveler's needs. When she'd made the reservation she'd booked the highest-end suites they offered, figuring the Jacuzzi tub might help Hunter recover from what she'd worried would be a hellish day of motion sickness for him.

Now she was glad of the luxurious bathroom for her own sake.

The Jacuzzi was wonderful. The bubbles created a kind of effervescence that reminded her of being in zero-g, if only because any blissful physical experience would have reminded her of being in zero-g.

She soaked for a long time, and when she was ready to get out, she shaved her legs more slowly and carefully than she ever had before, aware of the curve of her calf and the line of her shinbone and the challenge of the areas around the knee and ankle.

She'd brought one nice dress with her in case they went out to dinner or something, but it wasn't what she wanted to wear tonight. It was simple and black and appropriate for every occasion except the one she needed it for.

She was going to seduce Hunter Bryce, and she wasn't going to take no for an answer.

Well, unless he really did say no. It wasn't like she could force him or anything.

Oh God. What if he said no? That was a kind of humiliation she might never recover from.

But if she thought about that, she'd lose her nerve. And she'd been weightless today, damn it. Anything was possible.

She needed to focus on what to wear.

It wasn't like she had a lot of choices, other than the black dress. Jeans, a pair of navy cargo shorts, T-shirts, and cotton blouses.

After standing for what felt like a long time in front of her open suitcase—she hadn't bothered to hang anything except her dress and one blouse—she made a decision.

She dug into the zippered pocket on the inside of her case and pulled out a bra and panty set. It was pale pink satin edged with lace, and while it was simple, it also fit her really, really well. It wasn't the nicest lingerie she owned, but it was the nicest she'd brought with her, and it was, she hoped, enough to get the job done.

She stood at the full-length mirror on the back of the closet door and brushed her hair until it gleamed. She decided to skip makeup since her cheeks were pink enough without it—her pounding heart was delivering plenty of blood to flush her skin—but she put on clear lip gloss.

Her hands trembled so much as she applied it that she was glad she hadn't attempted a makeup job requiring more precision.

Then she put on the white cotton hotel bathrobe and went across the hall.

Chapter Nineteen

She knocked, and after a moment she heard Hunter's voice. "Yeah?"

"It's me."

There was a short pause. Then the door opened, and Hunter was standing there in sweatpants and no shirt, his bare chest as broad as a building and his shoulders like a professional athlete's. His face looked freshly scrubbed, as though he'd taken a shower, but he hadn't bothered to shave. The stubble that shadowed his jaw made her face tingle, as if she could already feel it scraping against her skin.

His expression was concerned. "Are you okay? What's up?"

Her heart was beating faster than it had before the first parabola. "I'm okay. I—"

She couldn't finish the sentence. She could barely breathe, much less speak. She crossed the threshold into his room, keeping her eyes on Hunter's as she reached behind her and pushed the door shut. Then she untied her robe and let it fall to the floor.

His eyes widened, and with one glance he took her in from her toes to the top of her head.

"Airin—"

She couldn't let him finish, because he might tell her to go back to her room. She closed the distance between them with two long strides, threw her arms around his neck, and pressed her mouth to his.

If he'd any ideas about sending her away, she knew the exact moment he gave them up.

He groaned. Then he moved her backward until she felt the door behind her, holding her up, as his hands slid into her hair and he angled her head to deepen the kiss.

Oh God, oh God, oh God.

The last time they'd done this, her ribs had been injured. But now they were healed. Every part of her was healed. And every part of her surged into him as he held her against the door, his body pressing into hers so she felt his hard erection against her belly.

He tore himself away, his eyes wild as they looked into hers. "If you stay one more second, I'm not letting you go until the morning. If you don't want that, leave now."

She was shaking like an engine straining for more speed than it was made for. "I'm not going anywhere."

He didn't say anything else. He just reached down to hook an arm behind her knees, and then he was carrying her to the bed, that boring hotel bed covered in its boring hotel bedspread that looked to her, right now, as glorious as a bower on Olympus.

He tossed her onto it and followed her down before she could catch her breath. His body covered hers, and as her mouth opened for him her legs fell apart, too, making a cradle for his lower body that he slid into as if it had been designed for him.

A low groan escaped him as he broke the seal of their mouths, kissing his way down her jaw to her neck.

Yes.

It was a cry of the body she'd only experienced three times before—the three kisses she'd shared with Hunter Bryce. But this was deeper and wilder, because this time she knew she wasn't leaving until morning.

Her pulse was beating like a hummingbird's wings. Hunter pressed his mouth to the place on her throat where it throbbed, and she arched her neck back to bring him closer.

If he revealed himself to be a vampire who wanted to drive his fangs into her jugular, she wouldn't refuse him.

She wanted to be consumed.

Just a few hours ago, she'd wanted nothing more than free fall. Weightlessness had felt like the most perfect gift the universe could offer. But now all she wanted was the heaviness of Hunter's body on hers. The weight of him pressing her into the mattress was the most exquisite force she'd ever experienced.

Except that she wanted more.

She wrapped her legs around his waist and squeezed, and he groaned again, that delicious sound that made her feel like a sex goddess.

And then he was moving against her, surging and retreating, his hard length pressing against her center and pulling away and pressing against her again until she was writhing beneath him.

"Oh, please," she heard herself say, and then she was saying it over and over again.

Hunter dragged his mouth from her neck to her ear.

"Wait," he whispered, and before she could tell him no, she didn't want to wait, she needed more of everything NOW, he had shifted down the bed so his head was at the level of her breasts.

Okay. This might work until they got to the other stuff.

She expected him to take her bra off, and she was ready to arch her back to help him. But then he bit her left nipple with her bra still on, and it felt so good she cried out.

He started to pull back. "Did I hurt you?"

"Yes. Do it again," she panted, putting her hands at the back of his head and tugging him down.

He didn't need any urging. He licked and bit at her breasts through the thin satin of her bra until the material was soaked through, and the sensation was so carnal and decadent that she twisted beneath him, not caring that she was moving like an animal and making small desperate sounds.

But when he shifted again, kissing his way down her belly to the place between her legs, she went still and silent. The only motion in her body was the quivering deep inside her, a kind of trembling in her very bones.

Hunter looked up, and their eyes met. She'd never experienced this before with another human being, this feeling like she was standing at the edge of an abyss that somehow felt like home. Her panties were soaked through, and she should have been embarrassed, afraid of what was coming next, but she wasn't.

At this moment, it felt like she'd never be afraid of anything ever again.

"Open your legs for me," Hunter said, his voice as rough as the scrape of his stubble on her skin had been.

It was the sexiest sentence she'd ever heard. Complying was the sexiest thing she'd ever done.

She spread her legs, and he was there between them, stretched out with his hands on her hips and his head between her thighs. Driven by a sudden need to feel and not to see, she pressed her head back into the pillows and closed her eyes.

He kissed her through her panties, and her hands fisted in the blankets beneath her.

"You're so wet," he murmured. "Jesus, Airin."

He grabbed her panties and pulled them off. Then it was just her body and his mouth, and oh God, it was the kind of good no amount of research could have prepared her for.

She was hanging on to the blankets like she'd held on to his hands in the zero-g flight—so she wouldn't float away.

His tongue was everywhere. Against her folds, inside her, and most especially on the center of all the exquisite agony that was making her moan.

It was going to happen. That thing she'd been trying to do for so long, during years of reading erotica and sex manuals and watching straight-up porn on the Internet. Nothing had ever worked. And now, after a few minutes between her legs, Hunter was making it happen.

But he wasn't in too damn much of a hurry. When he moved away from the heart of the action for the tenth time to tease at her slit and nibble on her thighs, she couldn't take it anymore.

"Go back," she panted. "Please, Hunter, please. Go back where you were."

She could swear she felt him smile against her skin.

"Here?" he murmured, and then suddenly his fingers were sliding inside her and his tongue was lashing at her over and over until . . .

The world seemed to split apart.

She hadn't known she was at such a dizzying height, to have so far to fall. Miles and miles and miles of falling and rising and falling again, and Hunter's hands on her body the whole time, steadying her, centering her, giving her a place to come home to.

Slowly she became aware that he was kissing his way back up her body, taking his time, until he lay beside her with his head on the pillow next to hers.

She turned on her side and looked at him.

Until now, she'd thought she knew his face so well that she could have sketched it on the back of a napkin with her eyes closed. But a man who could do what Hunter had just done had hidden depths, which meant there was still more to see.

He seemed equally captivated by her.

"I wish you could see your face right now," he whispered, reaching out to brush the backs of his knuckles along her flushed cheek.

"Why? What do I look like?"

"You look . . . satisfied."

"Satisfied," she said, sounding it out. She wriggled forward and nestled close to him, tucking her head in the place between his neck and his shoulder. "That's a really good word."

"Yeah."

Was that the feeling pulsing through her veins? Satisfaction? If so, she'd never been satisfied before. Because this feeling was entirely new.

And yet . . . she didn't think she would call it satisfaction. Because that implied that they were done, that this experience was complete.

And she didn't feel done.

A sudden rush of energy made her sit up.

"Whoa," Hunter said. "You look like you're back in the jet, ready to float up to the ceiling."

It was the same kind of giddiness, if not the same kind of weightlessness.

"There's so much I want to do," she said breathlessly.

He folded his arms behind his head and grinned up at her. "Yeah? Give me an example."

"I want to start by looking at you."

His eyes glittered. "That's okay by me. You should feel free to touch, too."

He was still wearing his sweatpants. They were tented at the crotch, and the thought of what was beneath the material made her hands curl against her palms.

"Will you take those off?"

His gaze flicked down to her breasts, still covered by her bra.

"If you take that off," he said, his voice husky.

They moved at the same time. She reached behind her back to unhook her bra, and he reached down to tug off his pants. As they tossed away their last vestiges of modesty, goose bumps swept across her skin.

"I've never seen a naked man before," she whispered, unable to take her gaze from the long, thick, proud erection between Hunter's legs. "Not in person."

"Well, I've seen a lot of naked women before," Hunter said. "Many of them in person." He paused. "But I've never in my whole life seen a woman as beautiful as you are."

She looked up at him, startled. "That's not true. That can't be true. Statistically speaking—"

His eyes burned into hers. "Fuck statistics. You're the most beautiful woman I've ever seen, Airin. And I want you so much I feel like I'm on fire."

Heat swept through her. "I . . ." She didn't know what to say. But she knew what she wanted to do, so maybe she could start there. "I want to touch you."

"You can do anything you want, angel. But if you don't mind, I'm going to stay really still while you do. If I let myself move, that'll be the end of foreplay. If I let myself touch you, you'll be on your back under me."

Her breath left her body, and she couldn't get it back. Her cheeks were so hot it felt like she had a fever. She reached out trembling hands and set them against his chest.

His skin was smooth, and the muscles beneath were like iron.

His breathing turned harsh.

"I want to touch your arms," she said, and he unclasped his hands from behind his head and laid them down, curling his fingers into the blankets like she had a few minutes before.

She slid her hands up from his chest to his shoulders, and then down those arms she'd dreamed about a hundred times.

She could barely span his biceps.

Her gaze swept along his torso to his hip bones. They were angled like runway lights, telling her, *Look down here, for God's sake. This is where the action is.*

After a moment Hunter growled, "If you think staring at me like that is going to make me any harder, the answer is no. It's not physically possible. I could drill through concrete right now."

She met his eyes again. "I want to touch you," she said, and he knew what she meant.

"You should douse me in cold water first or give me a leather strap to bite on. But okay."

She moved down the bed until she was kneeling by his hips. Then she reached out, slowly, and took him in her hand.

A long, low growl came from Hunter. When she looked up, his eyes were closed and his teeth were clenched tight, as if he really were biting on a leather strap.

He was hot and hard, which she'd known already. But what she hadn't imagined was how soft his skin would feel. She bent down and rubbed her cheek against him, and it was like velvet.

"Fuck."

She looked up at him again, and his eyes were hazel fire.

There were a lot of other things she wanted to try tonight. She wanted to spend hours touching him, finding out the things he liked. But right now, at this moment, there was really only one thing she wanted to do.

She moved back up the bed and put her hands on his chest again. She could feel his heart pounding against her palms.

"Hunter."

"Yeah?"

His voice was gravelly, and it played across her nerve endings like a calloused fingertip.

"I want that thing you were talking about before."

"What thing?"

"When you said—if you touched me—"

That was all it took. He reached up and seized her by the shoulders, and then he flipped them over so fast she squeaked.

Oh God.

He was supporting his weight with his arms, but he was so big and so powerful she felt pinned in place by the sheer force of him. She felt pinned by his gaze, too, which burned into her as though he could see into her soul.

Then he lowered his head and kissed her.

Her body surged into his as though she could levitate through sheer will. Their tongues thrust together as she looped her arms around his neck and pulled him down, down, until his chest crushed her breasts and his muscled thigh slid between her legs.

"Hunter," she gasped. "Hunter, I need . . ."

"Wallet," he said, rearing back and panting. "I think I have a condom in my wallet. Just . . . don't move, for God's sake. Stay right where you are."

He was back faster than she would have believed possible, and then he was ripping open the foil packet and rolling the latex over his rigid length, and finally, thank God, he was over her again.

"Please," she said, arching her back and wrapping her legs around his waist. "Please, please, please—"

"It's your first time, angel. We're going to take this slow."

"I don't want slow. I want—"

He leaned down and spoke right into her ear. "Trust me."

His whispered words made her shiver all over. Then he nudged at her entrance, and she went absolutely still.

Inch by slow inch he pushed inside. There was tightness and resistance but no pain, only pleasure, and when he was all the way home it felt like the fullness and friction and pressure and heat were secrets that could unlock the universe.

"Hunter."

He lifted himself up on his forearms and looked down at her, and the intensity in his eyes reverberated between them until it felt like they didn't need words to communicate anymore—only this, forever, for the rest of their lives.

When he started to move it was almost too much, and with every thrust hitting she climbed higher. She knew she wasn't going to come again, not this time, but the way she felt was a hint of things to come.

"Hunter."

She sank her nails into his back as she said his name, and he growled in response as his thrusts became rougher and more urgent. A moment later she felt him pulse inside her, and then he dropped his head onto her shoulder as he shuddered out his release.

They lay like that for a long time. The whole world was beating hearts and ragged breath and a heavy, rich, musky scent she knew was the tang of sex.

She wanted to float in it forever.

Hunter rolled away and pulled off the condom, tossing it in the trash before rolling back and pulling her into his arms. Then he tucked her against his chest and murmured into her hair.

"How are you feeling?"

She sighed. "This is the best I've ever felt in my entire life."

He chuckled. "Better than zero-g?"

"Yes." She paused. "What about you?"

He pulled back a little, enough that he could look her in the eyes. "If I could, I'd stay here like this forever."

His words made her feel hollowed out and shaky and joyful at the same time, the way she'd felt after their parabolic flight.

"I . . ." She swallowed. "I feel the same way."

And then, suddenly, she yawned.

Hunter chuckled again. Then he reached underneath them to tug down the covers, and once they'd slid beneath he pulled them up again, over their shoulders this time. Now they were in a warm cocoon of naked skin and body heat and that incredible sex haze, and she could feel her eyelids growing heavy.

Hunter reached out and turned off the light.

"Good night, angel," he whispered.

"Good night."

Chapter Twenty

It turned out that Airin snored.

It was a gentle and adorable snore, and Hunter could have listened to it all night. But after a while she shifted against him, making a kind of murping sound like a sleeping cat, and fell into a deeper slumber.

She stopped snoring. But he could still listen to her breathing, and he did. And with his eyes adjusted to the darkness, he could watch her sleep.

Making love with Airin was the best and worst thing that had ever happened to him.

He was no longer the ideal astronaut. Not as he defined it, anyway. Because now there was someone in his life he didn't want to leave behind.

He stayed where he was, Airin nestled against him, while he groped behind him for the phone he'd left on the bedside table.

He had to type the email slowly, using only his right thumb, because his left arm was under Airin's body and he didn't want to move it.

> Airin did great on the parabolic flight. She was born to go into space, whether you want to admit it or not. This will be the last report I send you, because I'm ending our arrangement. I understand I won't be part of the DelAres crew. But I'll be at Cape Canaveral when your mission launches, cheering

> them and you on. With luck, NASA will only be a few years behind you.

Another hour, maybe more, went by. Airin shifted again, and this time she yawned, stretched, and opened her eyes.

He watched her remembering where she was and who she was with. Then she looked up at him and smiled.

"Hi," she whispered.

He pressed a kiss to her forehead. "Hi."

"What time is it?"

"I think it's about three in the morning."

"Have you slept?"

He shook his head. "I can't sleep. I can't stop looking at you."

She blinked. "You've been watching me this whole time?"

"Yeah."

She stared up at him for a moment. Then reached out and traced the lines of his face with the tips of her fingers—his cheeks, his temples, his jaw.

He closed his eyes and leaned into her caress. "That feels good."

She brushed her fingertip across his lower lip. "Hunter?"

"Yeah?"

"Do you have another condom?"

He opened his eyes and smiled at her. "No. But, angel, there's a lot of other stuff we can do if you're so inclined."

She thought about that for a moment. Then she shifted again, sitting up this time.

"I know what I want to do," she said.

He rolled onto his back and clasped his hands behind his head. "Lay it on me."

She put a hand on his chest. "I want to talk about the future."

He raised his eyebrows.

"That's pretty diabolical. First you drug me with sex, and then you get me to have The Talk?"

She nodded solemnly. "Exactly. This is the technique I'll use with all the guys I—"

A wave of possessiveness went through him. "Don't talk about other guys."

One side of her mouth quirked up. "It was a joke. So can I tell you what I was thinking?"

"You're too intimidating sitting up like that. Lie down and you can tell me anything."

She slid down onto her side, her head pillowed on her arm. "Okay," she said. "I want you to know I don't expect anything from you. Anything permanent, I mean. Both of us have big plans for the future, and we shouldn't do anything to derail them. I've only just started the application process for medical school, and I have no idea where I'll end up. Meanwhile, you're at NASA's mercy. You'll be here in Hawaii for another year, maybe two, but after that? Maybe they'll send you to Houston. Maybe Florida. Maybe California to the Jet Propulsion Lab." She paused. "Maybe to the International Space Station. And I don't want to get in the way of any of that."

He was on his side, too, facing her. "I understand what you're saying."

"And," she went on, "I know you're not looking for a relationship. I know this because you told me. Several times. So I want you to know I don't expect that to change just because we've slept together."

He nodded slowly. "I see. So . . . what do you expect?"

"Nothing. I don't expect anything. Except . . ." She hesitated.

"Except what?"

"Except . . . I'd like to be with you like this again. For as long as we happen to be sharing a house. Or as long as we both want to," she amended. "With the understanding that either one of us can call it quits at any time, with no hard feelings. And we decide right now that we won't let things get weird and awkward again. We'll make a real effort to be friends, no matter what."

She looked so serious as she said that. God, she was so sweet . . . so sweet and so earnest. How the hell had he resisted her for so long?

Of course, he knew the answer. He'd resisted her because he'd understood, on some level, what would happen if he gave in to his desire for Airin.

He'd go up like tissue paper in a fire.

But Airin herself had talked about an escape route—the ability to call it quits "at any time, with no hard feelings." They didn't have to go too deep too soon.

He should be grateful for that built-in safety hatch. But he found himself saying, "There's something I want, too."

"Of course. I didn't mean to sound like I was setting the rules for both of us or anything. What do you want, Hunter?"

A wave of affection went through him that was as powerful as the lust that was already making him hard.

"I want you to keep an open mind."

She frowned a little. "An open mind? Open to what?"

For most of his adult life, his pillow talk with women had included a warning label. *I really like you, but I don't want to hurt you. I want to be sure we're going into this with our eyes open.* What Airin had just laid out were the ground rules he'd always set himself in the past. So the tack he was taking now felt a little strange.

"I don't want us to close the door on any possibilities."

"What do you mean?"

He tried again. "I don't think we should rule out the idea of a relationship. Not right off the bat. Shouldn't we see where things go? In a kind of structured way."

She blinked. "A kind of structured way? What would that look like, exactly?"

"We'd tell Val and Dean we're involved, so we don't have to keep it a secret. And while we're seeing each other, we . . . wouldn't see other people."

A slow smile spread across her face. "I know I don't have much experience in this area, but that sounds an awful lot like dating. Are you asking me to be your girlfriend?"

Shit.

"Yeah. I guess I am. But I agree with all that other stuff you said, too. I don't want to get in the way of your goals or your dreams."

"And I don't want to get in the way of yours."

"Okay then."

"Okay."

They lay still for a few moments, just looking at each other. Airin's brown eyes were warm, thoughtful, intelligent, and playful at the same time.

There weren't a lot of women who could operate on all those levels, especially when they were lying naked in bed with you.

A woman like that was someone you could spend your life with. A woman like that was someone you could go into space with.

But he wasn't ready to think about that possibility. There was too much uncertainty there, too much that scared him.

And anyway, there was something else he wanted to do right now.

He reached out and combed his fingers through the silken mass of her hair in one long, luxurious stroke. "Will you do something for me, Airin?"

He could read her response to his touch in the way her breath caught and her nipples puckered and hardened.

"What?" she whispered.

"Lie on your back and spread your legs. I want to taste you."

She closed her eyes and shivered. "I want that, too. But, Hunter?"

"Yeah?"

"After that, it's my turn to taste you."

His body hardened in one zero-to-liftoff rush.

"If you insist."

He trailed a hand down her body until he reached her center, where a trickle of moisture was already making her soft and ready.

"But first things first, angel. First things first."

Chapter Twenty-One

The next day they flew back to Hawaii. Hunter could hardly keep his hands off Airin during the flight, and when they came through the door of their house he had an arm around her shoulders.

Val and Dean were watching TV in the living room. When they looked up, Hunter saw the instant they figured out what was going on.

Val groaned. Dean, on the other hand, was grinning.

"Pay me," he said, extending a hand.

Val pulled her wallet from her pocket and fished out a twenty. "Just keep it down up there, okay?" she said as she gave the bill to Dean. "Remember you have housemates and that a closed door is everyone's friend."

They weren't particularly quiet, but they did close the door.

◆ ◆ ◆

He reached for Airin in the morning when he was still half-asleep, but she was already up and dressing.

"Where are you going?" he asked, watching as she buttoned her short-sleeved blouse. His fingers itched to undo every one.

"I promised Val I'd be back in the lab this morning. We're running tests on the new water extraction process."

He sat up in bed, letting the covers slide down to his waist.

"I bet Val won't mind if you're an hour late."

Her eyes traveled down his bare torso and back up again, and he winked at her.

She shook her head. "I can't believe you're using your masculine wiles to tempt me to neglect work."

"I can't believe you're resisting me."

She took theatrically slow steps toward the doorway. "I didn't say it was easy," she said, wiping imaginary sweat from her brow. "But didn't we agree work would always come first?"

"Maybe we should renegotiate that agreement."

She reached the door and blew him a kiss. "You're only saying that because you're still on vacation. I bet you'll be singing a different tune when it's your turn to go back to the lab."

"You might lose that bet. And since I don't have anything to do today but think about you, I should warn you I'm going to be full of energy when you get home."

She grinned at him. "That doesn't sound like a warning. It sounds like a promise." She blew him another kiss. "See you tonight."

After she was gone, he realized he was still smiling.

Life seemed pretty damn good right now, except for two things.

The first was that Dira had answered his email yesterday. I'll call you tomorrow at noon and we'll discuss it, she'd written.

There's nothing to discuss, he'd wanted to write back—but there was at least one good reason to keep things amicable with Dira.

She was Airin's mother.

So he'd talk to her in a few hours and explain that he wasn't comfortable with their deal anymore. He should never have agreed to it in the first place. He'd tell her that Airin was doing great and that enough time had gone by for them to restart their mother-daughter relationship on a healthier footing.

What he wouldn't tell her was that he and Airin were involved. That was a piece of information that could wait until Airin herself was ready to convey it.

The second fly in the ointment was the question of what—and when—to tell Airin about all this. He knew he ought to make a clean breast of things, explain what he'd done, and beg her forgiveness. That course of action seemed as simple and straightforward as doing the right thing always did.

But whenever he imagined that conversation, it always ended with Airin in tears or Airin furious at him . . . or Airin deciding she didn't want to be with him anymore.

And whenever he pictured that happening, he knew he wasn't ready to face the possibility of losing her.

So he'd wait. He'd tell her eventually, of course. When things between them were on a firmer footing. They'd only been together for forty-eight hours, after all. He could give it a few more days.

Or weeks.

◆ ◆ ◆

The call with Dira didn't go quite the way he'd expected.

She didn't try to talk him out of his decision. Instead she said, "It's been six weeks since we spoke in the hospital. Six weeks was all we agreed to then. As far as I'm concerned, you've honored your side of the bargain, and I'm prepared to honor mine." She paused. "Unless, of course, you no longer want a place on the DelAres crew."

The image of a landing craft on a rocky red plain filled his mind's eye. It was the *DelAres I*, and inside it was the first crew—the first human beings—to land on Mars.

A ladder extended from the craft to the planet, and an astronaut emerged from the air lock. Rung by rung he descended toward the surface. Then he stepped onto the regolith, making a footprint on the red soil.

His footprint.

The moment he'd emailed Dira from California, he'd known he was giving up that opportunity. To have it offered again was a shock.

He was standing at the living room window, looking out at the guava trees in the backyard. Could he accept a place on the DelAres crew now? What would he tell Airin if he did? How could he explain all this to her?

He'd have to tell her the whole story. Which, of course, he'd already decided to do . . . eventually. But what would Airin think about him joining her mother's company? Would she see that as a betrayal? What would it do to their relationship?

"You can't tell Airin," he heard himself say.

Silence on the other end of the phone. Then: "What?"

"I want to be the one to tell her, and not right away. I'll tell her in a few weeks, after we negotiate my transition from NASA to DelAres."

He paused, and a new possibility took root in his mind. The seed had been planted on the plane from California to Hawaii, when he and Airin had seen the first findings to come out of the biosphere mission. Janelle had emailed the report, reminding him of their conversation about couples in space, and he and Airin had read it together as they flew over the Pacific, holding hands under a thin airline blanket.

What if there was a way to have everything? His dream *and* Airin's dream?

"Have you read the first dispatch from the biosphere project?"

"What?" Dira sounded bewildered by the change of subject. "What are you talking about? What does that have to do with Airin? You haven't told me why you—"

"Just bear with me for a minute. Have you read it?"

Dira huffed out a sigh. "I haven't had time. I'm planning to review all the findings once the simulation is over. What is this about, Hunter?"

"Results are preliminary at this stage, but indications so far are that the two couples have done better than the four single astronauts. A lot better."

"And?"

"You said NASA has resisted the idea of sending couples into space. That's been true, so far. But now they're talking about making a change to that model, especially for long-haul missions. And I was wondering about the DelAres position on sending couples to Mars."

There was a long silence. Then: "We've thought about it, of course. Some on the team are in favor of the idea. It might be the best way to overcome some of the psychological difficulties of a three-year mission in space—or an even longer one. But why are you bringing this up, Hunter? Based on your profile, I would have thought you'd be against couples in space."

"I was against it. I always hated the idea. What if a situation comes up where you have to make an impossible choice? The safety of your partner versus the safety of another crew member, or the success of the mission?"

"Well, what if it does? What would you do?"

"I don't know. But it's something people can talk about and think about and plan for like any other aspect of space travel. Isn't that one of the things they're studying in the biosphere? Couple dynamics?"

"But what do you *think*? You're a pilot and a commander. A team leader. What's your instinct?"

Outside, a misty rain had begun to fall. The wind picked up, and the scent of Hawaii blew into the house.

He remembered what Airin had said the day she came into his room and told him she wanted to go into space.

The surface of Mars is as different from Hawaii as it's possible to be. Cold, dry, barren. No liquid water. No plants. No animals. No soft air against your cheek. No scent of flowers, no sound of raindrops.

He took a deep breath. "I think it's possible that the benefits could outweigh the drawbacks."

"How so? What do you see as the benefits?"

"I think Earth-out-of-view syndrome would be easier to handle if you brought a piece of home with you. Someone you love the way you love Earth."

Before Airin, he would never have used the word *love* in a conversation about space travel . . . or anything else, most likely. But then, even NASA used the word occasionally.

"One of the psychologists on the biosphere project has talked about this," he went on. "He's positing that a team on a long-haul mission might actually have a better chance of survival if they're fighting for—and with—people they love." He thought about the difference between a parabolic flight with Airin and a parabolic flight without Airin. "Plus, it would be more fun."

"Fun?" Dira repeated, as though it were a foreign word she mistrusted instinctively.

"Yeah. Believe me, it matters. Especially on a long mission."

There was another factor, one he didn't feel comfortable putting into words yet. When he imagined going into space with Airin—more specifically, to Mars—it made him think about immigrant families sailing across the Atlantic or pioneer families putting all their worldly possessions in a covered wagon before heading off into the unknown.

Being a lone-wolf explorer was very different. That was about glory and adventure, and while a part of him would always be attracted to those things, the motivation he was feeling now was bigger. Deeper.

Traveling into space with Airin would be about building something—building a future—with someone he cared about. Building something for future generations.

It was a terrifying idea in some ways. The best thing about being a lone wolf was the most obvious one: you didn't have as much to lose.

But he hadn't gotten where he was by letting fear rule his life.

"Well, Hunter, this is an interesting topic, and one that will no doubt be discussed a great deal in the coming years. Once you're part of the DelAres team, we'll seek your input." She paused. "By the way, you haven't yet formally accepted my offer. Do I take it that you wish to?"

"Yeah," he said. "As long as I can be the one who tells Airin about it—in a few weeks. After we figure out the transition with NASA."

That would give him time to tell Airin the whole story and to get her on board with the bigger dream.

The two of them going to Mars together. As a couple.

After a moment Dira spoke. "When we first talked in the hospital, I said I didn't want you to tell me anything about Airin's life that you or she would consider truly private."

"Yeah, I remember. You said I didn't need to steal her diary for you."

"Yes. Well. In that spirit, please understand that you may choose to answer this question or not, as you see fit. Are you dating my daughter?"

It was a question he should have been ready for. But he wasn't.

Dira wasn't an idiot. He'd told her he wanted to be the one to tell Airin about their deal, and then he'd talked about sending couples to Mars.

Shit.

Still, Dira would have found out eventually. Maybe it was better this way. Now she'd have time to come to terms with the idea before he and Airin told her formally. And he and Airin would have time, too. Time to figure out how to convince Dira that her daughter would be one of the finest astronauts to ever go into space.

But in the meantime, he wasn't going to talk about his relationship with Airin. It had only just begun, after all. They were still figuring things out themselves.

"Like you said, that's a private matter."

Another silence.

"Yes. Yes, of course. Well, Hunter, I suppose this will be the last time we talk—in this context, at any rate. Once you receive your contract and sign it, our conversations will be professional." She paused. "So I guess it's goodbye, then. Until we meet again."

She was letting him off the hook, at least for now.

"Goodbye, Dira."

Chapter Twenty-Two

Airin was smiling as she walked up the driveway to her house.

She'd been doing that a lot lately. Smiling.

On this particular occasion, she was remembering the dinner Hunter had taken her to a few nights before.

"For our one-week anniversary," he'd said, handing her a plumeria lei.

Their one-week anniversary.

This might be the first relationship she'd ever been in, but she'd watched enough TV to know that guys didn't usually celebrate one-week anniversaries. Not guys like Hunter, anyway.

She was a lucky woman.

She was also the first one home today, which was by design. She was going to cook dinner as a way to thank Dean and Val for everything they'd done for her—and to apologize for all the sex that had been happening on the second floor. She and Hunter had been trying to keep things reasonably quiet, but they weren't always successful.

Sex, it turned out, was as addictive as weightlessness. As soon as it was over, she wanted to do it again.

This had led, naturally, to thoughts of combining the two and many discussions with Hunter about the possibilities inherent in weightless sex.

Now there was an engineering problem you could really sink your teeth into.

They'd also started talking about the idea of couples in space. Their conversations had been mostly theoretical, and they'd skirted around the subtext. Would they still be together in ten or fifteen years? Would she be an astronaut? Would NASA select both of them for a Mars mission?

There were so many uncertainties, so many unknowns. But the fact that they were talking about this at all—and that Hunter was the one bringing it up—seemed like a really hopeful sign.

Everything these days seemed like a hopeful sign.

There was a UPS package on the front steps, the size of a thin book or a thick document. She grabbed it on her way in, noticing that it was addressed to her. She set her grocery bag on the kitchen counter and went into the living room, curling up on the couch in Val's usual spot with the package in her lap.

It was from her mother.

Well, the DelAres company, anyway. Which meant her mother.

It had been a few days since they'd last texted each other. She'd gotten used to not talking to her mother every day and to getting brief texts instead of long interrogations about her health and well-being. She was starting to feel more like an adult daughter and less like a permanently infantilized child, even though breaking away from Dira's influence had felt, in the beginning, as hard as breaking away from Earth's gravity.

But it was happening.

When she tore the package open, she saw that it was a document of some kind—legal by the look of it. She leaned back, set her feet on the edge of the coffee table, and began to read.

◆ ◆ ◆

She'd finished reading by the time Hunter got home.

He called out to her as he came through the front door. "I forgot to stop for wine, but I think we have a bottle left over from Dean's birthday party. If not, I can—"

He caught sight of her face and stopped dead.

"Jesus, Airin, what the hell happened? Are you okay?"

He was standing in the kitchen, looking at her over the counter. When she put the document on the coffee table with shaking hands, he came into the living room.

"What is this?" he asked, picking it up and sitting on the chair across from her.

"It's a contract," she said. "An employment contract."

She didn't recognize her own voice. It sounded empty, dead.

Exactly the way she felt.

It only took him a few seconds to see what it was. The guilt on his face told the whole story, but if she'd had any doubts, his next words would have cleared them up.

"Why did you open my mail?"

She hadn't known anything could hurt so much.

"It was addressed to me."

"Addressed to *you*? Why would—shit, of course." He closed his eyes briefly. "She knows we're involved, and this is her way of splitting us up. A brutally efficient method, too. That's Dira all over."

He called her mother by her first name.

He opened his eyes again and leaned forward, his expression intense.

"You have to let me explain. It's not—"

"You don't have to explain," she said. "My mother was kind enough to include a letter at the end of the contract, laying out exactly what you'd done for her and thanking you for the service." She paused. "You've been spying on me for her. In exchange for a spot on the DelAres crew."

His hands gripped his knees so hard his knuckles turned white. "It's not like that."

"It's exactly like that." She rose to her feet, every muscle in her body trembling. "I knew it in the hospital, right after the accident. I knew someday you'd resent me for screwing up your career. Is that what this was? Some kind of payback? Or did you just recognize an opportunity to get what you wanted most in the world?"

"Airin—"

Her head was pounding, and she pressed her palms to her temples. "Just tell me this, Hunter. Was sleeping with me part of the plan? Or was that just a bonus?"

His head jerked back as though she'd punched him.

"Never mind," she said. "I don't think I can stand to hear the answer."

"Airin—"

"Stop. Just stop."

How could she have been so blind? She'd been congratulating herself on her independence from her mother. She'd been feeling proud of herself—and of Dira—for letting the separation finally happen.

And all along, it had been a lie. Her mother hadn't let go at all. She'd been here the whole time.

Because of Hunter.

She was angry with her mother. Furious. But the thing that really hurt, the thing that was like a knife between her ribs, was that it was Hunter who'd made this moment possible.

It was Hunter who'd lied to her. Hunter who'd betrayed her. Hunter who, all along, had been incapable of caring for anyone as much as he cared for his own ambitions.

In this moment, she almost hated him. And as she stared into his hazel eyes, seeing the devastation there but not caring how sorry he thought he was, she knew there was only one thing that could have given him the power to hurt her so much.

She was in love with him.

On some level, she must have known it already. It seemed glaringly obvious now, and it must have been obvious to him, too.

Of course it was. Hunter had been with lots of women. He knew when one was in love with him.

Had he felt sorry for her? Was he feeling sorry for her right now?

God, what a pathetic fool I am.

Her mother had been right all along. If this was the real world, she wasn't ready for it.

The sound of gravel crunching caught her attention. "Damn it, someone's home. I can't face Dean or Val right now."

She surged to her feet and went toward the stairs, intending to go up and lock herself in her room for a while. But when she glanced through the screen door, she didn't see Dean or Val's car in the driveway.

She saw a long black limousine.

She froze. "It's my mother."

Seconds later, Hunter was standing beside her. "What the hell is she doing here?"

It took Airin only a moment to figure out exactly what Dira was doing here. "It makes perfect sense, actually. It's just the next step in her plan. Now that she's set off this explosion, she's here to pick up the pieces. To take me back home."

A minute ago, she'd told herself that her mother had been right all along. That she wasn't ready for the real world.

Well, here was her chance to admit defeat. To put the last six weeks behind her and go home with Dira.

She took a deep breath. "Fuck that. Fuck both of you, in fact. I'm going out the back door, and neither one of you had better follow me."

◆ ◆ ◆

Two hours later, she was doing her best to get drunk.

She'd taken the number twelve bus down to Leilani's in Waikiki. Kaleo was behind the bar, and she was on her second Blue Hawaii.

"Why so blue, Snow White?" he asked during a lull, resting his forearms on the bar.

"A color pun," she said, stirring the ice in her drink. "I see what you did there."

"I've got more where that came from. Trouble in paradise?"

"A Hawaii pun."

"Yep. So what's the story, gorgeous? Some man done you wrong?"

She thought about waking up with Hunter that morning. It seemed like a lifetime ago. He'd looked at her like she was every goddess he'd ever dreamed of, and he'd kissed her with so much passion and sweetness she felt transformed into the woman he saw in her.

Beautiful. Strong. Brave.

That part of it couldn't have been a lie. Could it?

No. Hunter had lied to her about Dira, but he hadn't lied about everything. She believed he felt something for her. Maybe not as much as she felt for him, but as much as he was capable of.

It was just that he loved himself more.

No, that wasn't it. It wasn't himself he loved, not exactly. It was his dream of going into space. That would always come first.

Well, why not? A love affair was a small, unimportant thing when you put it up against the first manned mission to Mars. That was future-of-humanity stuff.

She'd told him in California that she didn't want to get in the way of his goals and his dreams. And boy, she sure hadn't.

What was wrong with her Blue Hawaii? The alcohol was supposed to dull the pain in her heart. That's why she'd ordered it.

But it wasn't working.

"Could I have something stronger? A shot of whiskey, maybe?"

"Are you sure you—" Kaleo noticed someone over her shoulder and straightened up. "What can I get you, ma'am?"

A familiar voice spoke behind her. "I'll have what my daughter is having."

Two hours ago, she might have yelled at Dira if they'd come face-to-face. But now she just looked up, met her mother's eyes for a moment, and nodded toward the stool next to hers.

Dira took the seat and watched Kaleo as he poured a variety of liquids into a glass.

"It's blue," she said.

Airin didn't bother confirming that observation. "How did you find me?"

Her mother looked at her. "You're in my Phone Finder network. It identified this general vicinity, and Hunter figured out where you'd gone."

"You used a GPS tracker on me."

"I'll take you out of the network. I promise. After tonight, I'll never be able to find you again . . . unless you want me to."

Kaleo placed a cocktail napkin on the bar and set down Dira's Blue Hawaii. She leaned forward and tasted it.

"It's good." She took another sip. "I think this is the first time we've ever had a drink together."

Airin kept her eyes on her own glass. "You didn't exactly encourage alcohol in my life. Not even on my twenty-first birthday."

"No. I guess I didn't." A beat went by, and then Dira went on. "I had a long talk with your boyfriend. He spoke to me like no one else has dared to for years." She smiled grimly. "He read me the riot act for sending you that contract. And for a lot of other things."

Airin shook her head. "He's not my boyfriend. He is, however, your employee."

"Not anymore."

"You fired him already? That was fast."

"I didn't fire him. He quit."

Airin's head jerked around. "What?"

"He quit. He turned down my offer."

"But . . . that doesn't make any sense. I read the contract you sent. You offered him the one thing he wants most in the world—a guaranteed spot on the first manned mission to Mars. He already did what you asked him to do. Why would he reject the deal now?"

Her mother was quiet for a moment, stirring her drink. Then: "This wasn't even the first time he quit DelAres. The first time was two weeks ago."

Now she was really confused. "I don't understand."

"Hunter emailed me when the two of you were in California. He said you'd done well on the parabolic flight, and then he said he was ending our arrangement. He didn't give a reason, but he told me he understood he was giving up his spot on the DelAres crew."

In California. So after they became a couple, he'd cut ties with Dira. Only . . . he hadn't. Not really.

"But then why did you send a contract? Why did he—"

"Because I told him the job was still his if he wanted it. He'd already done what I'd asked him."

"Spied on me, you mean."

Her mother was frowning down at her Blue Hawaii. "I want you to understand why I did what I did."

"I know why," Airin said, her voice flat. "You couldn't stand the idea that I wanted to make a life for myself away from you."

"No." Dira paused. "Well, yes. There's some truth to that. But it isn't that I don't want good things for you, or that I—"

"It's just that you want to decide what's good for me and what isn't. You don't trust me to make those decisions for myself."

There was another silence, longer this time.

"Maybe I didn't trust you in the beginning," Dira said finally. "But I do now."

"Really?" Airin asked skeptically. "And what brought about this miraculous change of heart?"

"You did. But I didn't realize it until I came here, and Hunter made me see it." She turned to face her daughter. "He made me see *you*, Airin. How strong you are . . . how strong you've always been. How brave, how passionate, how committed. And I realized something I'm not proud of." Her voice faltered, and she took a quick breath. "It's your strength that made me so afraid. Because your father was strong, too. He was strong and brave and passionate and committed . . . and those are the very qualities that got him killed."

Airin had been twelve years old when her father died. Afterward, all her mother had shown publicly—and privately—was her pride in her husband and his service to his country. She'd told Airin she'd be there if her daughter needed to talk about her grief, but it had never once occurred to Airin to do that.

She remembered the nights she'd cried alone in her room, rocking back and forth with an old teddy bear her father had given her. Now, for the first time, she wondered if her mother had suffered that same lonely agony.

"We didn't help each other after he died," she said softly. "I wish we had."

Dira's eyes were bright. "I told myself I had to be strong for you, because of your heart condition. But the truth is, I was afraid. I was afraid if I let you or anyone see how I was really feeling, the grief would take over my life."

Airin nodded. "I understand that. But do you remember what Dad said once, about dying? He said it's not the worst thing that can happen to a person. The worst thing is not living a courageous life."

Dira smiled crookedly. "That's the kind of thing heroes say. But they're not the ones who get left behind." She reached out and put a hand on Airin's arm. "I couldn't bear to think that you might leave me, too. Even after the doctors said you were fully recovered, I just . . . wanted to hang on to you." Her lower lip trembled. "I know I don't say things out loud like your father did. I'm not expressive like he was. But you have to know I love you every bit as much. I love you more than any mother has ever loved her daughter. I love you more than anything in the world."

Tears stung her eyes. "I do know that. And I love you, too, Mom."

"I'm sorry for everything I've done wrong. I'm sorry I asked Hunter to do what he did. But, Airin—I want you to know—Hunter wasn't spying on you. He told me how your ribs were healing, how you seemed to be feeling, and about the work you were doing with Val. Nothing private. Only what you might have told me yourself if you—"

"If I'd wanted to tell you? But that's just the point, Mom. I wanted to be the one to set the boundaries between us."

"I know. And I know I violated those boundaries."

"Yes, you did. And Hunter helped you do it."

Her mother was quiet for a moment. "I know that, too. But if it makes you feel any better, he paid a big price. He lost you, and he lost his spot on the DelAres mission. Twice."

"But after the first time, you talked him into staying. Why?"

"Because I wanted him on my crew. I still do. I've reviewed his stats and his profile, and I've talked to the NASA team about him. He's the best man for the job. So I told him the spot was still his if he wanted it, and he accepted. But when he started talking about the biosphere project and couples in space, I realized that what he really wanted, the future he wanted to build, was for the two of you to go into space together."

He'd talked to her about couples in space, too. Was that really what he'd been hoping for? A future where the two of them could be part of the DelAres mission to Mars?

"That's when I decided to use our deal against him. Against both of you." Dira shook her head. "I was desperate. You seemed to be getting farther and farther away from me, and when I realized you and Hunter were together, I was afraid you might leave for good. I thought . . . if you and Hunter broke up . . . that you might come home." She sighed.

"All I've ever wanted is to keep you safe. And I thought that keeping you with me was the best way to do it."

"But I can't stay with you forever," Airin said gently. "At some point I have to grow up."

Dira sighed again. "So I've heard. You can thank Hunter for passing along that message loud and clear. He actually yelled at me."

She tried to imagine Hunter—or anyone—yelling at her mother.

"I still don't understand why he would give up his dream. If you were still willing to offer him a place on the crew, why would he—"

"Because of you."

"But—"

"When Hunter told me he was turning down the offer to join DelAres, he said he had a condition."

"A condition?"

"He told me to give his place to you. He said you're a born astronaut and that you deserve it more than he does. He sacrificed his chance to be first on Mars for you, Airin."

Hunter had given up his dream—and tried to make hers come true instead.

She remembered what Hunter had said after the parabolic flight. *I guess the secret is to go with someone you care about more than yourself.*

Dira continued. "Of course the terms of Hunter's contract don't actually allow for that kind of swap. A mission to Mars isn't a movie ticket, for goodness' sake. He can make all the suggestions he likes, but I don't have to accept them."

She wanted to yell at Hunter for making the deal with her mother in the first place, and she wanted to thank him for what he'd tried to do for her. Most of all, she wanted to tell him what she'd figured out back at the house.

She loved him.

But before she could do any of that, she had to think about the future.

Their future.

She met her mother's eyes. "You don't have to accept Hunter's suggestion. But what do you think about it?"

"I think I hate it more than any idea I've ever heard." She took a deep breath. "My God, I spent ten years fighting to keep you alive. And now that you've finally won that battle, you want to go to Mars? Do you know how hostile it is to human life?"

"So is Earth—at least in my experience."

Dira brushed that aside. "What you went through is an entirely different thing. Human beings are fragile creatures who have adapted very successfully to this planet. We don't know if we can survive on a world we're not made for."

"People thought the sound barrier would kill the pilot who tried to break it. We thought just being in space, being weightless, might kill us."

"Sometimes it does. You know all the ways space travel can kill you. Solar radiation. Asphyxiation. A reentry like the one that killed the *Columbia* crew. An explosion like the one that killed the *Challenger* crew."

"My own body tried to kill me for ten years."

Dira slapped her palm on the bar. "It's not. The same. Thing."

"Why not?"

"Because we're not designed for space. We're not meant to be there. Long hauls in zero-g decimate bone mass. Your heart doesn't have to work as hard, and it becomes less effective. What happens when you're back under a gravitational load?"

"You get stronger again. You survive. What else is there to do?" She paused. "And what about a one-way trip? The first Mars settlers, the ones who go there to live? My heart and my bones wouldn't have as much adjusting to do at one-third gravity."

Dira looked at her. "You really want to get away from me, don't you?"

For the first time in hours, Airin laughed.

"It's not that, Mom. Really. I just think some people are hardwired to want to *go* somewhere. To travel." She paused. "People like me and Hunter."

"So what's wrong with Paris or Tokyo? Why do you have to travel a hundred and forty million miles when it's so damned *dangerous*?"

She tried to find the right words to answer. "It's just . . . I don't believe the highest expression of our humanity is to protect our own existence. We don't get to opt out of dying, you know. All we can do is figure out what makes us feel alive." She thought for a moment. "You know what Bonnie Dunbar said once? That she'd trained her whole life to go into space, and if she died on a Mars mission, it wouldn't be a bad way to go. You know what Valentina Tereshkova said when they asked her about Mars? She was in her seventies, and she told an interviewer, 'I am ready to fly without coming back.'"

There was a long silence. When Dira spoke, there was no hint of the scientist in her voice.

Only the mother.

"You may be ready to go," she said, her voice trembling, "but I'm not ready to lose you."

"Oh, Mom." Airin put an arm around her shoulders. "Do you remember what Dad used to say? Children are lost from the beginning. Because they belong to the future, a place we can imagine but never see."

Dira's eyes were bright with tears. "God, you're so much like him."

"I'm like you, too."

"You think so?"

"Absolutely. That's why I'm going to be so good at what I do. And just think. If I join DelAres, we'll be doing it together." She picked up her drink. "How about a toast? To the cathedral we're going to build."

They clinked glasses, but Dira looked confused. "Cathedral?"

"Another thing Dad used to talk about. He said medieval cathedrals were a lot like the modern space program. Because it took generations to build them and faith in things you can't see."

Dira sighed. "I should hire you to do PR instead of the actual mission."

Airin tilted her head to the side. "Does that mean you're considering hiring me as an astronaut?"

"Maybe. If you pass the selection tests. And if your skills meet our needs."

Airin started to smile. "That sounds fair."

Her mother sighed again. "I can't believe I—" She broke off suddenly and gasped.

"What is it?" Airin asked, alarmed.

Dira jumped to her feet and pointed with a shaky finger at the wood below the bar.

"Look at that thing. My God, it must be four inches long."

Airin glanced down.

"Don't worry," she said, sliding off her bar stool. "It's just a *Periplaneta americana*."

"A what?"

"American cockroach. They grow 'em big in Hawaii."

She reached out and grabbed it in her bare hand, careful not to kill it. Then she walked it over to the door and tossed it out into the night air, where it flew away with a whir of insect wings.

"Do you have any hand sanitizer?" she asked as she came back.

Her mother was staring at her with wide eyes. Then, after a moment, she reached into her purse and pulled out a pack of wipes.

She shook her head slowly as Airin took one. "Bugs used to terrify you. Just a few months ago, you'd scream if you saw a spider the size of a pea."

"I know. But people can change."

"I guess they can." She paused. "You should remember that when you talk to Hunter."

She took a few bills from her purse and laid them down on the bar. "Thomas is waiting out front. I have a meeting tomorrow, so I should probably get going. Are you sure you don't want to come home with me? You don't have to stay forever."

Her voice was wistful, and Airin smiled at her.

"I'm sure," she said. "But I'd like to come for a visit in a few months, if that's okay."

"Always."

They went outside, where the limo was waiting at the curb. Thomas got out and opened the back door, but Airin spoke before her mother could get in.

"So . . . just to clarify. You said you still want Hunter on your crew, and you said you'd take me if I pass the tests. Does that mean there's a place for both of us on *DelAres I*?"

"I suppose so. Otherwise, I'll lose both of you to NASA."

She got into the back seat of the limo, and Thomas shut the door before going around to the driver's side. As he was getting in, Dira rolled down her window.

"Do you know what your grandmother would say if she were here?"

Airin took a step toward her. "What?"

"Don't fall for a pilot."

Airin grinned, remembering her grandmother's favorite story. "It's too late," she said. "I'm a goner."

The limo pulled away from the curb. The window rolled back up, and the last thing she saw was her mother's smile.

Airin stood on the sidewalk after Dira was gone, wondering what to do next. A few minutes before, sitting at the bar, she could hardly wait to go back home and talk to Hunter. But now that she was free to do just that, she wasn't sure she was ready.

She was starting to feel a little light-headed. Maybe the Blue Hawaii was finally hitting her.

She should walk around a little before heading home. That would give her time to clear her head and to think about what she wanted to say to Hunter.

She might be assuming too much about how he felt. When her mother had told her he'd given up his spot on the DelAres crew for her, she'd been sure he wouldn't have done that if he didn't love her.

But maybe he just felt guilty about making the deal with her mother. Maybe he thought he owed it to her.

Maybe he felt sorry for her.

The more she thought about it, the more depressed she felt. And as she walked, oblivious to the sights and sounds of Waikiki around her, her bright dream of the future started to seem like an improbable fantasy.

Chapter Twenty-Three

After Dira left the house to find Airin, Hunter left, too.

He walked down the driveway past his truck. His keys were in his pocket, but he didn't want to drive.

He wanted to walk.

He headed *makai*, seaward. He walked down through the lush Manoa Valley, past the university, through the busy streets inland of Waikiki to Waikiki itself.

He ended up at the beach.

It had taken him an hour to get there. That was a lot of time to think, but no brilliant solutions had presented themselves. He was a pilot and an engineer, a problem solver, and he couldn't come up with a single damn way to fix the damage he'd done.

The sun was setting, igniting the clouds on the horizon with red and gold. As he walked across the sand to the edge of the ocean, he waited for the beauty and majesty of the sky to work its usual magic on him.

But there was no magic.

He stood at the water's edge and stared out at the ocean. It was wide, trackless, stretching out beyond human knowledge. The Hawaiians, the Greeks, the Vikings in their longboats—all had taken on this great unknown with unimaginable courage.

Astronauts carried that mantle now. They were the explorers heading out into the abyss, carrying with them the spark of human curiosity and adventure. In a thousand years, their ships and tools would seem as primitive as the canoes of the ancient Polynesians did today.

All Hunter had ever wanted was to be a part of the journey. A part of mankind's great leap into the future.

That goal was so much bigger than he was. So why, now, did it seem small? How could he have outgrown something that had been a part of him for so long?

And if he'd outgrown his old dream, what had he grown into?

His phone rang, and for a moment he thought it was Airin. His heart leaped in his chest as he pulled it out of his pocket, but it was his brother's name on the screen.

He almost didn't answer. But they'd only talked on the phone once since the wedding, and it might be important.

"Hey, Caleb. What's going on?"

"Nothing much. Jane asked me today how you were doing, and I realized we hadn't talked in a while. Anything new with you?"

So . . . not important, then.

He started to tell Caleb he couldn't talk right now. Instead, he heard himself say, "I fucked up."

"My big brother? Not possible. What'd you fuck up? Something at NASA?"

"Not NASA. Airin."

There was a short silence. He'd told Caleb about Airin in an email last week, but he hadn't given much detail beyond the bare fact that they were involved.

"Okay," Caleb said after a moment. "I think you better tell me all about it. Unless you've got someplace else to be?"

"I've got nowhere to be."

He kicked off his shoes, sat down on the sand, and told Caleb the whole story.

It took a while. After he finished, he said, "That thing Airin thought about me. Do you think she was right?"

"Which thing?"

"She said our parents both left us, in different ways. She said if I go to Mars, I'll be the one leaving. I'll be leaving the whole world behind."

Caleb was quiet for a moment. Then he said, "I think she had a point, but I don't think she drew the right conclusion."

"What do you think her point was?"

"That what happened with Mom and Dad affected you. But it didn't make you want to leave other people behind. It made you afraid of wasting your life. It made you want to do something meaningful. Something that would last."

He thought about that. "Yeah."

Caleb went on. "But that's not the whole story with our parents."

"What do you mean?"

"I know things didn't end well for them. Obviously. But love isn't a waste, Hunter. It's the only thing that lasts. Not the way a building lasts or being the first guy to walk on the moon, but in a way that's more real than any of that stuff." He paused. "I know Dad was pretty screwed up, and Mom still is, but that doesn't mean love wasn't the best thing in their lives. They took a chance, and it didn't work out. But that doesn't mean they were wrong to try." He paused again. "When it comes to love, I don't think it's ever wrong to try."

A ray of the setting sun pierced through the clouds, making him blink.

That must be why tears stung behind his eyelids.

"Damn," he said after a moment. "It's weird to hear my little brother sounding so smart."

"If I said something smart, it's because of Jane. She's the one who makes me think about this shit."

Hunter took in a lungful of air and let it out slowly. "I want to try, with Airin. But I'm afraid I screwed up too bad. I'm afraid it's too late."

"I've got an answer for that, and it comes from you."

"Huh?"

"I said the same thing last year when I told you how I'd fucked up with Jane. I said it was too late to fix it. Remember what you told me?"

"No. Was it good?"

"Yeah. You said as long as you're alive, you can fix anything."

Silence.

"I said that, huh?"

"Yeah. So get to work, man. Figure it out. I'll give you a call tomorrow, okay?"

"Okay."

He slid his phone back into his pocket.

Figure it out, Caleb had said. Like it was that easy.

The sun was gone now. The ghost of red-and-gold glory lingered on the western horizon, but night was coming. Soon the sky would be filled with stars.

He still wanted to go into space. He still wanted to travel to Mars. But if Airin wasn't with him, none of it would mean a damn thing.

He'd rather stay on Earth with Airin than to go to the stars without her.

But what if she doesn't want me?

Well, that was her call to make. All he could do was tell her what he'd finally figured out.

He loved her. Nothing would change that. Even if she rejected him, even if she never wanted to see him again, she would still be his center of gravity.

Now and forever.

◆ ◆ ◆

Airin wasn't sure how long she walked before she ended up on Waikiki Beach.

She stood where the walkway met the sand, realizing where she was and remembering the last time she'd been here. Then she spotted Hunter.

He was sitting close to the ocean, right where the two of them had kissed that night.

The night that had changed their lives forever.

A thrill went down her spine.

She walked across the sand and sat down beside him.

"Hey," she said, wishing she'd come up with something more profound.

His head jerked around. "Airin," he said, as though he couldn't believe it. "What are you doing here? How did you find me?"

"I didn't. I was just walking, and I ended up here." She paused. "Then I saw you."

He was staring at her like he'd never look away.

During her walk through Waikiki, she'd planned a whole speech. She'd thought about everything she wanted to tell him. How angry she still was at what he'd done, how touched she was by the sacrifice he'd made, and how she couldn't imagine her life without him.

But now that she was here, now that she could say anything she wanted, words seemed to fail her.

I'm a goner, she'd told her mother, as though it were that simple.

But it wasn't simple. There was no engineering solution to her problem, and if there was an emotional solution, she didn't have the experience or wisdom to find it.

She bent her legs, wrapped her arms around her shins, and rested her chin on her knees.

It was a cool night for Hawaii, and when the wind picked up, she shivered. Hunter moved closer and put his arm around her shoulders, and the warmth and weight of him felt so good it made her throat ache.

The sun had set half an hour ago. Mars was visible in the sky to the west, hanging low above the horizon. She was sure Hunter was looking at it, too.

When he spoke, she knew she'd been right.

"The Hawaiians called it *Hokuula*. 'Red star.'"

"It was *Tiu* in Old English," she said. "That's where we get the word *Tuesday*—'Mars day.'"

"I didn't know that."

She leaned against him, and his arm tightened around her. They sat like that until Mars sank below the horizon, and the rest of the stars in the firmament grew brighter.

"Why did you turn down a spot on the DelAres crew?" she asked.

"You know why."

"No, I don't. That's why I'm asking."

He sighed. Then he shifted, turning to face her, and she did the same. They were sitting cross-legged on the sand, their knees almost touching, the ocean lapping against the shore a few yards away and the night sky a jeweled canopy above them.

"I turned it down because what I did was so shitty. And because if it takes me away from you, I don't want it. I don't want to go to Mars without you, Airin. I don't want to go anywhere without you. I love you."

He said it so simply, as though it was the easiest and most obvious thing in the world. But those three words did something to her, something she couldn't have explained if she had a hundred years and a million words.

"I don't know if you can forgive me for making that deal with your mother. But whether you do or not, whether you want to be with me or not, I'm yours. I'm yours forever. All I'm asking for is a chance to make it up to you. A chance to prove to you that I—"

She didn't move across the space between them as much as levitate across it. She was in his lap with her legs around his waist and her arms around his neck, and then she kissed him like it was the last thing she'd ever do.

It was a while before they came up for air. When they did, she put her hands on his shoulders and looked straight into his hazel eyes.

"I love you, too."

His eyes were bright. "I've thought about saying those words to you and what it would be like to hear you say them back."

"And?"

He slid his hands into her hair, and for every star in the sky there was a ripple of pleasure in her body.

"It's even better than I imagined."

She shifted in his lap so she could lay her head on his shoulder. "We're going to Mars, you know. You and me."

"We are, huh? With NASA or with DelAres?"

"DelAres."

"You think Dira will take me back?"

"Yep. She said she wants you to command her crew. The job's yours if you want it."

He kissed the top of her head. "Only if you're coming with me. Is there a place for you on the crew?"

"If I pass the astronaut selection tests."

He chuckled. "You'll pass them. I'm going to work you so hard over the next few years your head will spin."

She nestled closer to him, feeling the beat of his pulse at the base of his throat. "Is it weird that that sounds sexual to me?"

He chuckled again, and the sound vibrated through her body. "Nope. Do you remember the last time we were here?"

"Vaguely. What were we doing, again?"

"Breaking public decency laws."

"We never did get arrested," she murmured. "Maybe we should try again."

"Or we could just go back to the house."

"Or get a hotel room."

"So many possibilities," he said.

A wave broke just a few feet away from them, and it gave her an idea. "Do you remember when we talked about weightless sex?"

"Vividly."

"What if we start with a weightless kiss?"

"Angel, I am one hundred percent down with that. How do you propose we do it?"

She scrambled to her feet and held out a hand to help him up. "In the water."

He got to his feet and stood beside her. "A kiss in the ocean? Hell yeah. I can't believe we live in Hawaii and haven't done that yet. Should we go home and get our suits, or come back tomorrow?"

She shook her head. "I want to do it right now. In our clothes."

He grinned down at her. "Our phones and wallets might get stolen. The last time we kissed on this beach, you lost your purse. Are you ready to lose another one?"

She kicked off her sandals and dropped her phone and wallet on top of them.

"Who cares if we lose our wallets? That's just our identity." She gestured toward the Pacific. "That, out there? That's our essence."

Hunter looked at her for a second. "Okay, I'm in."

He dropped his phone and wallet beside hers. Then they walked hand in hand into the ocean, the water soaking their pants and then their shirts, the cotton clinging to their bodies and then ballooning out.

The air was cool, but the water was warm. The moon path stretched before them to the horizon, and where the waves crested, the silver light glimmered on sea foam.

"We lived near a lake when I was a kid," Hunter said. "I used to go there at night when the moon was full, and I imagined running along the track it made on the water."

"What did you think would happen when you got to the end?"

"I'd jump off. Out into the unknown."

"Can you still imagine yourself doing that?"

He turned to face her, sliding one arm around her waist and the other around her shoulders.

"Yeah," he said. "But this time, you're with me."

She put her arms around his neck and her legs around his waist. "I'll always be with you," she whispered.

His heart pounded against hers. He took a few steps farther out—deeper than where she could stand on her own.

Their mouths came together with an electric charge. Her body surged into his, and their kiss was sweet and salty and everything in between.

The ocean was all around them, cradling them in familiar mystery. But when they began to float, it didn't feel like the water was making it happen.

It felt like their love was stronger than gravity.

ACKNOWLEDGMENTS

Thanks to everyone at Montlake, especially Maria Gomez. Thank you to the amazing Charlotte Herscher for her insight. Thanks to my husband and son for their patience, support, and keen story sense, and to Tara Gorvine for being the best critique partner ever. Thank you to Dr. Heather Gallo for answering my medical questions, aspiring astronaut Abigail Harrison (@AstronautAbby) for answering my space questions, and my father for answering my military questions. Any errors you find are mine.

ABOUT THE AUTHOR

Photo © 2014 Target Portrait Studio

Abigail Strom started writing stories at the age of seven and has never been able to stop. In addition to writing for Montlake Romance, she has written for Harlequin and is also the author of the self-published Hart University series, the first book of which earned a 2016 RITA nomination. Her books have been translated into several languages, including French, German, Italian, Spanish, Dutch, and Turkish. Abigail also writes the steamy paranormal Blood and Absinthe series under the name Chloe Hart.

Abigail earned a BA in English from Cornell University, as well as an MFA in dance from the University of Hawaii, and held a wide variety of jobs—from dance teacher and choreographer to human resources manager—before becoming a full-time writer. Now she works in her pajamas and lives in New England with her family, who are incredibly supportive of the hours she spends hunched over her computer. Learn more about the author and her work at www.abigailstrom.com and www.authorchloehart.com.